# Ral, Space Colonizer

I0633343

## *David B Kingman*

**chipmunkapublishing**
the mental health publisher

David B Kingman

Published by
Chipmunkapublishing
PO Box 6872
Brentwood
Essex CM13 1ZT
United Kingdom

http://www.chipmunkapublishing.com

Chipmunkapublishing gratefully acknowledge the support of Arts Council England.

**Book Dedication**

I dedicate this book to my wife, Dottie Kingman, who cajoled and inspired me to complete it, always believing in the books underlying Nobel message of universal salvation.

David B Kingman

## About the Author

David Kingman was born in Morehead, Kentucky in 1942. He graduated from Miami Jacob's Business College with an extended two years of study through Urbana College. He has performed traditional country music on TV & Radio and has played in taverns, motels, and fairs for more than thirty years. For the past twenty years he changed his musical interest to gospel music. He served as vice-president of the Dayton Musician's Club in early 1961, and he also worked in Grand Rapids, Michigan as a studio photographer. In 1984, he served as a member of Dayton's S/E Priority Board, a community based organization. David served in Vietnam as a Photographer & Photo Lab Technician. After 23 years working in the Sales Division of a local cemetery, his biographical book, "The Shrines of Woodland", was published by the historic cemetery in Dayton, Ohio in 2008.

When David wrote "Ral, Space Colonizer" he realized that in effort to write a successful book he would need to write about familiar subjects, so mental health would be a given. He had lived with his demons and they needed to be tempered in the book with religious and philosophic thought in which David was well versed.

It is David's sincere desire that his science fiction book will not only inspire young and old to come to a personal relationship with their God, but also demonstrate to those that suffer with their own demons, they can also proudly walk this life with heads held high far above their mental health afflictions.

David B Kingman

# Ral, Space Colonizer

## Prologue

Old Ceylon a distant and ancient planet located deep within the Seventh Quadrant's star system, was in ancient times populated by space colonizers. In the early development of the planet a belief system was practiced in which the citizens worshiped the Unni, an awesome god. The colonies flourished and love for god and country became their anthem. After a few thousand years, a new government in its effort to develop higher learning and scientific advancements, prohibited the worship of the Unni, causing the colonies to fall into a state of decadence, wherein decency and morality became lost in the distant past.

For countless generations, old Ceylon's authority had gone unchallenged, however the destiny of this great planet was not to be destroyed by an enemy encounter but by one of the natural forces of its universe, a run away asteroid.

General Dreeska, military operations officer, recognized the danger of the impending asteroid far enough in advance that he had sufficient time to evacuate the colonies to a safe haven on one the recreational planets. When a new planet was discovered suitable for habitation, Dreeska was proclaimed governor and hailed down through the ages as savior of his people. Dreeska was adamant that the belief in the old Ceylonian god should never be resurrected and laid down harsh sentences to any that would dare speak the name of the banished deity.

The Unni called out a citizen that was born in New Ceylon, long after the death of Governor Dreeska, by the name of Atar, who would reestablish the ancient belief system, that was rejected during Ceylon's Golden Age. Because of their indifference to religion, the citizens of New Ceylon walked around with calloused attitudes. But Atar was different, he actually showed love toward his family and fellow citizens. He quickly moved up in the ranks of the military, eventually filling the empty seat of Governor Dreeska, that had been vacated by his death those many long years ago.

Atar desired that his son Ral, would one day rise to the same high position of power to which he had attained. The governor had no inhibition, when it came to moving his son up the ladder of success. This nepotism was not appreciated by those who had been passed over with more military experience, including Ragan, Ral's academy friend.

The Ceylonians, as well as their predecessor of old Ceylon, were known for their scientific ability to discover new planets for future colonization and Atar gave his son the gift of a fruitful planet, naming it the Feramas. This was Ral's first colonization but nothing is perfect and Ragan, whom Ral had appointed regent over the land rebelled, seeking to appropriate all power and wealth for his own.

Ral, in spite of Ragan's rebellion, continued to intervene in the affairs of the Feramas citizens by providing for their needs while hovering above the Feramas heavens in his starship. When Ragan caused the citizens to revolt, Ral in his moment of rage was ready to destroy Ragan and the entire planet, but Medoa his starship advisor explained that Ragan was needed by the Unni to bring into proper balance the positive and negative forces of the cosmos.

Ral, because of his strict background, found it difficult to believe in the Ceylonian god, even though time after time the Unni manifest his presence, and even with spiritual beings serving aboard his starship for numerous years, Ral continued his defiance. Because of Ral's transgressions against the Unni, the blessing that would have been his was transferred to his two sons, Kiah and Jedar. They would be chosen and honored to witness the ultimate destruction of all cosmological life.

The story is filled with love for family, religious fervor, exciting battles, and sexual interplay between Commander Ral and his ensign, Dreara.

After I began writing the book I realized that I had written into the book's characters, my own scarred personality, along with my mental health demons such as depression, fear, anxiety neurosis, panic attacks and suicidal ideations. Dottie, my precious wife can be recognized in the book as Dreara, Ral's skeptical wife. The book is filled with biblical concepts, illustrating how the God of creation is involved in the affairs of mankind, offering unlimited forgiveness, while leading them into the path of salvation.

# CHAPTER 1

For the past few months, science officer Dreeska, was observing an approaching asteroid, which was hurling toward the renown planet of Ceylon, and as a result of intense observation, he speculated that the collision would take place within six months. Immediately the academy began removing the citizens in an orderly fashion, before their home was hurled into sparkles of space dust. The approaching asteroid had a diameter of 2000 miles, being much larger than some of the well known astronomical objects that soared high above their planet, and as to be expected, Dreeska was placed in charge of the mass evacuation.

"Ceylon's power and glory will soon be just a memory." Mumbled one of his ensigns standing nearby. Dreeska was so lost in thought, he could not comprehend the words of his junior officer.

"What was that?" Asked Dreeska. His ensign repeated the words, as if he was just continuing his thoughts.

"I was just trying to say that Ceylon is the most prominent colonization in academy history. Sir, Ceylon is so powerful that it controls the entire united alliance of the Seventh Quadrant. Ceylon remains unchallenged except for the pesky Kronos Nation." Dreeska was pleased, his men still shared this unshakable loyalty for Ceylon.

"This young soldier displays the bravery and allegiance that will be imperative, if Ceylon is to hold on to its long reign of supremacy. Yes," Dreeska rambled on, "the land of our birth must be forgotten in time by its citizenship so that their hearts will remain resolute in the establishment of our future home."

## THE RECREATIONAL PLANET

The Ceylonians were transported by many of the outdated spacecraft that out lived their purpose as excursion ships. It seemed unusual to Dreeska that the fleet's last great adventure would be to transport the massive amount of anxious citizens to their temporary dwelling on one of the recreational planets. Dreeska knew the days to come would be most trying and difficult as the displaced citizens waited for one of the academy's neoteric planets to be made ready for habitation.

Recreational planets was esteemed by vacationing officers and appreciative citizens throughout the Seventh Quadrant, and the displaced citizens were greeted with open arms and gifts, as they disembarked their spacecrafts by the thousands.

"What an interesting wonderland," Dreeska sighed, as he leisurely strolled across the courtyard. "I have never encountered such delights as I behold here, they do not exist on Ceylon. Large luscious fruits grow everywhere in abundance and the females are much more pleasant to the eye than the masculine types on Ceylon."

The staff members assigned to the recreational planet were celebrated for their ability to influence the part of the brain that was responsible for stimulation of dreams and hallucinations. When each visitor signed in, there was nothing they lacked, for every pleasure was theirs to experience. Personal masseuse', pools, and spas were exquisite, but nothing could compare to the perfect holiday that was created in the deep chamber of their mind. The futuristic computers could decipher the most satisfying images that were locked in the subconscious, and create for those on vacation, the most wonderful escape from reality, that could be imagined. They could travel to places they had never been, or if sexual gratification was limited or lacking, there was no restrictions when it came to fulfilling their fantasy. Each evening at the appointed time, the visual episode so seemingly real, would disappear until a new one was invoked. The Ceylonians could only observe the excitement, because they were forbidden to even contemplate sex, but they were encouraged to take pleasure in the additional dreams and pleasures offered on the recreational planet.

Yes, Dreeska had requested permission from the Galaxy Exploratory Division to dock at this most celebrated wonderland but he absolutely realized that his military still needed to be trained in order to maintain supremacy over their adversaries. He felt assured that his men would not lose the zeal to fight for the honor of Ceylon.

Dreeska appeared forlorn over the eventual destruction of his home, but it was ingrained in the citizens, that what will happen will happen and therefore must ultimately be accepted.

No tears were shed as Dreeska and the citizens gathered on the far off distant planet to witness the awesome display of Ceylon's destruction. The multitude of gases hurled trails of colorful lights into the Ceylonian atmosphere and then Ceylon faded away without a whimper.

Time had passed quickly on the recreational planet, and the Ceylonians began to gather in mass, as they waited for Dreeska to announce his anticipated proclamation.

## THE DISCOVERY OF NEW CEYLON

"My honored and noble citizens, the Galaxy Exploratory Division has spotted a larger and much more evolved planet, which the council deems suitable for habitation. Bide your time it will not take long, but when readied, everything will be much the same as when you left your honored colonies on Ceylon."

Dreeska personally supervised the tedious arrangements of preparing for the departure of the military and the displaced citizens from the recreational planet, the academy fleet was sent first to establish strategic military positions, and scientist from the academy followed to prepare the way. The citizens had taken pleasure in their vacation, and a small number of them had even asked permission to remain, but Dreeska was determined that every citizen would be needed in order to maintain universal dominance over their enemy.

Dreeska, and the reluctant Ceylonians felt intimated when they stepped foot on the planet. It was almost as if they were being unfaithful to their former home, but preparations had already been made and the citizens soon adjusted to life on New Ceylon.

## DREESKA ELECTED GOVERNOR

The warring nations throughout the Seventh Quadrant had been surveying the state of affairs closely, keeping an eye open for signs of collapse in the military. The enemy respected Dreeska, and during their entire stay, not one dared to raise a hand against him.

Teams of builders were busy building dwelling places for the citizens. Dreeska believed this made the displaced citizens more productive. Dreeska then coordinated every essential operations for the establishment of New Ceylon.

Cheating and stealing became crimes of a former time. He also declared that theft, murder, and crimes against the government were all punishable by death. Dreeska had found it to his advantage to revise Ceylon's monarchal form of government to that of a ruling body comprised of twelve, revered and respected citizens.

Through an open ballot the council members would choose their governor. Dreeska was favored to win the election, after all, he was the one whose perceptive guidance was instrumental in keeping the Ceylonians safe and unchallenged by their galactic neighbors.

"Long live Dreeska!" Shouted the citizens in honor to his name. The statues of Dreeska stood in almost every major colony of the planet. Many also honored him by naming their province Sair-Dreeska, and his appointment to the governorship was the best thing that could have ever happened to Ceylon, because Dreeska loved the citizens. He believed he was doing his best in managing the affairs of its colonies, but some of his decisions would come back to haunt the Ceylonians in years to come.

After Dreeska ended his final death cycle, he was mourned by citizens throughout the Seventh Quadrant, his ashes were taken high above the Ceylonian heavens and scattered by the winds over the land that he held in such high esteem.

## COMMANDER ATAR RUNS FOR GOVERNOR

In the year 250,500 C. S. T., (Ceylonian Star Time) space colonization under the precept of Commander Atar had advanced to a high state of technology. Dreeska although having been dead for thousands of forgotten generations, retained power on the council through Gaunka, a distant relative. But Gaunka cared more for the pleasures of New Ceylon and only served as a token representative. New Ceylon was intensely interested in who would be next in line to hold this high and honored position of governor.

Ceylonian scientists were unrelenting, in their efforts to discover planets for future colonization. They never doubted that New Ceylon might succumb to a fate similar to that of old Ceylon, and Durran, an outlying planet, was selected as Ceylon's potential replacement.

Throughout the years, massive changes had taken place on Durran, teaching their citizens to live as Ceylonians and educating them in military tactics. Durranians had known for years that their slave status would forever prevent them from becoming property owners, they would never be called a Ceylonian, no matter how they tried. Slaves always found this to be true, and no one had ever dared to challenge the laws. New Ceylon was celebrated throughout the cosmos for its pursuit of knowledge, and due to the efforts of the

Galaxy Exploratory Division, they maintained their prominence as space colonizers.

New Ceylon was indeed larger than most of the habitable planets that fell under the supervision of this celebrated branch of the military. It had remained supreme and unconquered long before Dreeska was governor.

## THE NIGHT BEFORE THE ELECTION

A preliminary meeting of the Council of The Twelve was scheduled to be held behind closed doors. The seats of the eleven council members were arranged in circular fashion, with Dreeska's empty seat centered in the room. The members consisted not only of the wisest, but also the more wealthy and affluent of the aristocracy.

To work out their proper seating arrangements, every chair had a stream of colorful gases circulating throughout. The red chair, located in the center of the room had been sitting vacant ever since Dreeska had last occupied it. Not even Gaunka had ever chosen to sit there.

Ceylon had advanced technologically since the days of old Ceylon, and carnal pleasures that was practiced by their ancestors, for instance, eating the flesh of creatures, had been banned in the past and wholesome foods were now manufactured synthetically.

Each member of the council was approached by a humble servant, more often than not, a species from a planet, which had fallen under Ceylonian domain. The servant would enter the room, and after going through a cleansing ritual, he would walk over and place a piece of edible parchment in the mouth of the committee member. The constituent would then raise his choice of libation, turn in each direction of the table and salute. After eating and drinking, he consumed the vessel itself. These snacks tasted sweet, consisting of every known nutrient that enhanced the development of the mind and body. Bodily waste was now lost in the distant past, because the food intake was completely non-solid and water soluble.

Nutrients were released through the skin in the form of perspiration, emitting sweet smelling odors that varied according to the type of food digested.

It was also mandatory that each member wear a colorful bandana, which encased a computer chip located at the center of the forehead. This was designed to eliminate lying because it recorded electrical impulses. If a member ever thought of being untruthful, a shock was sent throughout the nervous system causing severe pain and partial paralysis.

The assembly members stood, when the committee officer arrived to preside over the preliminary ballots.

"My fellow members," spoke the committeeman, "the nomination lies between Commander Atar and our most esteemed committee member, Gemaal. Atar is a military strategist and is celebrated for his ability to find new planets for colonization. He is highly admired by our citizens as well as most colonies throughout the Seventh Quadrant."

"What can I express about Gemaal that you do not already know? But for the record, he is a citizen of high reputation in the political arena. Is it not Gemaal who has held Ceylon together by his superior ability to organize? He has united the sectors of our planet into a fine tuned machine. Yes, Gemaal has been acknowledged to be one our finest citizens. Is his devotion to Ceylon not beyond question?"

"Tomorrow, my fellow citizens, prepare your hearts and your mind for your decision will be scrutinized by philosophers throughout the entire Seventh Quadrant. Yes, honored citizens, get your rest tonight and tomorrow evening let the election take place."

The sounds of cheering was heard throughout every colony, because the greatest party ever to be held on the planet was about to happen, and indeed, be remembered as the most superb celebration in Ceylon's history.

### THE COUNCIL MEMBERS

That evening Keeksonn walked back and forth pacing the floor. "Glenna, my dear wife, help me decide which vote to cast for this most important ballet."

"Keeksonn, Keeksonn, my gracious and kind husband, whatever you decide I feel will be the best for our honored Ceylon."

"Please understand Glenna, (interpreted Sweetheart) this decision can have a vast effect on the quality of our existence here on Ceylon. Whosoever sits in the esteemed Chair of Dreeska will look with favor on those who support them in the honored position. Glenna, our dear friend Atar is conceivably the most honored citizen that ever graced the streets of our beloved homeland. He has been a valued friend, just as Mylia his wife, who has been so close that you are almost inseparable."

"Yes, Keeksonn, you are right, but what about Gemaal? I feel you are somewhat reserved concerning him."

"Yes, Glenna, Gemaal has politically done great things for Ceylon, but dear wife, when you look at all the deceit and lies that were instrumental in bringing him this far." Keeksonn paused. "Am I making myself clear?"

"Yes, but why are you so reserved about your decision?"

"I don't know Glenna, I just don't know. I am going to secretly speak with the council members in the morning. Perhaps I can determine which direction they are leaning toward the election."

"Fine husband, have a refreshing drink of Tanger before you retire for the night. It will help clear your head and relax you. I need to take care of you Keeksonn," his wife spoke jokingly, "after all, you may be Ceylon's governor one day."

## THE SECRET MEETINGS

"Council members come to order. We need to make some important decisions concerning tonight's election." Spoke Brudda, chairman of the committee, as the piercing sound of the assembly bell reverberated throughout the building. "I believe we are all in agreement that Atar is our choice for this honored seat but what if, when the time comes and the votes are tallied, the four that are not here with us cast their vote for Gemaal? Plus there is always the possibility that one of you might have a change of heart. You all know," Brudda spoke on, "what our fate would be if Gemaal attains such power and turns his wrath against us for voting against him."

"Yes, Brudda," spoke Keeksonn, "the council members have governed without the presence of a physical governor, since the death of Dreeska. But now the law has been challenged by evil cohorts of Gemaal and they demand the honored seat to be filled."

"Roll call." Spoke Brudda, while he fumbled nervously through his papers.

Baisha, Roprier, Gatalina and Keeksonn, all responded enthusiastically, "honored to serve." Then Keeksonn traded places with Brudda and he also replied, "honored to serve."

Keeksonn continued. "The absent members are Shashenna, Acerera, Quintoea, Panchar, and Leaoka."

Each member was able to rule, not only the assembly, but the governor's seat itself. Each member was also required to be married and their sons were compelled to be trained in the ways of the academy, an old law that had always been and no one ever dared to challenge. The Ceylonian hierarchy felt they must raise pure and untainted children to keep the master race supreme.

"Members of the council, may I have your attention! It is time to take our preliminary count." Cried out Keeksonn.

There was a deadly silence as each member placed his vote in the fire box, so named because as soon as the vote was tallied the ballots would automatically disintegrate inside the box. When each preliminary vote was analyzed by the computer it was, as expected, unanimously favored in the direction of Atar, and as the five council members departed from the meeting, Brudda sheepishly placed his hand on Keeksonn's shoulder, asking why the other members failed to show?

"I'm not really sure Brudda, but conceivably, Gemaal is involved stirring up dissention from among our ranks. I just don't know, but it can't be good."

## GEMAAL'S CORRUPTION ATTEMPT

All eyes were fixed upon Gemaal as he entered the room, Gemaal was of average build and he was not pleasant to look upon. Quintoea began chuckling to himself, when he began to recall that the young academy officers often mocked Gemaal calling him scarface. When Gemaal approached the podium Quintoea gazed intently into his eyes, as he began to speak.

"My honored and trusted members of the council," Gemaal spoke boldly, "although I haven't served on this council long with you, I believe we have made much progress, especially toward the development of our great homeland. It is for this reason that I have invited you to meet privately with me, for in each of you, I have seen signs that convince me that you are completely committed to the service of our colonies. If I am elected governor I will have all power, and if you back me in this election, you will be appointed as regents throughout Ceylon. There will be nothing you will lack, everything you desire will be yours for the asking. All you need to do is cast your vote for me. I assure you, Keeksonn, Brudda and the other council members have already expressed their confidence in me, and I will win this election in a landslide decision."

When Gemaal departed the room there was a deep silence, and Leaoka was the first to speak. "Acerera, you have served on the committee, longer than any of us. What is your feeling concerning this strange proposition?"

"Well Leaoka, I have read the history of old Ceylon, of the greed and the quest for wealth and power. It led to the down-fall of the planet. My next thought Leaoka, when we sit at the council table to make known our decision, we are required to wear the electrode head-band, which prevents us from making decisions based upon deceit, if we are untruthful we will suffer the consequence. Both Shashenna and Quintoea can vouch for me in this matter. Quintoea can even show his wounds that have affected his health to this day. It's impossible to lie or harbor deception under this condition."

"Acerera," spoke Quintoea, "do you believe Gemaal when he says the other members are in his favor?"

"No Quintoea, Gemaal never reached the position he now occupies by being honest. His reputation of dishonesty precedes him but I, Acerera, highly suggest we favor his election. If he wins and is aware of our decision against him, we will pay the consequences for our actions. Atar on the other hand, given his genteel nature, will not look upon us with disfavor if he should lose. Each of us has families, and admirable possessions," spoke Acerera, "but if found to oppose Gemaal, especially with his connections throughout the political arena, life could become very difficult. In defense of Atar, I must confess to you now, that he is the only citizen for this position and I truly would like to see him elected. His son Ral is young and ambitious and is a candidate for Starfleet, and if he ever learns to take life seriously, he could possibly be groomed to replace Atar as commander of the academy."

Ral because of his father's privileged position, knew each member serving on the council, after all, they were the leaders that often visited his father to discuss political issues and to play Pogron, a favorite past time game of Ceylonian nobility.

While the council members listened, and their questions were seemingly answered by the smooth glib of Acerera, Quintoea held his speech, and took it all in stride. After all he was a distant relative of Atar and was very close to the family. He also felt for the moment he best play along with the rest of the members.

Gemaal finally returned to the room and brought a bottle of Tanger to celebrate the occasion.

"Acerera," spoke Gemaal, "my informants tell me, there is a way the electrode head-band can be short circuited."

"Tell us Gemaal." They all cried out, almost in unison. "How do we override this dreaded machine?"

Gemaal continued. "You have heard of the Floacre Mind Meld?"

"Yes Gemaal, but the Floacre has developed this technique throughout many years."

"My children," spoke Gemaal, "gather round me and I will demonstrate. Start out by placing the small finger of your left hand between the eyes, at the area of the pineal gland. Keep pressing hard while extending the thumb, and applying pressure to the back of the left ear lobe. Now take the other hand and place your thumb and two of your fingers on the two acupuncture points located at the center of your partner's back, the power comes by the touching of each other in this fashion."

Gemaal explained they could gather this energy just before entering the voting chamber, and that the members of the committee could spent the rest of the afternoon demonstrating and practicing this method. "See you later." Each of them spoke as they nervously departed the room.

## THE ELECTION

Atar & Gemaal's photos were so publicized that practically every citizen throughout the entire Seventh Quadrant knew their face. Their pictures were produced by electronic holograms, the old antiquated paper images had been outdated long ago as a source of land pollution. While waiting for the proceeding to begin, Atar and Gemaal sat at their seats thinking their own complex thoughts.

Atar silently waited, wondering what exciting adventures might lay ahead for Ral, while Gemaal on the other hand, thought more of the prestige that he could achieve. "I could take the power of Ceylon further than anyone could ever imagine. Why, I could expand our domain deep unto the outer quadrants."

The candidates currently served on the council, but election rules dictated that those seeking election were disqualified from the voting process. This established rule left just ten members to decide the election.

"Attention!" Spoke Keeksonn. "I ask each of your servants to bring the sacred crystal and place it before you, but first, let's bow our heads so that our consciousness will be awakened and refreshed, and then let us proceed with this honored tradition."

"It is time to begin the election." Spoke Keeksonn, as the room became very quite.

"Baisha, place your hand in the crystal. Computer prepare crystal analysis for officer Baisha."

"Computer analysis, Lord Keeksonn." spoke the digitized voice. "Baisha cast his vote for Atar, and it is sealed and written in the crystal."

The election proceeded slowly as Roprier cast his vote for Atar, and it was sealed and written in the crystal. Gatalina, Brudda, and Keeksonn also went through the voting process and cast their votes for Atar. These votes were of no surprise to the constituency and the results were to be expected. The crowds began breaking out in an uproar disrupting the proceedings.

"Quite," Keeksonn shouted sternly, "do not let this election become a circus, for this moment will be remembered throughout our generations, it must be maintained as an election of dignity."

"Shashenna," spoke Keeksonn, "place your hand in the crystal." The computer replied, "Shashenna cast his vote for Gemaal and it is sealed and written in the crystal." Panchar also cast his vote for Gemaal and it was sealed and written in the crystal."

Acerera approached the crystal, large drops of perspiration formed upon his brow. "What if my nervous system is shattered to pieces because of my chicanery and I am permanently maimed?" Acerera believed his heart was about to stop, but he placed his hand slowly into the crystal.

"Computer analysis," spoke Keeksonn.

"Scanning," The computer responded, "Lord Keeksonn, Acerera cast his vote for Gemaal, and it is sealed and written in the crystal."

When Leaoka cast his vote for Gemaal, there was a sudden hush that fell from all those in attendance, as they gasped from the excitement of the moment, because they had already calculated that the next vote would decide the election.

"Quintoea! Quintoea!" His name was instantly broadcast throughout the Seventh Quadrant, and no matter what his decision, his name would forever be remembered as the citizen that changed his planets history. Every eye was on Quintoea as he walked up to the colorful crystal that had a hypnotic affect on those that gazed too long and deep into it.

"Quintoea, place your hand inside the crystal for analysis." Spoke Keeksonn.

The computer hesitated as if stumbled. "Lord Keeksonn, I am getting a discrepancy on officer Quintoea's reading. I must shut down to isolate the problem. The reading of officer Quintoea is indecisive, and is not to be relied upon or counted in this election." After a brief time elapsed the computer continued. "Lord Keeksonn, my system is now running at one hundred percent proficiency. The problem is attributable to a neuropathic disorder of council member Quintoea."

"Quintoea," spoke Lord Keeksonn, "because of this strange circumstance you are required to speak your candidate's name to each voting member. They will in turn repeat your answer so that there is no misunderstanding. Your answer will then be sealed and written in the crystal, and there recorded for all future generation to consider.

The name of Atar was spoken ten times by Quintoea and repeated by each of the council members. The computer responded. "Quintoea cast his vote for Atar," and then before the computer finished speaking, pandemonium commence breaking out across the planet.

Little did the members realize that the Floacre Mind Meld was just another foolish trick of Gemaal. He had merely bypassed the dreaded electroshock mechanism. The decision was contested by Gemaal because Quintoea, a relative of Atar, was responsible for the deciding vote and Gemaal felt that Quintoea's vote should thus not be counted.

Locked in his chamber, Gemaal was raging. "I was robbed. Atar, someday I will have my revenge on you and on that traitor Quintoea. Listen to me Atar! You will pay for stealing my position on the council."

No one was surprised when a few months later the Visual News Service of Ceylon reported:

**"QUINTOEA OUR RESPECTED AND HONORED MEMBER SERVING ON THE COUNCIL OF THE TWELVE WAS MURDERED BY AN UNKNOWN ASSASSIN."**

## CHAPTER 2

### ATAR GOVERNOR OF CEYLON

Ceylon had been the home of Atar, academy commander, for many generations, now it was governor Atar's desire that his son would move ahead in the academy and hopefully, replace him as Ceylon's governor.

Atar held this feeling in reserve, for he knew that his son was somewhat of a rebel, and the council only favored the youngest and most intelligent for advancement in the academy. It was deep-rooted in each cadet that allegiance to the council was paramount.

Atar reflected to himself, how Ral had always ranked near the top of his class and had been looked upon as a nominee for Star Fleet. Ral had recently been accepted into the Ceylonian academy, and Atar full of pride for his son, knew it was all possible due to his recent appointment as Ceylon's governor.

Atar was preoccupied, scrutinizing over the medals his son had accumulated. The trophies were proudly displayed in his den, with each accolade neatly encircling the large hologram picture of his son. Ral was the spitting image of his celebrated father, and his uniform dramatically did a lot to enhance that image. Every detail in Ral's picture appeared to be normal, but as Atar pondered over the picture, he placed his finger gently to his mouth. "The arrogance." That's what had been bothering Atar. He tapped his finger against his lip and repeated to himself, "it's the arrogance."

When Ral was a youth, he dared to be different, he thought not as the other young citizens of Ceylon. for them, sports was a game to be won at any cost, even at the expense of physical harm or death, but Ral seemed to enjoy the games, just for the pleasure of playing. "Although I can't recollect Ral ever losing a game," Atar thought even more intensely.

Atar remembered that Ral had studied Ceylonian history, but subject matter relating to the antiquity of old Ceylon had been censored by military leaders such as Dreeska, and even though the council had forbidden such idealism as possible insurrection, yet it had always held a certain fascination for Ral.

Ceylon's objective was to advance aspiring students toward higher degrees of scientific knowledge, but there was always a fear, if they ever failed in this regard, they could return to the conditions that lead to the fall of old Ceylon. The planet had achieved universal dominance, and no enemy had ever dared to challenge her military might, except for the pesky Kronos Empire, which offered limited opposition, this gave the Ceylonians more time to prosper socially by catering all education toward scientific and technical pursuits.

## RAL ATTENDS STAR FLEET ACADEMY

The academy looked very picturesque to Ral as he walked around the corner to the administration office. "I feel as if I am alive for the first time in my life, yes, matter of fact, I feel this may be my greatest day. I hope I do well with my entrance test, after all, if I am going to rise to great heights like father, I will have my work cut out for me. I can't believe father walked these very same halls." Ral was surprised to see a sports photo of his father prominently displayed on the wall. Ral filled with emotion, nervously began to wipe at his eye as if a speck of dust had blown in to it. It was then that Ral felt someone bump into him, the citizen seemed to be in a great hurry, then put out his hand to help Ral from the floor.

"Braka, is it really you?"

"Yes Ral."

"Well tell me my friend, what seems to be your big hurry?"

"Ral, I do not have time to speak with you, I am late for class, but I must ask you, how is your aunt Drekka? I have been on a training mission, and Ral, I really miss her. By the way, let me offer you my deepest apology."Are you hurt? "

Ral was silent as his mind reflected back to the times when Atar would assemble the family together. He especially remembered the wonderful times, when Braka would stop by to visit Drekka his father's sister.

"Ral, are you okay?" Ral was shocked back into reality.

"Yes, and I am also sorry Braka. Why don't you stop over this evening and visit? I will ask Drekka to attend but I will save the occasion as a surprise." That evening the young couple was able to reestablish their relationship, thanks to Ral's intervention.

Ral and Braka became room mates and began their training program. Time passed quickly, as the young cadets excelled in their studies, advancing to the next phase of academy training, and they were assigned unofficial rankings during this phase of instruction.

"Lt. Ral," spoke the instructor in his typical harsh voice. "You and Major Braka have passed your required examinations, but there is one more test, which will officially validate your acceptance into academy membership."

"Officer Peida, I am faithful to the academy and to the laws of Ceylon and if need be, will lay down my life. I also desire to excel in all my star fleet duties."

"Well said Officer Ral, and because you and Major Braka are in the top three percent of your class, tomorrow all these months of academy training will be put to the test. You greenhorns will be assigned aboard the starship Pnepe, and there you will be placed in combat situations. When you have your confirmed kills, then you will be officially classified, as star fleet officers. Congratulations on reaching this level of proficiency."

Peida showed a partiality toward Ral's training because Ral was the governor's son, and he also figured that he could possibly reap some future benefits.

The next morning, Braka began drilling his inexperienced crew in battlefield formations, and Ral appeared somewhat awed at the crew's respect for him. Braka could get productive work out of his junior officers, especially the females, who pranced about him like female birds, dancing for his favor. Braka commanded respect, but it was not brought about from fear, which was mandatory in the harsh academy training programs. Braka seemed to be a naturally gifted leader and Ral often felt that Braka reminded him of Atar, but he held too much respect for his father to admit that such feelings existed.

"Ral, assemble your crew," spoke Braka, "for this evening we are going to gain our acceptance into the academy."

"Tell me major," spoke Ral in a coy fashion, "do you plan to pay the enemy to walk up and surrender? With this inexperienced crew, we could never stand a chance against the Kronos females." Braka almost fell out of his seat laughing, it was another trait which Ral knew was different from the typical Ceylonian citizen.

"Where did Braka ever spawn from? He is so unlike the ordinary Ceylonians. He is kind, giving, generous and loving, and has demonstrated his fidelity toward father's sister." Ral waited on Braka to reply.

"Ral, later tonight the alliances from the Fourth Quadrant will be meeting, and while you were day dreaming about the days of old Ceylon, I was able with the help of the academy's computers to finally decipher the enemy's code. I was also able to determine the time and location of their rendezvous."

"Braka," Ral spoke with great concern, "have you given serious thought to this outlandish plot? Surely this is an undertaking for the advanced fleet. We have unskilled crew members, and our spaceship is not of the advanced design. The enemy you ask us to sacrifice our life for is not just one nation but the combined alliance. They will come down on us like fire and brimstone, Braka perhaps you should give this suicide plan a little more consideration."

"Ral, soon I will be part of your family and if I didn't think it was possible, I would not have accepted the assignment. Ral the enemy will be scattered throughout the various sectors before they finally rendezvous to discuss their options. You should have learned in your studies at the academy that the divided nations distrust each other, and if I am right each nation will not want to share its military plans, due to the fact that the plans may be stolen and the glory be internally divided."

"Tonight you will lead your squadron against the locations shown on the maps, when you see the arrival of the reserved team, then you will move against each of the isolated enemy positions."

Ral's heart was beating fast as his warship descended out of the belly of the Pnepe. Behind him followed four others in V-formation. Ral honed in on the enemy's position as he began to see their encampment lights. "How stupid can these primitives be? They party, and invite us to come down on them for destruction?"

Three of the enemy fighters appeared on Ral's left flank and he found himself completely engulfed in strong burst of light.

"It's an ambush!" Sweat profusely streamed down his face. "This is it! *I am* going to die! Father I wish I could have properly said good bye."

The night sky suddenly lit up like a festive holiday as it began blazing with the beauty of bursting lights, for the enemy were literally being blown from the sky. When Ral became composed, he looked over and saw Braka's warship approaching.

"You look a little peaked." Laughed Braka. "What do you say we head back and have a much needed drink of Tanger? I may be wrong young cousin, but did I just see you bend down and kiss your ass goodbye?"

"I will kill him with my bare hands. Braka, you piece of Ceylonian shit, you almost killed me and my entire crew." Growled Ral, as he journeyed back to the Pnepe.

By the time Ral found his way to the recreational room his nerves were beginning to settle down.

"Braka, am I wrong to assume that you used me as a decoy to draw the enemy into my position?"

"Ral during battle there are numerous chances that must be taken with the intention of accomplishing the mission. We were able to disrupt the activity of the enemy by deciphering their battle plans, and we confiscated not only two, but five of their starships for the academy's stockpile. That my little friend means that we will be promoted to major rankings in the academy."

"Braka, I realize you did what you thought was necessary, and I truly believe that you saved my life. I never imagined that I would be here talking with you or that I would ever see father again. Braka am I a coward? I froze in battle. I may have been responsible for the death of every soldier that joined with me in battle. Perhaps I should give notice before I am given academy positions I can never fulfill?"

"Ral every soldier needs an opportunity to prove himself. The commanders that go into battle just to kill and destroy have no ability to love. They kill to destroy the evil nature of their mind. Even in battle, you must have compassion for your enemy, just as you have compassion for your family. My answer is no, you are not a coward."

The academy recognized the talents of Major Braka and released him early from academy training in order to assign him to a Starfleet position, and he was free to marry Drekka. His male seed was preserved and stored by the academy as was the custom. It was the young couples desire that the name of Braka be perpetuated in the Ceylonian archives.

## RAL BEFRIENDS RAGAN

Ral had time, before he would be assigned further duty, so he signed up at the academy for additional credits. During this time, he would encounter Ragan, a fellow officer who would have a major impact on his entire military career.

The first evening at the academy, Ral decided to attend a scheduled musical program. He was surprised to see the auditorium filled with appreciative admirers, especially the young Ceylonian females, who eagerly waited for the feature act.

"Ragan! Ragan!" They began screaming, and after he came on stage and commence singing, Ral understood their enthusiasm, because he was also moved by the inspirational music of the young officer.

"This citizen undeniably has a lot to offer." Ral thought to himself. "I must meet him." This was to be the beginning of their early friendship, which found them almost inseparable.

Ragan was busy helping Ral study battle plan formations, he was also driving Ral crazy by looking out their window, singing into the Ceylonian skies. On the surface the two appeared to care for and respect each other. But Ragan was jealous, because Ral's father used his position as governor to favor his son. This infuriated Ragan who believed that he might be passed over by a lesser experienced officer. Ragan decided to keep his thoughts to himself, he needed to contemplate future plans for his military advancement, and for now, it couldn't hurt to maintain a friendly relationship with Ral.

The young officers received their orders and as they parted they made a solemn vow. "Friends forever".

The academy selected a lifetime partner for Ral, and soon they were able to settle down. The academy, within the appropriate time impregnated her with the seed tube, which contained his sperm.

The couple decided that if their newborn was a boy, he should be named Kiah, in honor of the young officer that had been killed by the giant Mokaz, during the surrender of the Zerena on the planet of Agreg.

## RAL DREAMS OF OLD CEYLON

Whenever time from his schedule allowed, Ral spent many leisure hours absorbing data found in the Academy Archives. When Ral approached the Visualization Chamber, a computerized voice requested, "subject, place, time." He responded, "Ancient Ceylonian History, Wars and Customs," as if he was guilty of some wrong doing. Immediately, he was living in virtual reality, intermingling with the primitive citizens of old Ceylon, as they went about the trials of daily life. When the program switched to the Ancient Wars of Ceylon, the visualization became so real that Ral found himself fighting side by side with the brave soldiers of old Ceylon. Ral's blood pulsated as he watched countless thousands die in the warfare. Then abruptly the program ended leaving Ral feeling somewhat despondent.

"This isn't real." He reasoned. "So why am I disheartened that I can never be part of it? Why am I so attracted to this barbaric madness?" Ral bemoaned the fact that he had never had the pleasure of what was known as Knuckle Battles in old Ceylon, a citizen to citizen confrontation. Ral was captivated with the idea of hand-to-hand combat and he whispered beneath his breath, "these were the true warriors, I wish I could have been there."

Modern day armies fought their battles with revolutionary technology. Lasers on starships had the potential to not only destroy enemy spacecraft, but mountains could be leveled to the ground as well. Even the hand lasers that were assigned to each soldier could destroy a number of the enemy in a specified radius, or render them completely defenseless.

Ral, realizing that it was closing time, said farewell to the curator, who looked suspiciously at the young officer, departing the room. Ral, filled with indecision and a multitude of unanswered questions, decided it would distress his father, if perhaps he revealed his feelings regarding old Ceylon, but he had nowhere else to turn.

Ral nervously spoke with his father, concerning his visit to the Academy Archives, as they relaxed in the family's holographic gardens. "Ral, I sternly advise that you are treading upon dangerous ground. I have been aware of your fascination for old Ceylonian history and I must admit, I have also delved into its past. It was truly compelling, but Ral, we are intricately intertwined with the future, there is no past, and you cannot go back. Be careful my son," Atar whispered, "the ideas you embrace could be subject to the council and its judgment."

## RAL'S ASSIGNMENT

Because of the astrological alignment of the planets, Atar governor of Ceylon, assembled the council members. "The Galaxy Exploratory Division has discovered a planet located in the outer region of our star system, this is unexplored territory and we must proceed with extreme caution. This planet is a rare find and may be our greatest discovery, it is also incredibly unique, because the land has been regenerated. It is abundant in trees and vegetation, and just as strange, land, sea and air creatures mysteriously inhabit the land. We must presume intelligence beyond the Seventh Quadrant may have regenerated the land and populated it with creatures from their zoological reserves. I will ask the academy to maintain surveillance to avoid a potential enemy encounter."

Atar colonized many of the habitable planets throughout the mid-range of quadrants and the majority had become successful beyond expectation. This colonization would be special, because the Feramas Project, so named by Atar to indicate that the regenerated land was still wild and untamed, would be given to Ral as his first colonization assignment.

## TEST SUBJECTS INTRODUCED ON THE FERAMAS

The Zorn planet had surrendered to Atar, desiring not to be annihilated by the mighty Ceylonians, and it was during the protocol of surrender that the Galaxy Exploratory Division stumbled upon a rare discovery, a male and female citizen, which they believed to be a treasured find. Atar had personally visited the Ceylonian museum and had examined the young couple. He especially admired the female, with the name of Repado, who they believed, was ready for child bearing. The academy determined that it was time to establish test subjects on the land, and the Zorn couple presently on display in the Ceylonian show case, would be the first to inhabit this unusual terrain on the Feramas. They were covertly taken to a remote region on the Feramas, and provided with instructions that would assure their survival until a temporary regent could be appointed.

# Ral, Space Colonizer

Before Ral could be appointed to take charge of a project, important as the Feramas, Atar realized his inexperienced son must prove himself to the council members, so he assigned Ral during the interim to command the Bracharian star base. During Ral's hiatus, Atar would keep his son informed of continuing development on the Feramas. Ral admired his father for discovering new colonies, and always dreamed of following in his footsteps as a space colonizer. He especially looked forward to his assignment, that would finally give him the chance to prove himself, not only to the council, but to his legendary father, whom he loved more than life.

The years passed slowly, and Ral bided his time. He had achieved extensive experience in commanding the hundreds of soldiers that were assigned to the star base, which was accordingly noted in the academy records

"Major Ral." Spoke the star base operations officer." The governor of Imperial Ceylon desires to speak with you. Sir, may I say? I have never conversed with anyone of such eminence, I am just about to shake out of my boots."

"Thank you for your comment officer, I will tell my father of your kind words."

The young officer must have been truly blessed, because he immediately returned to his work station, excitedly telling everyone that he had spoken with the most honored governor and that Ral was his son.

"Father, share with me some good news, when can I leave this lonely planetary system? I haven't seen Mylia and Kiah in what seems forever."

During the time his son was away, Atar had cared for Ral's family, but Mylia had become mentally unbalanced, and Atar was required to have her committed to Ceylon's mental institution. He did not reveal this information to Ral, not wanting to add any further trauma to his life, so far from home.

"I know you are apprehensive, but at the appropriate time, I will conclude your assignment and you will be fully commissioned to govern the affairs of the Feramas. But for now you will need to continue your training in an effort to please the council, and by the way, you must tell me whom you desire to appoint as your regent until you are ready to officially govern."

"I will give that serious thought father. I may be leaning toward Ragan my friend from the academy. I will get back to you in a few days concerning my decision."

"Ral take all the time you need, this could be one of the most important decisions you ever make in your military career, think long and hard my son. You must also give consideration to the fact that Ragan was born on Zylon. He is not a native citizen and the council may not look kindly to such an appointment."

When Atar was a young academy officer, he coerced the Zylonians into signing a declaration of peace, which had never been broken. Realizing they were not by nature a society bent toward war, the academy believed its interest would best be served, if they permitted Zylonian nobles to marry Ceylonian females. They were allowed to bear children under the same guidelines adhered to by Ceylonian aristocracy, and due to their Ceylonian genetics, their offspring were eligible for the Regeneration Process, thus extending their natural life-span. But for the Zylonians there was great regret, because they could never achieve the status of citizenship.

Ragan's father had worked his way through the ranks and had served as mayor of Zylon. Unfortunately, Ragan was conceived under the guidelines of this strict marital arrangement and not one day went by on Zylon that he did not curse the day he was born.
By the time Ragan reached young manhood the colonies on Zylon were predominately Ceylonian, which weighed heavily upon the mind of young Ragan.

"I possess the cells of the mighty Ceylonians, their blood pulsates through my veins. Why, after all these years of serfdom are my people still looked down upon, even by the lowest citizens of Ceylon?" This would be just one more piece of the injustice that would add to his hatred for the Ceylonians.

Ragan had never revealed this distain to Ral, who believed their friendship was based upon a bond that could never be broken. He was so blinded by their trust that he could not see the hate that raged within the heart of his friend.

Ral selected Ragan to be his regent in spite of his father's stern admonishment, that Ragan's slave status could possibly bring retribution from the council members. Ral remained adamant in his decision.

It would be the duty of Ragan to instruct the Zorn couple, not only in the laws and ways of the council, but also instill in them the appreciation of music. Yes, this would be taught to them by the master, Ragan the lord of music, who would soon enough arrive on the Feramas to become the provisional regent, while Ral remained temporarily on the Bracharian star base.

## RAGAN'S RAGE ON THE FERAMAS

Ragan journeyed through the cosmos, eventually reaching his destination sooner than expected. The creatures were startled by the deafening noise of the spacecraft, as it descended. The starship, energized by nuclear cells of Patriska, spit fire down on the planet, scorching everything within a circumference of a few miles. When the smoke had dissipated and the starship became silent, there could be seen the beautiful circling lights of red, gold, blue and amber, radiating from the outer rim of the command module.

When Ragan stepped on the brown soil of the Feramas, he was quickly overcome by the presence of a malicious force, so evil that it taunted his every action, and contended for possession of his mind. Ragan gave in to this diabolical manifestation of fear until he was completely possessed, losing all touch with reality. His eyes pierced deeply into the dark and gloomy Feramas skies, as if he was anticipating the arrival of Ral's starship.

"I am better than him! Screamed Ragan." Ragan shouted so loud into the heavens that the creatures by nature so tame, turned to run away, as if frightened by a thunder clap. Ragan hated Ral so much that his body began to violently shake. His fist were so rigid that the communicator he held in his hand shattered to pieces.

"The day will come that I will show Ral that I, Ragan, will not only rule the Feramas but the entire Seventh Quadrant and I will put on high what was once low. Yes, I will enslave the Ceylonians with all their pomp and superiority, they will pay for their injustice against Zylon."

The Zorn couple was never content dwelling on the strange planet but in time children were born unto them. The male citizen in discontentment, spent much of his idle time dreaming about friends and family he had left behind on Zorn. Eventually he just hopelessly gave up and stayed secluded and isolated from Rapado, the Zorn female and failed to further procreate.

The female of the Zorn Experiment was lovelier than any that ever graced the shores of Zylon, and then one evening, Ragan's melodic music captivated Rapado, and through his cunning he was able to seduce her.

The men of Zylon were notorious for their insatiable sexual desire, and the female in the proper time presented him with a male citizen. Ragan never laid claim to the child, he also did not admit to the birth of many other male and female offspring. If the council uncovered his folly, they would remove him to the tar pits that were monitored by the Agregleourite giants. The giants had gained such a reputation that many prisoners died by their own hand before ever reaching their destination.

Ragan's illicit offspring grew very evil, causing small clan wars to break out between the progeny of the original Zorn Couple and the offspring of Ragan.

Just before Ral completed his command on Bracharia, he began receiving reports that communications on the Feramas had ceased. Ragan had kept them uninformed by purposely destroying the starship's communication center.

Ral, long filled with suspicion, was forced to take action, by making his first journey high above the blue atmosphere of the Feramas, where with his second in command, a spiritual being by the name of Medoa, he viewed the disturbing disobedience in vivid detail.

"Ragan was personally selected by me, as my regent on the Feramas, Medoa, why didn't he keep the academy notified of these conditions?"

Medoa's voice thundered. "Why do you relentlessly ask me such questions, when the answers are so obvious?"

Ral's anger began to intensify. If this insurgence had been brought about by an adversary, perhaps he could understand, but his devoted friend from the academy, one that he had trusted with his life, had now risen up against him. The more Ral watched in disgust the more his anger would explode. Medoa walked over and placed his hand on Ral's shoulder and he became perfectly calm.

"I appreciate your special touch Medoa, my mind is now clear and I realize that such retribution as I am contemplating, will have to be brought to the attention of the academy."

Gigantic flames burst forth from under Ral's starship as he commanded Rogag, his bridge commander, to set coordinates to return to Ceylon.

## THE JOURNEY BACK TO CEYLON

While relaxing in his refreshing vapor bath, Ral seemed to pick up negative energy emanating from the Feramas. He realized that Ragan would not be much of a challenge, but for some strange reason, under the tranquilizing effects of the bath, his mind became flooded with stories, he had read of old Ceylon and of Unni, their god.

"I have read that the council had forbidden the citizens to worship Unni, but there must be more. They must have recognized a greater threat. Why did they fear him so? Could there be such a God out there beyond all distant quadrants?"

Ral had surreptitiously been a student of this early period of old Ceylon and was fascinated by their way of life, which was so diverse from his. The concept of a personal god superseding in the daily affairs of citizens, lay far beyond all imagination. Ral tried hard to understand his unorthodox thoughts, he had felt this positive force of good many times but did not want to associate it with such primitive superstitions.

"If Unni, the universal force of good actually exists, then Waki, the universal force of darkness, may consequently manifest a powerful negative influence throughout time and space. So if Ragan is under the influence of Waki," Ral struggled hard to reason, "then perhaps he should be left alone? For if positive and negative forces work together for good, to bring about the perfect balance of the cosmos, then Ragan may be needed on the Feramas to bring stability to these strong forces of energy? The council must never hear me speak of so much idealism, I could be compelled to walk into the molecular field to be destroyed. I absolutely must speak with Medoa concerning this matter."

Then Ral slithered under the refreshing sonic waves of his cosmic bath and dreamed of exciting battles of old Ceylon. "If only I could have been there," he whispered, "if only I could have been there," as he drifted off to sleep.

The next morning, Ral signaled for Medoa to join him for breakfast so he might discuss the troubling questions of the previous evening.

"Ral," Medoa spoke, "throughout your many generations colonization's have been highly successful, although none have risen to the scientific heights of Ceylon. Ral I sense within my spirit that you are greatly concerned, and you question if the Feramas Project is doomed now that Ragan has rebelled."

"Yes Medoa, but there are also other issues, please hear me out. In old Ceylon there was citizens that were loving and kind, but there were also thieves and murderers that dwelled among them. I recall that there were certain religious sects that boiled their children in wine, sacrificing them to their gods. The citizens who worshiped the Unni, forsook these heinous deeds, and practiced a life-style of good conduct. Wars still prevailed, but Medoa, the citizens that followed the Unni, sustained an inner peace even unto death. New Ceylon is a depressing planet, even our leisure time is carried out in holographic simulation chambers. Medoa, when I visit Ceylon the citizens never display the affections, reminiscent of what I have observed in the Ceylonian Reenactment Chambers. The citizens of Ceylon rarely speak, unless they require something for which they are lacking. What is missing Medoa? What am I searching for?"

"Listen carefully Ral. The citizens of old Ceylon displayed loving qualities but consider this. Old Ceylon and the Feramas are totally distinct and unique creations of the Unni. Old Ceylon was loved and blessed by the Unni until Dreeska shut out its glorious light, and without love the planet was destined for destruction."

"Ral, your comparison is correct, concerning the balance of positive and negative forces. They are essential in establishing exact relationships between good and evil. These forces are set in motion by the Unni, as he speaks, influencing nebula, star systems, planets, air, sea, water, creatures, and citizens in a continuous cycle of death and rebirth. Ral there is nothing that exists that is not governed by this variance of indestructible energy. If the axis of a planet alters by a few degrees the Unni will in given time, reverse the negative and reset the axis to its proper degree."

"Ral, if an asteroid hit Ceylon with all its destructive force would you believe that it was a planetary accident? I tell you that it was not by mishap, but that it was a necessary evil, set in motion by Unni. Even the hurricanes that run amuck and do their destruction on multitudes of planets are premeditated by his will to balance the negative and positive forces of his creation."

"Ragan is an instrument caught up in this constant struggle between these universal forces. Once hatred surfaced in his heart, he began to disrupt the perfect flow of energy, and unless he repents, the abundance of the negative influence will follow him into eternity separating him from the Unni's love. I know you cannot understand this deep concept but listen to me carefully. Ral, you are being lead by Unni to accomplish his great will, but take heed, the more you are influenced by his positive power the more you will find yourself under attack by the negative forces of evil."

"Ral just like old Ceylon, the Feramas is just as loved by our creator, so heed my prophecy. The Unni is even now altering the negative force that exerts its influence over the Feramas, and soon the Unni will stir you to send an ambassador to spark the fires of learning. The ambassador will accomplish this by teaching decency and morality, thereby enlightening the Feramas citizens in the ways of their creator. And even though his days shall be cut short, the envoy's seed shall bring forth a righteous leader that will bring them out of spiritual bondage, leading many into the glorious light of the Unni's love."

"Medoa I cannot allow myself to give credence to such ramblings. If I was to believe as you I could lose everything. I know there are things I do not understand, but the concepts you claim to be true, lie far beyond the scope of my imagination."

"Consider this Ral, the messengers that serve aboard this starship date back to the beginning of creation. We have journeyed through dimensions of time and space seeking to be of service to our creator, we are not as you. The physical entity that you see is not our true form. We are spirit and we will never die. Ral I pray that I have spoken just one thought that may increase the faith that lies sleeping within you."

"Thank you for your understanding Medoa," Ral responded somewhat puzzled, "you have given me much to think about."

## CHAPTER 3

### RAL'S HOMECOMING

That same evening, Ral had a perplexing dream concerning Mylia, the wife he left back on Ceylon. "Why is it that dreams are always so perplexing to me? It's as if they were trying to tell me some great meaning. I only know one thing," he thought to himself, "something traumatic is about to unfold in my life. Oh, I wish I could interpret the dream's meaning, yes I would give anything."

Ral ordered Rogag, his bridge commander, the very next morning to soar quickly back to Ceylon's portals. His curiosity was highly aroused about Unni, the Great Spirit. Ral wanted to converse with his father, and also to return to the archives and research early Ceylonian civilizations, to ascertain what Medoa had meant by his prior comments. Before Ral went to the archives, he would first present himself to his family, that he had not seen since making his long journey.

Atar could tell that his son was profoundly perplexed, as they strolled through the lush gardens, which were merely projected holograms. The singing of exotic birds, mixed with sounds of ocean breezes, resonated from the miniature speakers that were so small, they were invisible to the naked eye.

"What is troubling you my son?"

Ral again went through the entire thought process that he and Medoa had discussed the previous day, concerning the problems he was encountering on the Feramas.

"Ral, I have read accounts of the ancient days, but we are different in our nature. I cast vile and wickedness off as not befitting of modern civilization and when I was commander of the academy, there was nothing that could let all this negativity and wasted energy distract me. Ral, why is it, you always underestimate your ability to succeed? When you left Ceylon, you were at the head of your class, and for the duration of your early days at the academy, praises were spoken concerning the son of Atar."

"Ral, throughout the entire universe, there is nothing that you cannot triumph over. The stars by the myriads will reflect your glory. Yes Ral, I have heard of your failure thus far, but you will overcome, of this I am assured."

# Ral, Space Colonizer

"Ral abandon this foolish attempt to colonize the Feramas, any efforts in this cause could lead to a loss of credibility with the council. The philosophy of the messengers under the command of Medoa will lead to your destruction, Ral give it up before you fail. The concept of a benevolent god was contrived by the ancients to mislead the citizens into false hope. Old Ceylon needed an outside influence to believe in, they could not comprehend in their infancy that citizens have the inner power of mind to achieve anything they set their mind to accomplish."

"Their belief in the power of the Waki, answered to their satisfaction why the citizens were inclined toward evil, and the idea of the Unni answered to their liking, why things went well for them. Ral it is within you to make right and wrong choices and you must make the right choice concerning the Feramas Experiment."

"Father," Ral bemusedly shook his head, "your conversation has only influenced me to return to the Feramas, to try once again to look over the affairs of the planet. Forgive me father, but it's time for my chamber rest, which is much needed for my journey back."

Ral had not spoken to his son since returning home, and he had almost missed the opportunity, because his thoughts had been entirely upon his own problems. When Ral arrived at the governor's complex, those standing by were intently watching the Visual News which was presenting Ral's entrance into Ceylon's grand pavilion. Ral thought he appeared older on the gigantic screen than what his true age reflected.

"Perhaps I should give it up as father suggests. To be home with my family would be more than most citizens could ever dream of. The academy would surely offer more benefits than could ever be attained, traveling around the galaxies searching for new colonies to occupy."

David B Kingman

## RAL'S CONVERSATION WITH KIAH

As Kiah walked into the room, there was a coldness to his approach, moreover, he had not seen his father for more than 500 hundred C.S.T. (Ceylonian Star Time). Kiah was such a young child when Ral departed Ceylon that he barely remembered him, and he looked at his father with distain. Ral was cordial, but both citizen surmised, this may be their last time together. Ral remembered his previous conversation with Medoa, when they discussed the lack of emotions displayed by family members on Ceylon. He yearned to hold his son, but he knew this would never happen.

"Are you taking care of your mother, Kiah?"

"I would father, but she is dead. I believe shortly after your last departure from Bracharia."

Ral was physically shaken by the harsh words.

"Mylia is dead? Kiah, why didn't you tell me?"

"Why should I tell you father? So that you could return to state your affections? I can see you, weeping over her death capsule, to show the dignitaries how much you cared for her."

Ral could sense the bitterness in Kiah's voice, and kept his inner thoughts to himself. Ral knew no matter what he said that Kiah would defend his mother's memory, and he had not come back to Ceylon to argue with his son. He also realized that he must visit Malia's death capsule before his departure.

"Father, you are not the citizen I pictured." Kiah continued in an infuriated manner. "You do not have the spirit and fire that I had imagined, regarding your adventures. I thought you would be more like Atar, my grandfather. But you stand pompously before me, and can't even defend your thoughts concerning mother and me. Why don't you leave quickly, so I don't further mar my memory of Ral, Space Colonizer?"

They departed and Ral was shaking his head in disbelief. "I desired to return to my family these many years and now that I have I feel something inside me just died."

## RAL VISITS THE ARCHIVES

Ral jettisoned quickly to the Ceylonian Archive Center. He began to feel uneasy as those nearby looked upon his commander's uniform, that displayed his numerous medals of accommodation.

"What is he doing here?" They wondered. "He could stay at home and simply call, and one of the messengers would bring any requested documents."

In the seclusion of the Visualization Chamber Ral placed the disk in the metallic box, and watched picturesque displays of male and female citizens engaged in vulgar sexual behavior.

"They appear to be taking pleasure in this strange act, that stimulates their passion to blaze inside them. Look!" Ral whispered excitedly, "the citizens press their lips together, and cling tightly to each other in their sleep chamber. It seems they have an inner need for this type of relationship. We could never tolerate such disgusting things, what purpose could it serve?"

Ral asked the computer, "what is this emotion called?"

The words resounded in his headset. "It is a primitive form called love."

## RAL GRIEVES OVER MYLIA'S DEATH

That evening Ral abruptly awoke from a troubled sleep. He walked to the cafeteria and spoke, Pokar, and the dispenser began twirling, after being set to a high speed, the small diode lights soon began blinking indicating the beverage was prepared. The sounds of the dispenser had the affect of placing Ral into an almost hypnotic state of sleep. Ral barely heard Renna's voice as she softly spoke.

"Major Ral, I am required to remind you that before our departure, you desired to visit the outer Ceylonian tombs on Atra, all required paperwork has been submitted and accepted."

"Renna, I am still very sluggish, I can't seem to wake up." Ral spoke apologetically, still not completely recovered from his nightmare. Suddenly Ral's dream began to unfold.

"Ral became so excited that he shouted at Renna. "Renna, I remember now. The other day before I landed on Ceylon, I dreamed my wife, Mylia died." The dream rushed back into Ral's memory. "Oh yes," he recalled, "in my dream I saw Mylia sitting in a hospital chair and as the attendant pushed her closer and closer toward me, she was reaching for me pleading, help me, please help me. Then the dream shifted and I saw Mylia lying prone on a hard metal slab. Her body began descending into a warm solution of liquid in which she eventually became completely submerged. I remember thinking, that she is still alive, and will surely drown, but I did not have any in trepidation concerning her death. I just knew she was dead."

Ral felt his cold and uncaring attitude toward Mylia may somehow, reflect the same frigid feelings that Kiah had felt during their earlier conversation. Ral recalled the times when Mylia would accompany him to prominent social events. He never told her but he truly enjoyed the attention they received. "We did make a handsome couple. Why did I hide my feelings for Mylia?"

"She was always there when I needed her, she gave up everything to devote herself to Kiah, by making sure he received the compulsory training that would prepare his way into the academy. Yes, Mylia was constantly there alone, making things happen for the betterment of our family. I had always believed that if we had not married, we would have been the best of friends."

Ral had always been somewhat distant and cold toward his wife, but it never penetrated his mind, why he would also abandon his son. It was apparent that Ral believed Kiah would grow up and fail to remember, everything Mylia may have spoken against him. But suddenly he realized, that this would never happen, and he was deeply distressed. Ral, troubled over Mylia's death, set his mind to visit her on Atra's death colony, which was located just inside the Seventh Quadrant.

The flaming starship made its descent into the Atra loading zone. Ral, feeling somewhat pensive, gazed at the commotion as the dock workers prepared for the arrival of the high ranking academy officer. The first thing he noticed was the floating capsules holding the dead. Officers were situated in a more isolated location, and their capsules were aligned in rows of thousands reaching into the skies. The capsules of lower ranking officer's descended, until the last capsules were reached, which contained the wives of prominent politicians and high ranking academy officers. It took the capsules a few moments to arrive. Ral pushed the button and a computerized voice spoke, "name of deceased?"

"Mylia," he responded, "wife of Ral, planet of Ceylon."

"Breathe upon the glass for vapor identification." Spoke the computer. This was an outdated means of identification and Ral could not believe that the Colony on Atra would not have adapted genetic identification technology, which was now in common use. After Ral's breath pattern was approved, the small screen appeared and a hologram of Mylia appeared before him.

"My name is Mylia, born on the planet of Ceylon, which is located in the Seventh Quadrant. My parents were Doeka and Strika also from Ceylon. I am married to Ral, an officer in the academy, and we have one son, Kiah. Because of my mental condition, I spent the last few years of my life confined to a mental institution. Those were lonely days and I had many opportunities to reflect concerning the love I held for my family and my country."

The recorder ended and Ral placed his head in his hands, his anguish was just too much. "Mylia was incarcerated in a mental institution! She must have been so terrified before she died. Why didn't father let me know? If I only could have loved her." Ral kept repeating the words. "If only I could have loved her."

"Mylia I know you cannot hear me, unless that part of you still exists and remains, that was spoken of by the religious sects of old Ceylon. And now I ask your forgiveness, if not for your sake at least for mine. Mylia maybe I could accept your death, if I can somehow feel that you have forgiven me."

Ral was startled by the re-emergence of Mylia's image on the screen and the words she was speaking. "If I have ever offended any citizen during my life, I ask forgiveness. I do not desire to be buried with bitterness in my heart against any, and that includes the council, my son and my husband, whom I had loved during the years he desired to remain away from me. Ral if you are listening to my words, at least I have this opportunity to ask you to watch over our son. I must finish now, but remember, I forgive you Ral and I will always love you."

Ral began to tremble, and if it had been the custom for a citizen to cry, this would have been the time. He sighed deep within, repeating the following remorseful lamentation. "Forgive me dear wife, forgive me. Mylia was such a wonderful citizen." Ral watched as the image disappeared from the monitor.

"Prepare for capsule descent!" Sounded the computerized voice and the multitudes of death capsules began to move slowly upward and sideways, until eventually, Mylia's capsule appeared in front of a special linen backdrop. The scarlet and blue colors gave a royal appearance to the setting. Mylia looked as if she was the same youthful citizen that Ral had married so long ago. The Ceylonians had created a method of rejuvenating skin tissue and felt the age of fourteen thousand Ceylonian years to be the perfect age, setting it as the standard for the rejuvenation process.

The capsule was impregnable and once sealed, could never be opened. Preserving the dead was important to the Ceylonians, and a honor guard was ordered to spend continual watch over the death colony. This was a strange custom when compared to the idea that millions of lives were forfeited in the molecular field and their cremated remains were scattered into the far reaches of space.

Ral watched as Mylia's capsule began slowly to move back in perfect unison with the rest and then quickly soared to one of the higher locations without making a whisper.

The automated voice then thanked the visitor for taking the time to visit, and continued its message.

"There is only one entry concerning Mylia of the planet of Ceylon. She appears to have died of natural causes precipitated by her long bout with mental illness, along with a prolonged state of loneliness. She has had five visitors since her encapsulation."

"I wonder who they were? Perhaps Kiah and some of the academy officers and their wives."

Ral became mindful that he must depart to Ceylon, for he was required to say farewell to his father, before his journey back to the Feramas.

## PREPARATIONS TO LEAVE CEYLON

It would be a cordial farewell, as Atar made arrangements for Ral's departure, the reporters failed to show, because Ral had not returned a hero, and Atar did not desire to have Ral singled out for such foolishness as the Feramas Project.

Atar used his authority to appropriate the finest starship for Ral to command, and it was recommended that his crew be replaced with officers, experienced in updated starship navigation.

"Thank you Father, I know it was your influence that made all this possible, and I promise to keep you informed of my status on the Feramas." Atar never responded, but gently nodded his head in the affirmative.

Ral became excited, because the 6035 Tri-Star was highly publicized for featuring the most innovated transporter of it time. It was with intent, designed to dematerialize, transport and reassemble crew members within the range of a galaxy. Transporters of the past were responsible for many health issues that could occur during the transportation cycle, especially metaphysical psychosis.

"Ral," thundered the voice of Medoa, "in order for you to be assigned duty aboard this starship, there had to be experienced officers that were passed by. I have some good news for you, only an academy commander can be sanctioned to operate a starship of this magnitude. I have your certificate of promotion, signed by the governor, your father, and he wishes you well. Ral was in a state of shock, not believing that he had been promoted to Commander of the Academy. You truly are destined by the Unni, to be part of his great plan. Ral for now, just stay faithful to the laws of the council, and you will continue to be successful in all you seek to accomplish, but, every citizen must be tested and the Feramas may well be your ultimate test."

Ral, for the moment was awe struck as the mighty Tri-Star was passing planet after planet with unprecedented grace and speed. He knew it was a grave responsibility to be commander of the crew members whose lives were dependent on his navigational skills.

"Medoa, I would like to meet with each of my officers. We must not let our defenses down." Spoke Ral, almost apologetically. "Medoa, please instruct ensign Borkia to put together an extensive program, because I will soon test my officers in a simulation war game. Medoa please send Rogag to my chamber."

Medoa brought Rogag the Bridge Commander to Ral.

"I salute you Commander Ral, and it has been an honor to serve under the son of Atar."

"Please major, my objective with meeting my officers is to know each one personally, so that we may be able to work together, if perchance, battle should occur. Thank everyone for me Medoa, later I need to relax in my study to hone up on the workings of this complexity of a spacecraft. Also Medoa, don't forget to send Borkia to my quarters for his tutoring expertise will be of great benefit to me. The war games will take place in the morning at first light of the Krondor sun."

Rogag looked at Medoa with a puzzled look on his face. Medoa realized that Rogag had never encountered such a star fleet commander especially one that looked upon his crew with kindness. Rogag returned to the bridge scratching his head in disbelief.

Early that morning, as to be expected, Borkia sounded the sirens and the shrilling sounds echoed, piercing through the halls of the starship. His officers commanded their stations in accordance to Starfleet manuals, and the games went off as expected.

That evening Ral and Borkia held dinner for the officers, and Ral realized at that moment, that they were becoming very close friends. They spent hours during the evening, chatting about what could have gone wrong, and planning what alternatives they might have employed to overcome the enemy during the simulation war game.

Rogag gave the Tri-Star praise for its highly sophisticated computer system, and suggested that the results may not have been so predictable, if they had not relied so heavily upon the computer. Without it, perhaps the enemy may have had a slight chance.

Ral listened intently to the words of his bridge commander with keen interest.

"Ral contemplated. "What would have happened if we had encountered the enemy on their own ground? Yes a battle just like I experienced back in the archive of Visual Wars?" His blood became hot with anticipation as he rehashed the idea over and over.

Medoa gazed intently in Ral's direction. He had a sincere respect for the commander, and had vowed to protect and guide him until the day he would return to the spirit world of the Unni.

## RAL'S FIRST SPACE BATTLE

Unbeknown to Ral, Teegra the commander of the Kronos warship was watching the Tri-Star passing within a short distance of their command post.

"Bastards," shouted Teegra, "the bastards streak through the Kronos air space like they are gods that control even the air we breathe. It is time we give the Ceylonians a taste of the space crap they has been feeding us these long many years."

Atar had long been respected by the Kronos, but he was only so honored, because of the iron-clad rule that he maintained in controlling his galactic enemy. The Kronos were infamous for their persistent insurrections and inhuman behavior, which had long been a thorn in the side of the Ceylonians.

"I have heard," exclaimed Teegra, "that Ral, Atar's son, has been assigned one of the more recent academy starships, surely this is he. Ral is young and inexperienced in warfare and this may be our chance to pay back the Ceylonian injustice."

"Aha, I have figured out the young commander's routine, the latest Ceylonian warships are so fast, they are required to dock occasionally to energize their nuclear pods and to permit their crew to refresh themselves on the planets of leisure. I also discern that by the waning light of the Kronos moons, that Ral will be susceptible to our swift attack. And perhaps if we catch him unaware, we may conceivably, claim the starship for our glorious homeland." Teegra sat back in his plush commander's chair, with an air of satisfaction on his face. "Engineer start engaging the cloaking shields to conceal us till the appointed time."
"Cloaking shields in place." Replied his officer.
"Rest now my warriors", spoke Teegra, "for soon the tenth hour will be your redemption from our hated adversary."

"Shields up, fire!" screamed Teegra. "Ral and his young crew have been caught with their pants down. They drank their fill of fermented Tanger and have now fallen asleep. What fools these Ceylonians?" Teegra was excited, beyond all his expectations. "This will be Ral's folly as if the Feramas wasn't a big enough spectacle."
The Kronos commander was correct in his summation that his enemy may have been caught somewhat unprepared but Ral was unconcerned, knowing full well that the Kronos had no idea of the awesome power, he could unleash upon the inferior vessel that had come against him.
Ral froze in his tracks, crying out in anticipation. "This is my opportunity to see what it would be like to have a one-on-one fight, just the way they took place on old Ceylon's battle fields. The Tri-Star's shields cannot be penetrated. Renna unlock all force fields and reduce all weaponry that would make us superior to the Kronos, we will fight them on their own terms as an equal."
The officers were aghast. "Commander Ral, you can not do this illogical act. We have vowed to protect this crew and vessel with our lives, and you desire to go contrary to the laws and leave this entire ship open to danger?"
Medoa came quickly to Ral's defense. "Commander Ral has authority to command this starship in any manner he chooses as long as he accomplishes his mission. You officers are in jeopardy of

insurrection. If there is a problem with the commander, you have the right to file a protest with the council upon your return to Ceylon."

The Tri-Star took a direct hit which rocked the ship and the crew just as in the simulation war games, manned their post with the utmost precision, and as Ral gave orders to return fire for fire upon the feeble Kronos spaceship his eyes widened with delight.

"What a feeling," shouted Ral, "what a sensation! I feel like I am alive for the first time in my life. If only father could have shared my exhilarating experience, then perhaps, he may understand what I have been trying to say. Oh yes," Ral remembered, "because of Borkia's wonderful job in training the crew, I will have Medoa to submit a request for his promotion to captain.

The morning came, and the Kronos vessel crippled back to its home base. After all, Ral who was not a hardened warrior had no desire to destroy Teegra, his mind and mission was on the Feramas. The battle had been won and Ral felt somehow that he should have an award to display on the wall of Atar's trophy room. The battle was relived over and over in his mind, as the Tri-Star ripped through the solar heavens looking more like a flaming comet.

Ral had Rogag, his bridge commander, to set course for the Feramas, with the commander proudly at the helm, still boasting about the victory, he had won over the foolish Kronos commander. Yet Ral felt this may not be their last encounter.

## RAL APPROACHES THE FERAMAS

50 C.S.T., (Ceylonian Star Time) had passed since Ral's last departure from the Feramas and he was anxious to return. Ral reasoned, the Zorn couple by this time, would have had sufficient opportunity to fill the land with productive offspring. Ral could not forget his last hasty departure, and the more his thoughts tarried on the failure carried out under the leadership of Ragan, the fire once more began to rage as he ordered Rogag, full speed ahead.

The atmosphere above the Feramas was misty as Ral gave orders to send out visual scans from high above the brown planet. A mist had gone up continually, long before it was first discovered, and in the proper course of time, the moisture that had accumulated in the atmosphere, would without question, burst in a thunderous explosion. This phenomenon was not unique to only the Feramas, but any planet at this particular phase of its development. The time of the Feramas deluge could be accurately ascertained with complex calculations.

Ral aware of the total devastation that could be unleashed upon the inhabitants, realized that at some point in time, it would be imperative that he return and intercede for their protection.

"Commander Ral there is a message from your father and it sounds extremely urgent." Spoke Renna in a serious but automated tone. Ral responded slowly, because his mind was caught up with the challenge of intervening in the affairs of the Feramas.

"Commander Ral, please answer, priority mess...." Ral cut Renna off before she finished the sentence.

"Renna, lock all security codes, and screen the following communication."

"Your orders will be carried out as requested." Softly spoke Renna.

Ral and Atar spoke for a long period of time and everyone realized something serious was in the air, when they observed Ral's state of mind. When the two citizens concluded their conversation, Ral slowly walked to the ship's public address system.

"Attention! Attention! Have all senior officers report to the main deck at the third hour," spoke Ral despondently.

The time passed by swiftly and the officers all gathered round. Anticipation was in the air, and then Ral entered the room, which became extremely quiet.

"Fellow citizens, my father, the governor of Ceylon has informed me of a change in our mission. The Venduras colonies located in the sixth quadrant has revolted and is at this very moment waging war against, not just its neighbors, but against the Imperial Fleet. You know my feelings concerning the Feramas Project, and I would give anything to continue my present mission," Ral spoke disparagingly as if he had just lost a dear friend in death, "but I must be faithful to my country and my father, and most certainly, we will depart for the Venduras with the arrival of the Feramas sunrise."

"Captain Borkia, I have talked with my father concerning your training ability, and he has sealed orders for you to remain on the Feramas in my place. He agrees with me that only a citizen with your unique abilities to teach and educate the masses could carry out such a demanding task. Borkia as much as I need your services on the Tri-Star, I must think about the survival of the Feramas citizens.

That is why I have confirmed my decision to send you, so until I return from the Venduras, you will have full authority to teach the Ceylonian Law Codes to my people."

"I have arranged for your immediate departure in the early morning, but listen closely my friend, for there is conditions taking place on the Feramas that could pose a threat to your safety and you will be away from the academy's protective care for an unspecified period of time. It is also reported that Ragan is becoming more and more of a threat in his quest to rule over the land."

"Borkia we have monitored the activities on the Feramas and have ascertained, there is a clan of citizens that oppose Ragan and his wicked hoards. They are called the sons of enlightenment, dating their ancestry back to a prophet called Chaldoc. It is also reported that Ragan has begun murdering the prophets of this clan. If you align yourself with the brotherhood of these pious citizens, they may be able to protect you from those that are in opposition to them, a clan called the The Sons of Darkness."

"Borkia, the academy informs me that it could be years before I can return to join you, but for now my friend, your services are extremely essential to the development of the colonies."

The morning came much too soon as Ral, who was feeling a bit melancholy, began making plans for Borkia's departure to the Feramas. Ral's thoughts weighed heavily upon his mind.

"Since the day he rose up against me, I have calculated my retribution against Ragan and it has consumed my every thought. Kiah my own son has forsaken me and now Borkia my best friend has been taken from me. I have sentenced him to defend for himself in a hostile environment against the machinations of Ragan. I feel if I don't soon get away that my head will burst asunder. Medoa page Borkia to the bridge."

Borkia arrived with all his survival gear in hand.

"Captain Borkia reporting as ordered sir."

"Borkia I have prepared a list of items that can only be requisitioned through higher channels. I will not leave you totally defenseless against the wiles of the enemy. All supplies will be transported to you when you are safely established on the Feramas."

## CHAPTER 4

### BORKIA ON THE FERAMAS

Ral watched as Borkia eagerly stepped onto the transporter pad. Borkia, as well as numerous other officers that had experienced this mode of travel, felt a little trepidation, that either the transporter might not properly work, or else when they materialized they might wind up imbedded in side of a mountain, regardless it had happened before. But he had the satisfaction of knowing that this transporter was of the latest design, and that the academy records reflected not one single accident.

Borkia began twirling at a high rate of speed and quickly disappeared, as Ral wondered if he would ever see his friend again. Ral bowed his head and spoke to Rogag. "Set course at warp speed to destination, the Venduras colonies."

Ral looked back toward the Feramas as the Tri-Star soared through the heavens.

"I have not forgotten you Ragan. Bide your time till I return for that day will be with my entire wrath, and the day of my return shall be a day to be remembered throughout your generations."

Borkia found himself somewhere on the Feramas surrounded in vegetation and immense trees. The air was extremely humid and Borkia's first considerations was that he was lost. It was a strange sensation for Borkia, because on Ceylon, trees and green plant life were artificially created and the closest thing he could compare it to was hologram visuals that gave the sensation that you were actually there. But this planet was different, he could pick the fruit off the trees, smelling and tasting them. Even the air had a clean refreshing smell and a nearby brook, when touched, offered an invigorating refreshing to the body.

"If only Ceylon was as energizing as this." He exclaimed. "This is wonderful, it makes me feel as if I am alive."

Then the sound of talking was heard in the distance and Borkia made haste to the nearest hiding place. After all he was an alien in this land, and the academy's mission was his first priority.

"Majia," Borkia heard someone call.

"Yes father," she replied.

"Gather more sticks for the fire, the meeting is just about to begin." Spoke her father in a humble and gentle way.

As the maiden approached the hiding place of Borkia, he was suddenly taken aback. There in front of him was the loveliest young female his eyes had ever beheld. He backed off gently into the brush so as not to be observed. The maiden returned to her father and performed some local ritual, which was unknown to Borkia. He could not take his eyes off the maiden as he watched through the entire early morning hours until the meeting was concluded.

Keeping secluded Borkia made detailed notes describing the assembly of fifty men as they offered animal sacrifices to their deity. The maiden's father, Zehon, appeared to be a priest or some kind of a prophet.

"Majia," spoke her father, "soon we must make plans to select for you a companion from among our people."

"Please father! I have dedicated myself to Rhadda, the Great Spirit, and my life is to serve here with you. I need no male citizen, but rather, I choose the life of a priestess."

Dorkea arose. "Fellow citizens of this righteous assembly we must be careful, for our enemy walks among us disguised in sheep's clothing. Why! He could be here now masquerading as one of the sons of Chaldoc."

"Aha." Silently spoke Borkia to himself. "So these are the Sons of Chaldoc that Ral mentioned."

The brush suddenly became alive as enemy warriors began infiltrating the Chaldocian camp. Those that resisted their advances were knocked to the ground and beaten.

"I will teach you religious fools that you cannot defy our laws which warn against such religious assemblage." Spoke one of the intruders.

"Gather them together," cried out Brugula, "we will march them to our encampment, and by the time their journey ends, there won't be many of them left, and they will wonder why their god has forsaken them."

Borkia was trying to collect his thoughts in order to see what course of action to take when suddenly he heard a scream. One of the men called Victar, had taken the young maiden, and began dragging her deep into the thicket. Majia screamed as the barbarian began ripping off her sheepskin clothing.

"No! No! My body is dedicated to Rhadda. I have taken a vow of chastity." Begged Majia.

Her persecutor never tried to muffle her cries, for there was no one among the Chaldocian that dared stand against him. He stood tall above the unclothed female citizen and as he stood removing his warrior's robe, he anxiously began mounting the young maiden. The cries of her father was heard in the distance. "Oh great Rhadda, help my daughter in this our darkest hour."

The barbarian, due to his awkward position, was taken by surprise when Borkia who was a hardened veteran of many conflicts picked him up by the hair of the head and threw him into the brush. When the barbarian landed, there was a sudden thud, like the sound of a ripened melon bursting open and Borkia didn't have to look to know that the enemy's head had just exploded against a rock.

Borkia was awed at the presence of the lovely maiden, as she lay naked on the very spot her abductor had left her. Her long hair, that was ruffled from the attack, lay gently across her breast. Borkia gazed intently at the maiden taking a long silent look.

"Kill me," screamed Majia, "you killed to have your way with me. Kill me now you barbarian pig, then you can do with me as you will, at least my soul will be free and pure."

"Victar where are you?" Before Borkia could comprehend where the sound was coming from, he looked around and found he was surrounded.

"Well, what is this?" Exclaimed Tonkor, their leader, as he walked over and kicked the lifeless body of Victar. When the body rolled over his brain was exposed, the gray matter oozed down the rock and streamed into a small puddle on the ground. At this point, time seemed to stand still. The intruders spent their moments gazing at the nude body of Majia and the citizen dressed in the immaculate white uniform. Suddenly swords were drawn.

"You imbecile, you will die your death a thousand times."

Majia started to scream as the warriors raised their swords to charge.

Twenty barbarians instantaneously lay dead on the ground, and Majia shocked back into reality, walked over to Borkia, who remained stalwart in his defensive position.

"Are you our God?" She asked. Borkia never responded as the maiden began wrapping her garments around her, and began to bow in reverence to her liberator. She then accidentally touched the lazier, which was still extremely hot from being fired so many times in succession.

"Oh!" She loudly cried out as she slipped and stumbled against him. Borkia quickly caught her and drew her into his arms and there was a fire that lit inside that he had never felt before.

"Are you a God?" She asked again. "Our fathers have been telling us that one day Rhadda, the Great Spirit, would come down to us from out of the sky, that he would deliver us from the hands of our oppressors."

"You are partly right," spoke Borkia, "it is Majia? Is that your name?"

"Yes." Majia quietly spoke.

"I did travel here from a land far out in distant space but I am not a god. I am a representative sent down to teach the citizens of your colonies how to live properly in observing the laws of my country."

"Sir, for some strange reason, I feel safe in your presence and although you speak strange and illogical words, I would like to invite you to join with my people. We will sit with you and try to reason out these strange new laws you speak about."

"Majia, oh Majia, your safe." Spoke Zehon, as they entered the camp.

"Father this is Borkia, a distant traveler. He saved me from the Hunsha. I must confess Father, I am no longer worthy to be a priestess for Victar the Hunsha attacked me and has violated my virginity. This stranger saved my life and I ask that we treat him as one of our own, for the duration of his stay with us."

"Yes, yes, young man, thank you for saving my daughter. Now come, sit at our fire and tell us from where you came and the purpose of your journey."

Borkia began that evening to teach the law codes of Ceylon to the citizens on the Feramas.

The word quickly spread to Ragan's headquarters.

"Who is this intruder that has entered my domain?" Ragan spoke angrily as he paced back and forth.

"He tells the citizens that he is from another colony far out in distant space." Spoke one of his men.

"Describe to me his uniform." Thundered Ragan.

Before finishing his description Ragan cut him off.

"He is a Ceylonian officer sent to counteract my activities, he shall not prevail, not in my world. Five hundred rubies to any of my warriors that bring his head back to me on a pole."

The henchmen began running around in circles.

"Five hundred rubies, the pig is as good as dead." They begin to cry out.

"Borkia, please wake up." Majia shouted as she shook him from his sleep. "The black force has put a contract out on you, five hundred rubies to the man they say that kills you."

"Majia," Borkia placed his strong hands on her shoulder, sternly looking into her eyes. "Put the word out that the Ceylonian warrior offers 1000 rubies to the man that kills the black force."

"Where will you get that kind of wealth?"

"If you have such wonderful faith in your god Majia, then try to have a little faith in me, for I have learned great knowledge in my country, which I can use to help advance the Feramas to great heights."

"I believe in you Borkia." Majia took Borkia by the arm and walked with him all the way to the camp. Her father, Zehon the priest, realized that his daughter was slowly falling in love.

Borkia, advanced the children of light to great heights, and Majia, now free from her vow of chastity, married Borkia according to the local custom. Many nights they sat together under the large shade trees, where he would tell her stories of his home on Ceylon.

"Majia, I can't wait until I can take you aboard the starship and show you the boundless wonders of the heavens." Spoke Borkia as they lay looking up into the billowy vastness of the Feramas sky.

"Yes Borkia, I would love to travel there to visit your home and meet with your family. Would they accept me? I would be so afraid. Borkia now that we are alone, I have something to confess to you."

"Tell me mama, what is this deep dark secret?"

"Oh Borkia!, I don't know how you are able to do it, but you always seem to know what I am thinking. Well anyway, you are going to be a father."

"I thought so", said Borkia, "and that is truly wonderful."

"He will be our first born," Majia smiled as she continued expressing her thoughts, "which means he must be presented to the chief priest, to live a life of servitude to the Rhadda. We must also provide for him a name that is pleasing to the creator, something that shows humility. Boeski, how does that name sound Borkia?"

"Very nice Majia. By the way, what is the meaning of the name?"

Majia quickly replied, "One that is born out of poverty. "I feel this to be a humble name."

"Yes Majia, I agree." Spoke Borkia as he gently smiled at his wife.

## THE DEATH OF BORKIA

The birth of the child was truly a blessing not only for the young couple but the entire clan felt like this little one belonged to them. There was just something compelling about the newborn's demeanor. His countenance and radiance told everyone that their child was born for some great purpose.

Then, five years after the birth of Boeski, Borkia journeyed to out-of-the-way encampments to teach the Children of Chaldoc concerning the great laws of Ceylon. Borkia failed to return home and many long days they diligently searched, but he was no where to be found. Zehon gathered together the shaman from the various tribes and they united their spiritual powers. When they finished their meditation they began dropping sticks, and as the sticks fell they pointed in this direction and then that direction, until eventually the shaman were standing at the top of a great ravine. Suddenly the head priest stopped.

"Here! The presence of Borkia is in our midst but I am receiving troubling messages." The head priest then bent down and began to write in the sand with a stick.

"I am not understanding these strange symbols and what message they imply, but I feel evil vibrations all around us."

"Look!" One of them cried out. "There is something over there."

Zehon walked down the hill, and there under the brush he saw the form of Borkia's body. At first glance it appeared to be the result of an accident. Zehon had surmised that Borkia had and fallen into the ravine, but the shaman knew when the smoke from the fire burned black into the heavens an evil presence was responsible for Borkia's death.

## THE PROPHET, SON OF BORKIA

"Boeski, where are you?"

"I am here mother, you shouldn't worry about me. Don't you know that I am doing the work that Rhadda called me to do?"

""Yes, I know Boeski, and your father would have been very proud of you."

"Tell me something mother, father was not a member of the Chaldocians was he?"

"No, Boeski, he was not a believer in the Rhadda. It has been twenty years since your father died, and now that you have risen to great heights in the priesthood, I feel it is time for you to know the truth concerning your father."

When Majia finished telling the story of her encounter with Borkia, Boeski feigned to be dumbfounded.

"Mother, you are telling me that father came from another world? That is blasphemous." Boeski cried out. "Mother, the creator that made us dwells in the heavens and you are trying to tell me that my father, was some kind of a god? Mother, I understand that father was intelligent and very scientific minded, but Zeradin the sage that travels through this land is also wise in all things. Mother, Zeradin has taught me the deep things of Rhadda, and I could never hold a light to the vast knowledge that he holds concerning universal truths and the telling of stars. Mother, I know the earliest records tell of gods that were space travelers, who came down and intervened in the affairs of the citizens, but these were myths handed down from our ancestors to appease the small ones with interesting folklore."

"Boeski your father was the most honest citizen I have ever met. I did not question him then , nor do I now."

"Go on Mother, I will listen to you because you have never lied to me, and I feel you truly believe what you are saying."

"Boeski, your father loved you, without question, and he would have been so proud that you have become one of the most respected citizens throughout the Feramas. I know he would have enjoyed sharing his vast knowledge of the universe with you."

"Mother, I am honored that you and the esteemed leaders have such confidence in me, but I can do nothing on my own. All power is given to me by Rhadda and it is to him all praise and honor is due. Mother, I am still waiting for you to share the information with me concerning father. Please I am interested in what you have to say, perhaps my spiritual eyes will be opened, if I stop listening with my mind and begin to listen with my heart."

"Boeski, your father often spoke of his friend Ral, who is commander of a starship, at least that is what he called it. He also stated that his commander friend was off on an extended journey though the heavens and that he was to return for him. Boeski, father yearned to take us aboard the starship and show us the complexities of the heavens. He was going to take us to visit his home on a planet called Ceylon, a distant land somewhere far beyond the stars."

"Mother don't speak of this any further, for it is time for your rest, and we will speak of these things another day. Rest for now dear mother."

"You too my precious son."

Zeradin the prophet had already revealed the information concerning Borkia to Boeski, shortly before he was anointed as a prophet and Boeski at that time was afraid to confront his frail aging mother, believing it best to keep the information to himself. Boeski had also encountered the old books of his father from which Borkia had taught the ancient law codes of Ceylon. Boeski had chosen not to believe the foolish hearsay concerning his father's connection as a spaceman. Boeski's greatest displeasure was that his father's laws were completely contrary to the holy laws that the great spirit had handed down to Chaldoc on Zidio, the sacred hill.

Majia, was determined to convince Boeski of his father's love, and Boeski felt obliged to indulge his mother as the sun began setting in the sky.

"Ok mother," let us reason together. Father could have arrived from a sector on the Feramas that was not familiar to me or to any of the members of the priesthood. You told me that you never saw the spaceship, isn't that true? So what you believe to be true is taken from father's conversations. Please mother, you must know that I am right."

"Boeski, if your father had not died so violently at the hands of paid assassins, and if you had gotten to know your father and loved him as I do, then perhaps you would understand. To you he's just a fleeting thought, but to me his widow, he lives on in my heart and mind. Boeski, these past twenty years the priesthood has been your father. Oh Boeski, if you could have known him."

"Goodnight mother." Boeski reached down and kissed the forehead of his mother, whom appeared older than her true age. For after Borkia's death, she lost the desire to continue on in life without him. Boeski stroked his mother's hair and just as she fell asleep, he whispered, "I love you mother, I love you."

Majia lived only a few days, and the name of her husband was upon her lips as she spoke these last words: "You will see your father again my son." Boeski assumed she met in the spirit realm of the Rhadda.

"Yes mother, we'll also meet again."

"No Boeski!" Before she finished speaking she was dead. Boeski with all the strength that was within him, reached down and picked her up high above his head and cried out a primeval scream that came from deep inside his inner soul.

"Rhadda, bring her back to me!"

The clouds began to move across the heavens, and thunder that started from a gentle roar, became the most frightening sound ever to be heard on the Feramas. Then, just as sudden as the thunder occurred, the sun shine appeared through the darkened clouds, and a colorful rainbow arched across the sky. Suddenly there was a calm and peace that Boeski had never felt before, and he took this as a sign that his mother was at peace, and he buried her beside Borkia, somewhere in the pleasant land of the Feramas.

Today, after many generations, Boeski the prophet walks the land, always with a look of sadness on his face. After all, he had by far outlived all of his contemporaries on the Feramas. Boeski had finally become accustomed to watching each succeeding generation die out and a new one begin. For some unexplained reason, Boeski the prophet, the seed of a Ceylonian officer, could not die. In fact, most of the citizenship believed the prophet to be a god, but Boeski adamantly denied their foolish assumptions, telling them that he was the voice of a greater prophet that would someday come and walk among his brethren.

David B Kingman

## RAL RETURNS TO THE FERAMAS

Ral once again entered the Feramas skies and his heart was beating so heavy that he thought he might need a pill to calm down, realizing many changes would have taken place throughout the land. Ral, deservedly received recognition from the academy for his many accomplishments during the Venduras Campaign, but he had never forgotten about the Feramas and its citizens. Ral retired to his rest chamber and after drinking intoxicating drinks of Tanger, he fell into a deep sleep and a troublesome dream began to unfold.

In the dream, Ragan was entertaining the lovely females of Zylon, while Ral, inebriated, was dancing with one of the Zylonian females. He suddenly spun her around for the unveiling of her mask, when confronting him was the face of death. Ral's dream continued as if everything was normal and to be expected, he even continued to dance with death's lady, until the music stopped, and he waited eagerly for the anticipated kiss.

When their lips met, Ral suddenly awakened in a sweat, he did not need an interpreter to reveal the dreams hidden meaning, and became aware that he was greatly troubled concerning the fate of his friend Borkia, whom he had left behind to defend for himself on the Feramas.

Medoa gazed intently, as the computer scanned the activity taking place on the Feramas.

"Ral, conditions have not improved, because evil continues throughout the Feramas, and Ragan's control is stronger than ever. This convinces me that Borkia was not successful in his endeavor to spread the laws of Ceylon, and I would surmise that Borkia perhaps, did not survive."

"Medoa, I will totally destroy the Feramas and its inhabitants, take Simka and Treeka and speak with these rebellious citizens, tell them, that they have been sentenced to be exterminated due to their open rebellion."

"Commander, the messengers will carry out your words as you have ordered. I only ask that you listen closely to what I have to say. It is true that Ragan has turned many from the laws of Ceylon, but you are also treading on dangerous ground. I know you believe that you're right, but you are not god! Do you remember when Atar proclaimed that the Feramas was already regenerated, and that land, air and sea creatures, strangely inhabited the land? Commander, it all came into existence by the Unni's creative power. He regenerated the land, not you. And if you had not compelled slaves to populate the Feramas, the Unni would have inevitably created citizens in his own image and placed them on the land, but he would have done so in his own predetermined time."

"Ral, because you are not yet a believer in the Unni, many of your transgressions may be overlooked, but the Unni has been drawing you to him, and I believe you have felt his presence. You may not understand, but the Unni will soon begin to unfold his plan for your life."

"Ral, not all citizens on the Feramas are evil, there is a remnant that honors the Unni's laws and do not hearken to the voice of evil, will you destroy them also? If you annihilate all flesh, your project will become a failure. I know your true feelings for these colonies, and I feel your displeasure at their disobedience. If you are determined to destroy all flesh, do this one thing in the name of our friendship, preserve the citizens that has upheld the laws and kept truth alive." Medoa was speaking concerning the Sons of Chaldoc.

Ral placed his hands to his head as if he was confused. He had always had complete confidence in Medoa's decisions, but his rage lessened when Medoa walked over and placed his strong hand on his shoulder.

"You are always able to do that to me Medoa, I may not agree with you, but I will place the assignment in your hand."

"Commander," spoke Medoa, "you have taken the death of your friend very hard, and you will come to accept the reality of it in time, but for now the Unni has need of your strength."

The Gyro-craft descended from the bowels of the Tri-Star, appearing as a whirlwind coming out of the clouds, as an awesome fire infolded itself, with glorious brilliant colors of amber, blue and green. The messengers wore metallic uniforms which sparkled, each one the color of burnished brass. The messengers lay side by side in a prone position across the horizontal bar of the Gyro-craft. Simka and Treeka, consorts of Medoa, enjoyed these rare excursions, their spirit craved freedom, and to be out in the open expanse away from the Tri-Star, was indeed an additional blessing.

Boeski felt he had seen as much as any citizen in his long tenure on the Feramas, but he was totally shocked to see the flaming chariot soaring down from out of the sky.

Simka saw the prophet bathing beside a brook. The Gyro-craft circled the naked holy man and then, Simka reached down and grabbed Boeski by the hair of his head as the Gyro-craft soared high above the ground with Boeski screaming at the top of his lungs.

"Help me! Put me down!" The prophet felt like an eagle flying high above his lofty perch, and as he looked down at the land and water below him, he was about to gain a little composure in his flight, until he remembered, he was nude as the eagle's behind. By the time he shrieked out his loudest, "put me down!" The Gyro-craft landed gently on the side of a hill, where Medoa exited the craft and walked over to Boeski. The prophet began trembling so hysterically he could barely compose himself. Medoa then, as was his custom, placed his hand upon Boeski's shoulder and said, "Be calm," and Boeski became completely relaxed.

"Prophet, great destruction in a little while, is about to be unleashed upon the citizens of this land, for their iniquity is out of control, and you have only a brief time to gather your followers and save them from the imminent destruction."

If Boeski had any doubts about the great spirit, they were dispelled that day, because he recognized that these beings truly were sent by the Rhadda. It took Boeski a few days to make his way back to his people, and although he was very tired, that evening, he began spreading the calamitous message of Medoa to his followers. Many of the Chaldocians could not fathom the strange message of Boeski, and the non-believers as expected, jeered him and tried to impede his plans. It wasn't long until the appointed time was nigh upon them.

"Children of Chaldoc, Boeski cried out, "it is now time to flee into the Rhadda's Ark of Safety, before we perish in this great destruction."

The message spread quickly throughout the Feramas and Ragan was beside himself and boasting, "what destruction? There is no invisible god that is going to destroy my domain. Tell the dim-witted citizens to worship me and I will protect them from their day of wrath."

Ragan was speaking under his breath, for he knew that this threat could only come from Ral, and Ragan realizing the danger at hand, secretly began making plans to relocate to a highly secret and remote sector of the land.

## THE CHALDOCIANS ABOARD THE TRI-STAR

Ral had appointed a time and place for the rendezvous and the prophet was very successful in uniting his followers to assemble without question. Suddenly the Tri-Star descended from seemingly out of nowhere and the Children of Chaldoc were aghast.

"Boeski save us, because we cannot stand before the awe-inspiring power of the Rhadda."

A bright intense beam was emitted from the Tri-Star, and as the citizens stepped into the light, the others watched in awe as their comrades were gliding effortlessly inside the starship.

When the citizens were settled inside, they noticed the lack of sound, and then watched in bewilderment as the Tri-Star departed the Feramas, appearing as a lightning flash, until they were far out into distant space.

The messengers reported that all conditions had been met and the land was now ready for destruction. If Ral had any regrets it was too late, for once an academy commander initiated an order it could not be rescinded.

## EVIL DESTROYED ON THE FERAMAS

The prophet learned to write, and documented every detail of what he had observed. How exited he became when he saw the galaxies, planets and myriad of stars. Eventually he had collected an entire set of writings describing his adventure. He had become very skilled in the study of the stars and the complexities of the cosmos, while living aboard the Starship.

The nuclear compound of Patriska was dropped from the Tri-Star, destroying major portions of land throughout the Feramas, especially where the citizenship had settled, taking with it, many of the creatures of the sea, land and air. Ral then sent a shrilling sound throughout the atmosphere, and so penetrating was its sound, that all citizens and creatures within its radius perished.

The Patriska had been released in order to burst the water reservoirs, that had stored up in the atmosphere since the planets regeneration. Ral watched as the moisture accumulating above the atmosphere, joined forces with the erupting explosions from beneath the sea, and vast numbers of those that inhabited the Feramas died in the murky waters that covered the land.

"The Feramas," spoke Medoa, "is now purified by fire and refreshed by water, but before the Chaldocians can be placed back on fruitful ground, the land must go through a period of restoration, and the Children of Chaldoc will be required to remain aboard the Tri-Star until the appointed time."

Ral enjoyed interacting with the Sons of Chaldoc on the Tri-Star and learned much about their way of life on the Feramas, and the prophet was able to educate Ral in the ways of the Rhadda. Ral as usual, took everything in stride, but for some strange reason he felt an inner compulsion that something exciting and wonderful was about to occur.

## CHAPTER 5

### RAL'S ROMANCE

There was not much left for Ral to accomplish at this stage of the Feramas Experiment, and as Medoa had implied, the land should be left alone for a period of time to restructure itself.

Ral keen on physical exercise, felt a Starfleet commander should always be in top condition and spent much of his free time in the activity room. After a vigorous workout, Ral spoke, "computer, shower on," and when he stepped into the bathing compartment an invigorating pressurized spray of atomic particles instantaneously killed off all bacteria, and accordingly identified and recorded all foreign pathogens, which may have been present.

Gone were the days of bathing in water as was practiced in old Ceylon, water was just too scarce to be wasted, requiring the cherished liquid to be imported from various regions throughout the quadrants. Water restrictions had been enforced so long that the citizens had forgotten what fun was. No swimming, no boating, not even fishing, even physical exercise had been banned in effort to reduce water usage. So it was no wonder that the general population was calloused, cold natured and embittered, trying to survive in such an environmentally unfriendly society.

Ral finished his shower, and then lay completely naked on the air sauna bed, which sprayed his entire body with highly prized, exotic streams of fragrant bath oils. Ral was in a state of ecstasy as he lay dreaming of single handedly fighting off the entire fleet of Teegra the Kronos and his hoards. He was just about to put the hook into the nose of Teegra, when he was awakened from his rest.

"Commander Ral, Commander Ral." Repeated Dreara, the ensign of Tri-Star activities. Dreara, unlike the average Ceylonian female was somewhat attractive, and as she bent over the air sauna bed to awaken Ral, her firm large breast lay almost exposed in front of his mouth.

"You had better be careful Dreara. I was just dreaming and I envisioned you there with me, in a garden filled with all sorts of wonderful delights. You were lying nude on the ground and behold, there I was naked standing in front of you, looking into your eyes. The sun was burning me from behind and feelings were awakening inside me that have been hidden for many generations. Have you ever had such desires Dreara?"

"Commander Ral, females of Ceylon learned to control such primitive passions long ago."

It was getting late, and Ral softly spoke, as the light faintly dimmed.

"Dreara, I have observed wonderful videos of old Ceylon, where the citizens enjoyed moments such as this, moments when they were alone sharing with each other and exhibiting forbidden behaviors, which appeared to bring them great pleasure. Dreara, you don't have to participate with me in this my fantasy, but I have this longing to be with you."

Dreara spoke and the larger sauna bed began to unfold. Ral watched as she unbuttoned each of her star-fleet lapels and her top fell silently to the floor. The lights were just bright enough for Ral to observe, while sparkles of light, danced and encircled Dreara's breast. Ral feeling somewhat timid, was reserved when it came time for his love dance. Dreara recognizing his dilemma stepped gingerly over her discarded clothing, she then aggressively sat upon Ral's chest, looking deeply into his eyes. The sexual scenes from Ceylon's Visualization Chamber began rushing back into his mind, it was all coming back to him as they pressed their lips for the heated kiss.

"Commander Ral! Not so hard, that hurts."

"I'm sorry," spoke Ral, "this is a new experience for me."

"I know." Dreara spoke sweetly.

Ral filled with passion climbed on Dreara with anticipation and the exotic scenes, he had enjoyed back on Ceylon, once again vividly reappeared. And soon Ral was in a state of rapture, going in and out of reality. For an instant he would stop and consider his actions but the attraction was too strong, and he would return with even greater vigor. The soft gentle sounds coming from somewhere deep inside of Dreara, were now resounding louder and louder, till suddenly there was utter silence.

"I will never forget this experience," Ral gently whispered into Dreara's ear.

Ral, you are my commander and your word is law. If I had denied your request, would you have condemned me to one of the penal colonies?" Dreara playfully winked at Ral, realizing that as a Ceylonian female, she had no right to complain regarding anything that he would ask of her. "Ral," Dreara added in afterthought. "I also shall not forget our moment of love making."

Ral did not respond as he finished buttoning his uniform but then very unexpectedly, he looked back and smiled at Dreara as if everything was going to be alright.

The Children of Chaldoc were still wondering when Ral would return them to the Feramas, and the prophet approached the commander as he was sitting at the helm of the ship.

"Commander the citizens on the Feramas pay homage to you as if you were their god, yet I stand here and I see flesh and bone, just as I am, are you a god commander?"

The commander placed his hand confidently upon Boeski's shoulder.

"Prophet, my people came to your planet from a distant universe. Atar my father is legendary throughout the galaxies as a colonizer of lands very similar to yours. The scientific departments on Ceylon have made vast numbers of planets like yours habitable. They have also made it possible for creatures to inhabit the seas and the air. Even you my friend, are the result of our experimentation. Your first ancestors were also as I, but of another distant planet called Zorn. Whom do you pray to? Do you burn your sacrifice to me? Who you say is as mortal as you. Write in your books all the wondrous things I will show you."

"No commander! These are questions that need reasoned out. The Sons of Chaldoc many generations ago were spoken to by Rhadda, who gave us his laws. It is to him we offer our sacrifices. Commander, we knew that our God would come someday, as it is written and release us from our oppressors, but your arrival was so marvelous that it startled us for a while. But now my spiritual eyes are opened to the truth and I know you are not the one that we are awaiting, but I feel within my spirit that you are not here by chance and I welcome your intervention."

"Consider this, Commander Ral. When you regenerate the barren lands on distant planets, do you accomplish it by introducing plant life and vegetation that was previous alive in your scientific laboratories? Were the cloned creatures and citizens that you placed upon the planets, genetic copies from preexisting living molecules of DNA? Commander you are not a god! It was Rhadda who made all that exist from the very beginning of his marvelous creation. Can you create a universe, a planet or a star? No commander, it was all brought to life by the great spirit whom you call the Unni."

"Prophet, I am somewhat amazed at your boldness and to be frank, I am not accustomed to having my subjects speak to me in such a fashion. If this encounter would have taken place on Ceylon, by all right, the academy would have cut your body asunder and had you cremated in the Molecular Field."

"Is that what you are going to do to me commander? What about the Chaldocians that are here with me, are they also to share this unspeakable experience? If this is your intention, commander, why even bring us aboard this great sky vehicle?"

"Prophet I don't know. Even at this very moment, I cannot explain to you why I am here playing mother hen to this miserable and forsaken planet."

"Ral I have observed you and I find you to be a man with a kind heart, and the spirit of good lies within you. You my friend are destined for some great purpose and that is yet to be revealed to you. With your approval commander, I will now go to my people for a time of meditation. I do ask this one request, would it be possible for you to prepare conference monitors to be audible throughout the Tri-Star? For the Children of Chaldoc still need to know that I am alive and well and accessible to provide for their spiritual needs."

Ral marveled at the prophet's words. "Truly, I have never encountered a citizen like the prophet. When I speak with him I feel wonderful, and when he leaves my presence, I feel like a light went out inside of me. I must speak with Medoa concerning the prophet, I must figure out these multitudes of unanswered questions that burn deep inside me."

## RAL HEARS OF ATAR'S DEATH

Ral had not been informed that his father was dead and that Gemaal replaced him as governor. Gemaal sent Leaoka, his envoy to inform Ral, but this was only done so the council would not be to upset before he firmly secured his position as governor.

When the ambassador was transported on the Tri-Star, the crew wondered about the purpose of his visit.

"Commander Ral, spoke Leaoka, "your father's ultimate life cycle has come to an end, and the council request you attend his memorial service on Ceylon." Ral never spoke another word but turned aside from the envoy and walked to his chamber to be alone.

The citizens of Ceylon infrequently showed emotions when family members died, and somehow Ral felt deep inside of his inner self, that he was not a true Ceylonian. Too much had happened and Ral wondered what changes he might eventually consider.

"Send in the prophet, Medoa."

'The prophet entered, somewhat puzzled as to why he had been summoned once again, so hastily.

"You asked to see me commander?"

"Yes prophet, come in. I have observed how you embrace, and shed tears after the death of your fellow citizens, even though they live so few years on the Feramas and their dust quickly returns to the ground. Prophet my people teach that the body at the end of its final regeneration just ceases to exist."

"My father has completed his final life-cycle, what do you believe is the answer prophet?" Can you teach me of your beliefs? Can a god as your people believe I am, be taught of these things?"

"Commander, Rhadda lives in all things and all things are made by him, and Ral, because you are his creation, he asks that you express his love. When you have love, you reflect the very essence of the Unni's spirit, for he is love. Ral, I was taught to abide by your Ceylonian law codes as a child, but it so happened that the Children of Light have been following a higher set of commandments, the laws of the Spirit."

"You are perhaps the wisest citizen of all your generations, because you only, have stopped to consider these great truths. This is the reason you feel different about Ceylon, commander you have always been different, and this is why you could never accept their ways. Medoa is comprised entirely of spiritual essence, he discerns from where he came, and Ral, he knows your heart, just as well as I. And we both are full aware that you are destined to change the laws of the council, and to re-unite citizens throughout the far reaches of space with their creator."

"That reminds me prophet, I have some good news for you. The academy has given the Chaldocians clearance to return to the Feramas, but if I allow the citizens to retain the experience of their journey, Medoa informs me that it may possibly alter the destiny of the planet."

"Ral, I do understand your request, but before we depart, may I ask one more request?"

"What is that my friend?"

"That I may continue to travel with you, so that I may learn all the scientific knowledge that is possible, in order to be a blessing unto my people?"

"Yes prophet, so be it. I know that in you there is no guile, and your request is only for the betterment and development of your people."

"How long do you anticipate our return?"

'"It will not be too long, I will let you know when the time is right."

"I'll keep you in my prayers commander."

## GEMAAL'S DEPLORABLE DECISION

Meanwhile back on Ceylon, Governor Gemaal was taking his stroll through the Ceylonian gardens. Conditions seemed fairly normal for the time of year, but something was wrong and Gemaal could not put his finger on it. He was beginning to have suspicions, even before the soothsayers and the doomsday prophets began to proclaim, their great planet was soon to encounter great destruction. Dreeska, long ago had began preparing the planet of Durran to be Ceylon's future habitation, in case such an unfolding of events were ever to occur.

"Gemaal was then interrupted by his aide. "The council has issued a priority message and they say it is now official concerning the likelihood of Ceylon's impending destruction. The date of the asteroid's arrival is yet undetermined, it is just too far away to make an accurate prediction, but we are keeping a constant vigilance and you assuredly will be updated of any changes or alteration in its course." Gemaal began to weigh his course of action. "If the clock is truly running out for my beloved Ceylon, then perhaps it is time to prepare for evacuation to Durran. Yes, millions of lives could be saved and I would be hailed as the savior of my people, just as Dreeska, when he protected the citizens of old Ceylon." Gemaal continued to reason. "But if the calamity was so sudden upon us that a mass evacuation was impossible, what would I do? What if plans were set in motion and Ceylon should survive? I would then be considered a fool. It would be a no win decision. Perhaps I should wait until I see more visible signs, then I shall reveal my plans."

"Atar! Atar!" He shouted to himself. "Now that you have finally passed on, I still can't find peace in my life. I hated you for stealing my seat on the council. If only I could have had those early days of your clad-iron rule, then I, Gemaal, would have brought Ceylon to greater heights than could ever have been imagined. Atar!

Atar! If you had not died, I would have destroyed you myself, just as I did to that traitor Quintoea."

"Why am I talking to the memory of a dead man? Atar, now that you are gone, can you hear my confession? Can you now see how I yielded my influence to keep Ral from advancing in the academy? I even convinced the council to confine your rebel son to that forsaken Feramas planet. Why Atar, why would I succumb to such chicanery? Because I hated you and I hate you more today than I ever did. As far as I am concerned, Ral will be demoted from what little authority he now holds, and plans are already in the making to bring your rebellious son down even further into obscurity."

"It is only for the sake of your grandson Kiah, that I have allowed Ral to keep what limited status he now enjoys. Atar, Kiah faithfully serves under my command and has advanced through the ranks. Perhaps I feel like I have stolen something that was very dear to you. But it appears in the end," Gemaal sighed, "that you may have won the final victory. Yes, even in death it seems you exert your sway. Is this your cloud of doom which hangs over my beloved home? Are these decisions I contemplate the same you would have made, my old enemy? Why do I feel you are out there, watching everything I do? I almost feel you are in charge of these affairs, could it be you are? And perhaps, even in death, you have won the final battle."

## DREARA'S SURPRISE

"Hi, Ral," spoke Dreara in a soft feminine voice, "I have been waiting for you to stop by the recreational department, for I have some news that may be of interest to you."

Ral had left the prophet only moments before and his mind was not on Dreara's conversation.

"I am with child." There was a sudden hush that filled the room as Dreara continued her sentence. "Ral we have conceived this little one in a unique and wonderful way that is impossible for me to express, and I deeply wonder why am I blessed above all Ceylonian females to bring about a citizen in this fashion? Ral I have bypassed being injected with the seed tube, and I also understand that this is of no concern to you, but commander, this little citizen will always be a sweet reminder of our special moment together."

"Dreara, I hear what you are saying but for now we must consider the consequence of our actions. Many generations ago the council declared that all bearing of children would be placed in the hands of the scientific department. Dreara the numbers implanted in your hand shows that you were conceived under their guidelines. The fact that you are an academy female officer, testifies that your mother was one of the millions injected with the seed of a prominent Ceylonian aristocrat."

"Dreara long ago the scientific department, set exact limits on how many citizens are needed to inhabit the colonies. If there are too many, they are required to forfeit their lives in the molecular field, and Dreara, we could be called into account for our actions. The council is going to call the shots, the little one will be taken from you and be registered with the statistical department's life-long identification number."

"Ral you have explained the situation quite well, but how will you inform this to those in power?"

"I will take charge of all the preliminary work, I will also speak with you later in your chamber."

Ral walked the long corridor toward the communication's center, and suddenly he felt, as if his brain was about to explode. Pressing his hands to his head, Ral tried hard to relieve the pressure causing his troubled and incoherent thoughts, he then passed by the medical lab where Doctor Rhear observed his behavior.

"Commander Ral, is something wrong?"

"No, I'm fine doctor, just had some things on my mind."

"Please come into my lab for an examination, you do not look to well commander."

Ral desiring to have someone to confide in, sat down in the plush air-chair and waited for the doctor to speak.

"Cut out the small talk commander, I have not served in the academy without learning something about how things work in the complicated mind."

"Dr. Rhear since the beginning of the Feramas Experiment I slowly began to change. Thoughts and beliefs I had grown up with suddenly began to take on a different perspective. It is almost as if someone or something has been trying to control my thoughts and action, and I have never known who to turn to except for Medoa, who is wise in all things. Yes doctor, there has also been forbidden & complicated matters that have been haunting me, thoughts so complicated, I feel my brain is about to explode."

"Doctor Rhear, Dreara is going to bear a child, which was conceived when we lay together in a time of passion. And for some strange illogical reason I feel bonded to, not only Dreara, but to this little one who will soon enough be born."

"Commander." Dr. Rhear spoke harshly. "Let me stop you right there. You will need to reason out these primitive feelings that have long been banned on Ceylon, so heed my advice. If the council should get word that you have done this deed, they may look with disfavor toward further colonization efforts, and your entire career could be in jeopardy."

"Doctor, I am very aware of everything you say, but there is something else that I must confess. I feel more and more that I am becoming isolated from my home, my people and their ways, every day I feel more kinship toward the prophet and the Chaldocians, I feel more comfortable with them than all the rigid laws of Ceylon."

"Ral do you understand that if your confession had been told to me outside the confidentiality of this office that I would have been duty-bound to report your actions, and I assure you that the council would have imposed harsh punishments. Ral I have always been your friend and ally as I was your fathers, so I implore you to be extremely careful. Do I have your promise? Place your arm on the table, this shot will relieve your headache and allow you to get some needed rest."

"Thank you Doctor, I have too many things to accomplish and too few star years to carry them out, and now I must prepare to return the Chaldocians to the Feramas and when that is all settled, I must begin making plans to return to Ceylon for my father's death ceremony."

## THE CHALDOCIANS RETURNED TO THE FERAMAS

The sun was shining brightly and Ral was anxious to see the Chaldocians off on their return home. They had undergone a mind modification program, which eradicated the entire experience of their intergalactic journey. This disheartened Ral, because those he had befriended could not recognize him as they passed him on their way to the transporter station.

They were relocated to the same region from which they were taken, and temporarily things appeared strange to them. But in time they were able to settled down and soon everything returned to normal. The prophet, as promised, retained all the memories of his galactic adventures, and henceforth, his heart would be forever tied to his friends aboard the Tri-Star.

Because of Boeski's advanced age and spiritual nature, the citizens of the Feramas never questioned that he was a prophet, but in due course of time, they began to take his tales of space travel with the proverbial grain of salt, and it wasn't long until his stories were delegated to the status of village folk lore. Boeski had amassed a wide following and righteous disciples sat at his feet, recording every philosophical thought that he uttered.

Time passed quickly and Ral sent word that it was once again time for the leader of the Chaldocians to return to the Tri-Star, and Boeski eagerly awaited his arrival. This time, Ral would make arrangements to rendezvous with the prophet in a more obscure area

Ragan, because he was gifted with Ceylonian intelligence, escaped the deluge and returned to the populated areas following the movement of the prophet by having his evil cohorts once again mix among the Children of Chaldoc.

"You are the Children of Light," spoke Boeski, "and your father beholds you always from the heavens, he will return for you, if you will stay faithful to his laws. Remember and take heed, how it is written in the law that your father in the heavens looked down on great injustice, which was so vile that he destroyed the Sons of Darkness in his murky vengeance, but in his goodness and mercy he miraculously preserved alive the Sons of Chaldoc, which remain unto this day. My scheduled time is nigh and I must leave you for a season, but I have left you other prophets whom have the same spirit, hearken to their voice and encourage each other until my return."

Ragan watched, and was filled with disbelief as the citizens murmured, concerning the prophets departing words. Ragan dared not to reveal his presence and chose not to speak, for he feared the citizens may have stoned him on the spot where he stood. Ragan kept his words under breath, but if one were standing close enough, he would have heard these words: "You speak lies prophet friend of Ral, and I cannot believe I have let you live this long." Ragan also understood, in spite of his hatred for the prophet, he needed more time to re-establish the previous power and authority that he had lost due to the major destruction that was heaped upon the Feramas.

Boeski waited on a predetermined mountain top with the companion that was to succeed him as prophet.

"Behold the whirlwind from the heavens has come for me, weepiest not, my faithful servant, for I will return and visit with my children in times of need, but for now, rejoice that I am honored to be a vessel in the service of the Rhadda."

The Tri-Star hovered high above the mountain, where the prophet was waiting. The noise of exploding Patriska coming from the nuclear reactors, sounded like the rushing of many waters.

When the smoke dissipated, the streaks of flashing colorful lights left the lesser prophet virtually in shock, especially when the beam of light shone down on the ground, where Boeski was waiting.

Treeka and Simka appeared, almost out of nowhere, riding on the Gyro-craft. Boeski walked over and lay prone on the metal bar, which extended across the vessel's underside. Treeka pushed the button and the locking bar snapped around the prophet's body as the Gyro-craft began its ascension toward the belly of the Tri-Star. The messengers preferred this mode of transportation, rather than utilizing the Tri-Star's transporter, because they felt it could alter their molecular structure during the process, they were also able to energize themselves by pinching their nose and spinning, which was so much easier.

## SAFE ABOARD THE TRI-STAR

When Boeski stepped off the transporter dock, he looked deep into the eyes of his friend. He walked over and embraced him, surprising Ral, because this was not the custom on Ceylon where men seldom touched, except in the traditional patriotic locking of arms, and stiff slap on the shoulder. But Ral felt comforted by the embrace and when he backed off, there were tears flowing from the eyes of the prophet.

"Why are you crying?" Asked Ral.

"Because commander, I have grown close to, not only you, but also to many of the crew on this starship and I have found them to be wonderful and beautiful citizens. It is part of our nature to feel close to those who we have grown to love, and someday, you will come to know this feeling, which can only come from the Rhadda's love."

During the long and wonderful years, Boeski acquired a great understanding of scientific technology, while living aboard the Tri-

Star, and Ral decided it was time for the prophet to make the most of this knowledge, by advancing the development of the Feramas.

Boeski's principal assignment was in a desert area, where the leaders of the citizens erected large monuments to perpetuate their own immortality. Boeski accomplished this feat with the help of the Tri-Star, by means of the magnetic pull of the starship's atomic boosters, which enabled extremely large stones to be stacked, higher than the hills of Ceylon. Many of these structures were used by cults that practiced a form of mystical religion. Boeski also worked in this region accumulating papyrus scrolls and books of learning from major provinces throughout the colonies. He was able to develop a library, which became one of the most remarkable accomplishments of its time.

The prophet assisted in the advancement of the Feramas, and Ral often reflected, how he could have been blessed with such a wonderful friend. But the years passed by slowly for Boeski, and once again, he felt it was time to return, at least for a short stay to reunite with his people.

**THE DEATH AND RESURRECTION OF THE PROPHET**

Ral had been so absorbed with his duties that he had not given much consideration to what was taking place on the Feramas. For a long time he had realized that Ragan was continuing to gain power and control, but he had failed to take into account that the diabolical and evil force contending for the soul of Ragan was also growing stronger with each passing day.

Ragan waged war upon the Sons of Chaldoc, especially the prophets, which had been taught at the feet of Boeski. Cruel and Maskra, Ragan's elder sons, purposely defiled the outer courtyard of the Chaldocians by offering forbidden and vile beast in front of the assemblage. They further scorned and disrespected the law codes by repeatedly performing incestuous and detestable acts of sex inside the holiest sanctuary of the temple.

Ragan's henchmen once again infiltrated the Chaldocians disguised as believers, while dressed in their cloak. The evil workers continually planted seeds of doubt causing dissention throughout the clans of righteous citizens.

"Your prophets speak lies, their only desire is to keep you locked in bondage, imposing unneeded restriction, to keep you from enjoying the gifts of life that are free for the asking. Are you slaves or are you free?"

The citizens hearkened to their words, and began furiously screaming at the prophets.

"You prophets have spread your filthy lies too long!"

At that moment, Boeski was transported to the courtyard where sacrificial animals were being slaughtered. Boeski turned to wave farewell as a symbolic gesture toward the Tri-Star.

"Look! Screamed the citizens, the great leader has returned, death to the prophet!"

Boeski heard their words in disbelief, and suddenly, Ragan revealed himself from his concealed position. When the prophet saw Ragan surrounded by the screaming citizens, he realized that his life was in danger. Boeski calmly raised his arms toward the heavens and cried out.

"Faithful children, love your enemy!"

Ragan with all the hate he could muster, cast everything to the wind, while lunging at the prophet with his dagger, stabbing him repeatedly, and with each mortal wound, he cried louder and louder, "damn you lying prophet, spread your filthy lies no more!"

Boeski lay dead at the foot of the sacrificial alter, while his blood flowed rapidly into the basin, which was already filled and overflowing with blood from the recently slaughtered animals, and Ragan with sword in hand, pointed to the sky screaming.

"Ral! Here is your sacrificial blood, come down and I will give you a taste of this prophet's blood mixed with your own. Then I will divide your stinking body into pieces and feed it the fowls of the Feramas to devour."

The Children of Chaldoc were aghast, each with their face in the dirt, crying. "Father saves us, Father save us!"

Ragan feeling his power growing, cried out to the heavens, proclaiming that he, Ragan, shall be the supreme commander of the Feramas and the entire Ceylonian Empire.

"Emergency, Commander Ral, please respond!"

"Yes Medoa, I am receiving your signal, transmit."

"Ral, rebellion is rampant on the Feramas, and commander, Ragan murdered your friend the prophet and now stands challenging your authority to rule over the land."

Ral infuriated, shouted, "alert status! Prepare to blow this rebellious traitor and his evil followers into space dust. I will pursue

Ragan through the far reaches of space for his dastardly injustice." It then dawned on Ral that his friend was dead, tears for the first time began running down his face and an emptiness emanated from deep within his heart.

When Medoa turned on the large monitor showing the land surface. Ral look in disbelief at Boeski's lifeless, blood soaked body.

"Unni! Unni!" Ral cried out, beating his chest in torment. If you can hear me, please restore life to the prophet! If you are as powerful as the messengers say you are, then prove it"

"The citizens cried out, look! The prophet began moving in his own pool of blood, and slowly began rising into the air. As the prophet slowly descended to the altar, the frightened citizens fell, humbling themselves, as they looked upon the resurrected prophet in his blood drenched robe.

The prophet began to speak. "Brothers and sisters, remain unyielding in your spiritual belief, keeping your thoughts always upon the Rhadda, his word is true and if you stay faithful, he will come to you."

As Ral and Medoa gazed at the scene on the monitor, they could barely believe their eyes. The citizens all joined forces and began throwing rocks at Ragan and his band of henchmen. Ragan made a speedy retreat to his hideaway, where he once again began making serious plans to destroy Ral, and his friends on the Feramas.

# CHAPTER 6

## RAGAN MEETS WITH THE KRONOS NATION

Ragan humiliated and defeated, prepared to depart to the planet of the Kronos, to convince them to unite against the armies of Ceylon. If he was successful in this endeavor, Ragan believed he could begin to slowly establish his power and authority throughout the Seventh Quadrant.

Teegra the Kronos commander met with Ragan reluctantly, in spite of everything, this was the academy officer that had helped suppress his people by keeping them under Ceylonian bondage.

"Seize him!" Teegra ordered his chief captain. "Bind him so I may decide if he is telling the truth."

That evening, Teegra held the wildest party, ever held in their region of the planet. Teegra under the influence, danced with Ragan, which was their custom. Kronos were known throughout the Seventh Quadrant for their barbaric acts. They boiled their infant females in milk and ate their succulent organs as a delicacy. They also sacrificed their children to Truno, their god, by throwing them from high sacrificial alters unto very honed, jagged spikes. Large containers lay just beneath to collect the blood, which was used in their ceremonial feast.

The Kronos females served just one purpose, to bear strong sons, teaching them to reap injustice on their enemy, which was the custom of their barbaric and ancient ancestors. This primitive nature went beyond normal reason, they even reaped havoc upon their own kind. This was the reason that the Kronos were never successful in keeping control over their enemy, they were just too busy fighting among themselves.

Ragan was embarrassed for making a fool of himself with Teegra, and realized that the Kronos leader was indeed a primitive fool, who would not be of assistance in his plans to take control of the Ceylonian Empire. Ragan felt obliged to play the game a little longer, just in case, there may be a thread of hope that Teegra was half as smart as he presented himself to be.

"Teegra write for me a letter of acceptance, that I may go and speak with each of the strongest alliances that have fallen under the servitude of the mighty Ceylonians."

"Ragan, the Zecra recently formed a treaty with the United Alliance, just outside the Sixth Quadrant. It is rumored that the Zecra have been making plans to overthrow the Ceylonians. Go in haste Ragan, I will signal Gormia that you will be arriving."

The Zecra citizens in their early history were a break off of the Ziana colonies and Ceppra, Teegra's sister, was given to Gormia, the Zecra leader in marriage to seal the peace between their planets.

## RAGAN & THE ZECRA

"Ragan, tell me why you have traveled so far to visit with me." Spoke Gormia suspiciously.

The two strangers were eyeing each other, trying to find something, a word, a look, anything that would give them the upper hand in their encounter. Gormia the Zecra's high leader felt it best to break the ice and speak first.

"We have heard of your bold attempt to unite us against the mighty Ceylonians." The more Gormia spoke the more composure he gathered. "Ragan your fame is unprecedented, you are renown throughout the Seventh Quadrant for your pure and evil nature, but what do I see before me? You look just like an ordinary dog citizen, and you are more hideous, than any obnoxious slime that I have ever encountered. You dare come to my nation and stand before me in such pomp and propriety as if I am to bow down and kiss your ugly Ceylonian ass."

Ragan decided not to speak a word, he had already come to the conclusion that Teegra the Kronos had deliberately set him up.

"I will certainly deal with the Kronos later," contemplated Ragan, "but for now, I will develop a plan to get through this ordeal with the Zecra."

"From the bizarre reports I have heard, I figured you to be something of an awesome spirit. So tell me you outcast Ceylonian swine, are you more powerful than Puell our god, who can change the direction of the winds, or can you speak to us from deep inside our precipitous volcanoes? What tricks can you draw from your sleeves? Perhaps you're more like unto our magicians and tricksters. Can you change me into a deformed and hideous creature Ragan?"

"If you can't, then tell me you grafted in Ceylonian piece of garbage, why would the great Zecra listen to the likes of you? If this was not the evening of the sacred festival dedicated to our great god Puell, I would boil you in the kettle and then hang you from a nearby tree, so that each of our starving children could gaze upon your fair and succulent body, and taste of your roasted flesh. Seize him!" Screamed Gormia. "Bind him and prepare him to meet with the governor before the evening feast begins."

They swiftly carried Ragan off, suspended upside down on a pole, which conceivably had been the spit for roasting flesh. As Ragan was being escorted from the transportation area, he thought to himself, "how strange, this all came about without offering one single word in defense."

Ragan was tied to a strong tree and secured tightly with cords of the strongest material on Zecra, and as Ragan watched the festival taking place, he thought, "how primitive these citizens, how could I have ever considered an alliance with such heathens. I have studied the mind of Ral, my hated adversary, and I know of his fascination for the barbaric people of old Ceylon. But these citizens stink, they are also without any manners, food slobbers disgustingly down their chin, as they rip their meat apart with their hands, eating it virtually uncooked."

Ragan began having strange feelings that slowly came over him, and wondered, if it might have been the drink. "Perhaps I was drugged," he reasoned, "yes, probably for them to gain the upper hand to tie me up."

Sounds coming from the roaring volcano were intensifying as the Zecra continued to dance, getting wilder and louder in their screams, which was begining to affect Ragan, and he seemed to be getting weaker and weaker.

The Zecra females began dancing and tossed flowers as the governor approached the festival. The volcano suddenly thundered, and as spurts of lava and ash spewed from the erupting crater, the skies lit up, as the Zecra watched in fear and wonder at the colorful light display taking place before their eyes.

Suddenly the Zecra bowed before the great statue of Puell, crying out to their god that the volcano should be appeased. Ragan was beginning to feel that he was soon to become a living sacrifice, unless he could figure out a plan to outsmart the primitive Zecra. Ragan breathed a sigh of relief as he listened to the screams of a mother, as her infant was tossed into the crater and the cries became silent.

"How strange," thought Ragan, as the volcano ceased its roar and the flames abated. "Interesting," he thought, wondering if it happened that way each time a child was offered.

The governor walked over and looked at Ragan as if he was a museum show piece from the Interplanetary Zoo. "So you are a soldier and also a singer, that is indeed quite a combination. Sing for me Ragan, my people are involved in celebration. Sing, drink, make merry and be gay."

Ragan never moved, while the governor slowly poured a libation of sacrificial wine on his head, the warm liquid burned into Ragan's eyes, leaving a putrid smell in his nostrils.

"Strip him! Let the females come and feast their eyes upon his pearly skin, let him give them pleasure before he dies his horrific death."

Ceppra the younger sister of Teegra the Kronos, began to stroke her fingers down the bare chest of Ragan, the stench of her breath and the stinking odor from her body caused him to finally turn his head, the disgusting smell was just too unbearable.

Ceppra's sex organ, and her four breasts were completely exposed. The practice of nudity was enforced to keep the colonies permanently overpopulated. This law had been enacted to ensure replacements for citizens that were killed in battle. And even though food supplies were diminishing, and the colonies were experiencing starvation, the Zecra never associated their dilemma with the sexual attraction of their female dress code. Ragan's mind was so clouded by the drugs, he began to believe that Ceppra's hideous body was voluptuous and beautiful, the attraction was so great that slobber was beginning to ooze down his chin.

Ceppra thoroughly enjoyed the sexual escapade, and just as he climaxed in sexual bliss, she withdrew herself and summoned the young intoxicated male citizens to come and share in the orgy.

The effects of the drug was beginning to wear off as Ragan began to rebel against his attackers, but the Zecra had even greater plans for the fair body of Ragan.

## RAGAN POSSESSED BY WAKI

The more Ragan cried out against their advances, the more angry he became, until suddenly, his eyes became ablaze. The cords which bound his hands and feet, miraculously fell to the ground. Suddenly, as if incarnated by some uncontrollable force, he reached his hands toward the advancing Zecra, and strong spurts of energy emanated from his fingers, electrocuting every Zecra standing in his way. Ragan was surprised as thunderous words began to spew out of his mouth.

Waki's voice was frightening beyond measure, as he began to speak through Ragan. "Hear my words and behold Puell, your pathetic god."

The Zecra began trembling in fear as they watched.

"Look!" Cried out Gormia. "Puell is moving from his lofty seat, he is coming to help us. Save us, Puell, save us," The eyes of the Zecra standing beneath the colossal statue widened in disbelief, and then all of a sudden, they lay crushed beneath their fallen idol of stone, which was shattered to pieces.

Ragan's head flipped back as the Waki once again began to speak through him.

"This is just a taste of the devastation I will unleash against the stupid citizens that refuse to follow me. My servant Ragan shall lead the Ceylonians to their destruction. Hearken to my words, you ungrateful Zecra, I, Waki, am your god. I am the one that supplies your needs, not this pathetic piece of rubble, you call Puell."

"Behold your skies." The day was hot and the bright sun burned into the parched soil. "Is that a small dark cloud, exclaimed Waki?" Rain for the first time came down so hard that in just a very short span of time, the Zecra cried out, "run to higher ground, less we perish."

"Silence!" "Behold there is a rainbow in your sky? Is this not your sign the rain is through?"

As suddenly as the rains began, the storm ceased abruptly. Each time the Waki performed his miracles, Ragan's body twisted and gyrated with the consequence of great pain. Waki caused a great burning heat to scourge the land of the Zecra, and with their hands on their throat they groaned with immense pain, and if the Waki had not released his hold, all the Zecra would have perished.

"Hearken unto me and I will perpetuate your evil, making you infamous throughout the vast quadrants." When Waki finished speaking, the energy was drained from Ragan, causing him to fall to his knees.

"Citizens of Zecra," spoke Gormia, "Ragan bows to the great spirit, everyone must pay homage to the god of Ragan so that we will survive on our colony and receive the power to conquer all things."

With support from Gormia and the United Alliance, Ragan was able to form a plan of attack against the Ceylonians. The United Alliance ambushed a Ceylonian patrol vessel in the inner region of the Seventh Quadrant, completely destroying the ship and its entire crew. The news reached Ceylon just moments after the destruction.

## RAL DISPATCHED TO THE BATTLE

Renna the Tri-Star computer, switched on the alert sirens, which echoed throughout the starship. Renna then classified the call, top secret, and directed it to Ral's private chamber.

"Commander Ral please respond, alert status. Commander Ral, there is a top priority message from Keeksonn, chairman of the Ceylonian council."

"Renna standby to record, and scan your memory banks for any communication leaks."

"Affirmative commander, you may now proceed with your communications."

"Ral, it's great to hear your voice but my message is urgent. The United Alliance located in the Sixth Quadrant has declared war upon us, destroying our academy starship, which was patrolling the defensive boundary. Listen to me closely commander, I am ordering you into I.C.D., (Immediate Combat Defense) and I am also placing the entire Ceylonian fleet on alert status. Kiah has been placed in charge of our star-base, just in case the enemy should break through our protective ranks."

"Keeksonn, keep me informed, I will prepare my men for battle, and will soon be back in communication with you."

"Ral, I will tell the academy fighters, you are on the way.

Ral had been concerned with the events taking place on the Feramas, and now that he was once again off to war, he realized that Boeski would be left alone on the Feramas to defend the forces of good over evil. Ral realized that there was also a chance they may never meet again, but for now, he must think about the task at hand, and Kiah was his primary concern.

"My son Kiah in charge of the Academy Star-Base?" Ral was having problems with Kiah's recognition, it hadn't seemed that long ago, they had spoken their last words on Ceylon.

"To your stations!" Shouted Ral. He was extremely excited because he knew top priority alert status was only given when the council declared a state of war. The Venduras Campaign had turned Ral into a seasoned fighter, but now, he was feeling more and more intimidated.

"I wish the prophet was here, for some strange reason I feel I need his strength to guide me. Why do I feel something is wrong?"

## RALS FIRST LIFE CYCLE ENDS

The Zecra and their newly formulated alliance would have little chance against the academy fleet, and Ral realizing the council would be monitoring his capability to command, suddenly began to worry. Ral had barely finished his thoughts as the Zecra spacecraft penetrated into Ceylonian territory.

Braka, Ral's uncle was in charge of the academy's fortified perimeters. Ral always felt their relationship was more like brothers, the bond between them was just too strong. Throughout their time at the academy, the two were almost inseparable, but Braka's marriage eventually came between them. It was also about this time that Ral met Ragan and soon their relationship came to an end.

"Greetings dear nephew, are you ready for battle?" Ral was surprised to hear Braka's voice, especially after just thinking about their good times at the academy. But suddenly, Braka's words faded and there was no more sound.

"Braka, Major Braka, please respond!" Ral, after feeling the initial explosion, knew within his heart that he would never hear the voice of his friend again.

When death resulted from explosion, the atomic elements could not be gathered for restructuring in the regeneration chamber. Ral wondered about his own death, especially after watching fellow officers, being brought back to life in this manner.

The Academy's Fleet was overcoming the United Alliance and was down to the enemy's last spaceship, which was under the command of Gormia, the leader of the Zecra Nation. Gormia would have to fight alone, even Teegra his brother-in-law had deserted him early on to cowardly return to the safety of the Kronos colonies.

After being inspired by Waki, Gormia set course to return to Zecra for refuge, but for the moment, he was able to slip out of sight and conceal his position from the Tri-Star.

Commander Ral was somewhat confused, wondering where Gormia was hiding.

Ral asked his navigator to search the computer banks for identifiable meteorites in the vicinity.

"Commander," spoke Leardar, his navigator, "ARZ5031 asteroid lies directly ahead and compositional analysis indicates an overt abundance of synthetic metals to be present."

"Ral screamed, fire lasers!" Sensing the imminent danger with great in trepidation.

When the meteorite burst into trillions of pieces, Gormia's spaceship mysteriously appeared, firing laser after laser. The Tri-Star shook like a tree of Ceylon caught up in a tremendous storm. Gormia had scored a direct hit on the belly of the powerful warship, catching Ral completely unprepared, as he was suddenly thrown vigorously against the cabin's support beam and lay motionless.

Gormia sensing his victory, bowed and gave reverence to the god of Ragan as he continued his journey home.

"What fools these Ceylonians, they are not as mighty as they make out to be. I will make plans to form new alliances and then I shall put a final end to the Ceylonians long rule of injustice."

## CHAPTER 7

### RAL'S DEATH EXPERIENCE

Ral was suddenly becoming aware of his strange dilemma. "What is happening? I feel as if I am dreaming, where am I?"

Ral was now floating, just inches from the ceiling of the command room and it seemed strange to Ral that he was bouncing off the ceiling like a ball. He could see everyone quite clearly, but the crew appeared to be very despondent, each of his officers were standing at attention as if they were awaiting inspection of the ranks. Over by the control center, Medoa and Treeka were standing by idly chatting about some event that just happened. Then Dreara walked into the room with Doctor Rhear, who seemed to be comforting her.

"I am sorry about the death of your husband, Dreara."

At first the words didn't register with Ral, until he realized his position. Then Ral, as if he was looking through a slight haze, began to visualize what the crew was looking at. He saw the form of someone lying prone on the couch, and he began to gaze intently at the citizen.

"That is me lying there, what am I doing sleeping, while everyone else is walking around?" Ral then became aware that the sleeping citizen was indeed himself, but for some strange reason, he was content with his environment. "Am I dead? Yes, I am dead."

He heard Rogag speaking. "He was the most gracious and loving citizen that ever walked the streets of Ceylon." Ral also heard two officers standing nearby, telling how they were blessed to have known such an understanding commander.

"The crew really cared for me, so many tears from a group of hard core Ceylonian officers." Spoke Ral in a confused state of mind.

But the hardest was to see Dreara crying bitterly, almost to the point of collapsing from exhaustion. "Ral! Ral! You are my life and the only love I have ever known, take me with you. Ral don't leave me!" The primordial screams of Dreara, touched all that were present, and they wept for the wounded soul of Dreara.

Elaborate funeral service were held each time a Ceylonian noble died. Frankly, the regeneration process was not as yet full proof, and thousands of Ceylonian officers never made it past their first regeneration.

Ral realized that if he could, he would pull Dreara close to him, and tell her how much he loved her. He also knew that within every fiber of his essence, that theirs was an undying love, but now from his lofty position, everything felt and looked different.

Ral felt a force pulling him closer to the ceiling, and the feelings he was having were of ecstasy. He then sensed a glow of light surrounding him, and the feelings of love was stronger at this moment than the temporal callings of those he was leaving behind.

"It's dark, pitch darkness. I have never experienced such an empty void, no, not anywhere throughout the galaxies, where am I?"

Ral was now totally absorbed in the blackness, which had engulfed his awareness of the past events. A pin point of light began to appear in the distance. Somehow Ral became fixed on the light, being drawn to it, as if a magnetic force was pulling him toward a greater luminosity.

Two entities began speaking in the darkness, within a short distance of Ral's new position.

"This soul must return." Suggested the first speaker.

"He can't go back he must stay." The second entity seemed to disagree with the other's opinion.

"The spirit of this soul entity is extremely strong, it should have never reached to this higher spiritual plane, he is a Ceylonian and has been called for a divine purpose, he must be returned."

The second entity, once again questioned the other. "Why are the Ceylonians different than the other soul entities?"

"Their scientist, acting conversely to the laws of the Unni, developed a regeneration process to extend their natural life cycle. When each diverse life cycles end, the souls of the Ceylonians are temporarily held in a state of limbo, it is then during the spinning of the chamber that the soul is unnaturally forced to reunite with the body. When these citizens ultimately expires, they are brought here, where the final step of their spiritual development is determined. Frankly throughout all their generations there has only been a few that every made it to this level of spiritual awareness and they were the citizens that lived on old Ceylon, before the banishment of the Unni was mandated. This citizen has truly gained favor in the eyes of the creator, so let us prepare for his return."

Atar had just recently ended his final life-cycle, and his essence was still dwelling in the spiritual realm, where Ral, was temporarily detained. Atar's spirit passed by Ral many times, but according to the rules of the higher order, he could not communicate with his son. Ral somehow felt his father's presence and began to speak softly, "Father, Father, Father." Ral's words drifted into the darkness as he forcefully, was pulled downward. He wasn't certain why, the only thing he knew for sure, he did not want to leave this place of such wonderful peace and love.

Once again Ral was hovering just below the ceiling, but this time he found himself in the regeneration room. He saw Medoa and Doctor Rhear standing in front of the opened chamber door and then his thoughts went blank.

## RAL'S REGENERATION

"The son of Atar, our past honored governor, has ended his first life-cycle." Spoke Dr. Rhear. "Prepare his cremated remains to be placed in the chamber. The process is very complex, if conditions are not in compliance according to exact specifications, his atomic makeup will be altered and the entire process will lead to failure."

The chamber began twirling so fast, that Ral appeared to be standing still, all eyes were on him, as his eyes flashed open.

"Father, where am I?" Rambled Ral in a state of confusion. "Mylia, where is Kiah? Where am I?"

"Commander, you have just been reborn into your second life-cycle. You were killed when Gormia the Zecra and the United Alliance engaged you in battle." Spoke Dr. Rhear.

"I was killed? I don't understand. Zecra, what is a Zecra?" Ral queried. "Who was talking in the darkness? There was a great light."

"Commander it will take many days to get back into synch with your surroundings." Spoke Dr. Rhear. "It has a lot to do with the chamber's high velocity spin and its affect on your equilibrium."

When Ral awakened from his nap, Medoa was there at his side, he had not left the commander alone during his entire ordeal.

"Welcome to the land of the living commander," thundered Medoa.

"Medoa I am glad to see you. I had the strangest dream but I can't seem to bring it to mind, all I remember is that it troubled me greatly, can you reveal its meaning?"

"No Ral, not at this moment, the dream will be revealed to you when the time is right, and if you learn to wait upon the Unni, he will reveal all things to you."

"Medoa, father was right, dying is like going to sleep. I feel as energetic as I did when I was a recruit at the academy."

"Yes," spoke Medoa, "you should feel great because every cell of your body is now brand new."

"Commander," spoke Dr. Rhear, "you must now continue your rest, because you are on a mission to return and honor your father's memory on Ceylon, and when you awaken in the morning it will all start coming back to you, and when you are feeling able, we will depart for Ceylon."

## RAL'S SECOND TRIP HOME

When the Tri-Star docked at Ceylon's port, Ral was busy checking his appearance before the large mirror, located just inside the terminal. He stared intently at the mirror, looking at a younger version of himself, and he came to the conclusion that he felt better than he had in many years. While observing his image, Ral almost caught a glimpse of his death experience, but the vision was just to fleeting.

Ral grinned as he walked away from the mirror, and as he became more comfortable with his new image, he spoke out loud, "this dying is incredible," which startled a curious citizen standing nearby.

It had been numerous years since Ral's last trip home, and he surmised that Ceylon was not the homeland that he remembered. He noticed that innovative changes had been instituted by governor Gemaal, such as the modern system of transportation. The citizens were now transported throughout Ceylon by computer highways, a elaborate system, which was erected high above the city. When the citizens entered at ground level, they stood erect inside a capsule, protective straps held each one securely around the ankles and waist as they held on for their 200 mile per hour ride to their destination. Since the invisible highways were instituted there had never been one reported accident.

Ral noticed that clothing was now paper thin and could be worn during any season. The advanced synthetic structure of their clothing protected the citizen from Ceylon's extreme heat, or they could walk into a snow storm and still be protected from the affects of the elements. Ral thought that all the changes he observed were wonderful, but in spite of Gemaal's efforts, it was not the changes that troubled him.

"Father is dead and the citizens act as if he never existed." Ral then saw a gigantic photo of Gemaal and hate began to fester in his heart. "How could Ceylon have let this evil citizen ever take the place of father? How can they forget him so easily?" Ral considered this all with a look of disgust on his face.

Little did he realize that the eyes of Gemaal were watching, recording and documenting every move the son of Atar made as he continued his walk throughout the city. The citizens looked at Ral's multi-decorated medals, recognizing, he was indeed the son of Atar. They also realized that he was there for his father's, Honor of Death, but they couldn't care less, because they were involved in their own affairs.

Each citizen had his assigned job, working approximately three hours, and then after work, they returned home to settle in to their repetitive and boring routines. Ral felt they acted more like the Ceylonian androids, which were already doing eighty percent of the labor throughout the Ceylonian colonies.

If the Ceylonians had taken the time to seriously consider the matter, they would have deduced that it was the computerization of every aspects of life, that had destroyed the social and moral fiber throughout Ceylon. Without each citizen's personal computer, very little could be accomplished. All that a citizen had to do was sit at home, type a simple command, and the world was at his beckoned call.

Every aspects of banking and finances were electronically prepared by specialized computers, and the citizen's monthly pay was automatically deducted. When they required food, clothing or any item from the computer catalogue, they just typed an itemized list and their order arrived air speed to their door. The foods came in packets, which contained the highest nutritional value, and the bill was automatically deducted via the finance depository.

Each citizen was listed in the national census, which was an elaborate surveillance system that practically put a stop to crime, thus, eliminating their need for law enforcement. Any legal actions fell directly under the jurisdiction of the council, which dictated all law enforcement policies. If the citizen broke a major law, an officer entered the violation into the computer, and then give notice for the offender to appear. When the citizen arrived, he voluntarily walked into the molecular chamber to forfeit his life, thus by so doing, he consequently forfeited his remaining life-cycles.

The Ceylonians did retain a few luxuries such as browsing the archives for interesting books, or they could enjoy listening to one of the public readers who had spent years memorizing, word for word, one entire novel. The reader would then for the rest of his life, read the book, over and over, on one of the busy street corners to appreciative audiences. The citizens also attended musical programs in the Hologram Pavilion. Ral immediately became aware that there was a deep void in his heart , a fire had gone out and a love had died inside his inner self. He felt this would be a short stay and perhaps the final visit to his homeland.

The National News Agency was broadcasting that Kiah, the grandson of Atar, had been appointed as regent of the academy, a position formerly held by Ral, and his father. The thought flashed through his mind, "what does the future hold for my son"? Ral felt Kiah's next promotion might well be to replace him as the academy commander", however, he felt satisfaction that Kiah was continuing to advance through the ranks, rather than someone less deserving.

Ral reflected, concerning his wife Mylia and the wonderful times they had shared on Ceylon, but now she was gone. He could almost feel her torture as she suffered in anguish in Ceylon's mental institution. This feeling had haunted Ral continually since he left the Atra death colony, leaving him with a feeling of torment, which he would take to his grave.

Ral could not get his father off his mind, it was as if Atar was trying to speak to him, and this hastened his desire to depart. Ral returned to the docking area, but at the moment, he could not leave without making his required audience before the council.

There was a hand few of old friends that joined Ral during Atar's memorial service, but he had surmised the likelihood of this happening, and left before its conclusion. Only Keeksonn extended his hand in friendship, and by the time Ral returned to the Tri-Star, he was tired and his countenance waned.

"Medoa assemble the crew to standby, we will be leaving in the morning at first light." Ral had already suspected that with his father's death, Gemaal would never again show him the military consideration in which he was accustomed.

"I no longer have any reason to stay Medoa, even Kiah did not request to meet with me, I still recall the hatred he held for me, but Medoa, I do wish him well?"

## MEDOA CONTINUES TO TEACH RAL

"Medoa meet me in the hologram chamber and project for me the sweet serene sounds of the Feramas, where the trees reach toward the heavens, and the ocean's mighty waves are raging up to the shore lines."

Ral actually reached toward the feathered creatures, as they soared through the skies, singing their alluring songs. Ral closed his eyes, believing that he was one with the universe, when Medoa stood, disrupting Ral's peaceful moment of bliss.

"Ral long ago, you asked me to have the Unni dispatch his messengers to the citizens on the Feramas and I told you that it was already done. Commander Ral, the messengers have always traveled to where they were invited, the Unni asks that his followers, vocally make their petitions known to him. Belief in the Unni was banished during the later, "Golden Years," of old Ceylon, under the precepts of Governor Dreeska, and as a result of his bias, the Unni left the Ceylonians to live their lives reprobate in self made prisons."

"So this is why they became so cold and calloused?"

Yes Ral, if it was not for the kind and understanding heart of Atar, the Unni would have destroyed New Ceylon long ago, with its contrived pomp and power. Ral I know you question me and you wonder how I discern these things. My answer is simple, love is virtually nonexistent on Ceylon, and there is no recognition of the Unni. When you have love, you will have consideration for others, and you will be able to forgive others, no matter how much they have hurt you. Ral all spiritual laws are embodied into one great law and that is the law of love, and those that exhibit spiritual love will recognize the Unni, because he is love."

"Commander, it was not happenstance that old Ceylon was blown asunder by the asteroid, the Unni altered space and time to make it happen, just as he brings about the death of galaxies, stars and planets in order that new ones can be born. When the citizens, without regard to their environment, poison the land, air and water, the Unni is embodied in the form of destructive hurricanes, tornados and wild fires to remind them of their injustice against his creation."

"Ral, the Unni is the totality of everything that exists. He is the air you breathe and the water you drink. He is the composition of all galaxies, planets and stars, and commander, he is in every cell and molecule that makes up this entity called Ral. What I am trying to get across to you is this, New Ceylon is soon to meet a similar fate as its sister of old. This destruction will rock the heavens as the Unni continues his plan for the ending and beginning of all things. I know you are concerned for your family, but since the death of Atar, Ceylon is beyond saving. Even though there is no turning back, rest assured, your sons will be spared until right before the destruction."

"Medoa I can't seem to get father off my mind, and lately I feel more and more, that he has been trying to speak to me, was it my imagination?"

"Ral, your father has cast off the chains of mortality and is now pure spirit, enjoying fellowship with the Unni, and yes, he is able to manifest his presence to you, if you are attentive to his voice. Your father was Ceylon's greatest citizen, and Unni has placed him in the hierarchy of the messengers, assigning him to help fight the Waki's dark forces. Ral if you were able to conform to the Unni, you would be able to finally peer into my world, then you would believe all things that I have been telling you these long many years."

## RAL DREAMS OF THE UNNI

That evening Ral began dreaming, and once again his body began to rise, floating around the room.

"Ral pondered if perchance he had died again. He had such serene feelings that he did not want to return to his body. Ral then felt a tug, pulling him upward as he soared into a beam of pure light, and Ral approached a majestic throne. Beside the throne there was a messenger holding a book, which contained rules of conduct that were unfamiliar to him, and the voice thundered, "take the book and eat."

"Sir, just in case you don't know, I am a Ceylonian officer in command of many citizens. Spoke Ral boldly."

Just as sudden as Ral spoke his final word, the messenger forced the book into his mouth. Ral swallowed the book and was surprisingly pleased, when it tasted sweet like fresh honey out of the comb. He furthermore felt compelled to kneel, which had always been taught as beneath the dignity of a Ceylonian warrior. Ral stared intently at the form, which was enclosed in immense light, and the clarity of the heaven's was orchestrated with unadulterated musical harmony, as the alabaster throne sang in unison with the myriad of messengers as they bowed and worshiped in his presence.

"Ral you believe that you are dreaming, but this is not a dream. I have summoned your spirit at the request of Medoa, as he is known to you, he is my emissary of the highest order. I am called by many names throughout my unlimited space, I am the life-giver of all that was, that is, and that is to be. I am the healer and protector of my creation. Yes Ral, I am Unni, the life force that you have been searching for. I have looked into the heart of Atar, and I have known your heart also. Your father shares great privilege in my spiritual armies, as Medoa has informed you, and your father, although he never actually believed in me, believed in my principals, which are based upon love."

"But I have also held you dear to my heart. My spirit has long been guiding you, to bring you to this time and place, for I have need of you, to help advance my children on colonies scattered throughout the galaxies."

"If you will be faithful and follow the principals that I handed down to Chaldoc on the sacred mountain, I will bless you in my never-ending kingdom. When you awaken in the morning, you will not recall our conversation, but through my eatable word, which you have tasted, I will leave a bit of my spirit within you, to guide you, and if you seek my ways, you will be opened to my words."

"I will leave you with some encouraging words. Before you ask Dreara to be your wife, I will have moved upon the council to accept your petition to keep the child, the young one shall be called Jedar. Ral, because of the hardness of your heart, I shall appoint him to replace you, so that he shall accomplish my divine mission. Stay faithful Ral, stay faithful, and I will be a lamp unto your feet."

## RAL AWAKES

The aroma of freshly brewed Tanger permeated the room. Ral awoke, vigorously rubbing his eyes. "What was I dreaming of? I can't remember, but somehow I feel it was very important."

"Commander, priority-two level message, please respond. Renna to commander Ral!"

Ral sensing the urgency of Renna's repeated calls, finally walked toward the ship's message center. "Yes Renna," shouted the commander in a loud tone.

"Commander, my message can't be transmitted unless your tone is presented at a much lower decibel." The soft and feminine voice of the computer instructed.

"Sorry Renna, please transmit."

"Commander, there is an urgent message from Keeksonn, he desires to inform you that the council has approved your request, the infant you applied for is scheduled to be assigned to you. Pardon me commander, but I have never heard of such a request to be so honored, it just isn't done." Implied Renna in a questionable tone. Ral had a pleased look upon his face, but yet he was perplexed.

"How could my application reach its destination so soon? It was too recently presented, it should have taken months." Ral also considered, he did not believe anything would become of it, and that he was really only doing this for Dreara.

"I will never be able to figure this out. I wonder if Medoa had anything to do with it, or maybe this had something to do with the strange dream that has so perplexed me? Perhaps, perhaps," Ral reflected as he stroked the new growth of beard that was beginning to grace his presence with the sense of advanced maturity.

"Commander." Spoke Renna in an abrupt tone. "If I may conclude my message, I would be much obliged. The council will be dispatching their private physician to supervise the berthing of the forthcoming arrival."

Passing by the communication center, Medoa saw Ral, and noticed the pleased look on the face of his friend.

"Medoa have the supply officer prepare the sleep chamber for Dr. Louska, he will be transported on board in the morning. It is a great honor to have such an acclaimed physician in our presence."

Medoa remembered Dr. Louska as a skilled physician who would perform his task with a gentle manner, and Ral's child would be assured the finest care.

"Ral, I will ask the ship's crew to make the doctor's stay as comfortable as possible. See you later commander, it appears things are going your way."

"Thank you Medoa, but in some way, I suspect that you are behind all these happenings."

## DREARA ENCOUNTERS RAL

Ral had a feeling that he was about to meet Dreara, he had noticed lately that these strange foretelling feelings were becoming stronger, especially after the outlandish dream that had left him so puzzled. Almost as soon as he had pictured her in his mind, she was there in front of him, and when their eyes met, Ral pulled her close embracing her, and as they kissed, Dreara backed off.

"What's wrong Dreara?"

"Nothing," she replied in a playful mood. "but aren't you worried about what the crew will say, and commander, how about the rumors, such as how the son of Atar has weakened at the hand of a Ceylonian female?"

Ral never said another word but pulled her to him in a brisk fashion, and she realized that something wonderful had happened to Ral. Dreara was experiencing the same sensual feelings she had felt when she became impregnated by Ral in the recreational room.

"Ral, it's getting awfully warm?" Dreara pretended to be embarrassed. "I need to return to my chamber and take a refreshing sauna bath." Dreara lovingly winked at Ral as she hastily departed.

Ral knew that he not only wanted Dreara for love making, but he desired to share the rest of his life with her.

Unbeknownst to Ral and Dreara, two messengers, Treeka and Eparda, had been observing their heated sexual conduct. "These citizens are blessed exceedingly." Expressed Eparda. "They press their lips together while holding each other close and Treeka, their atomic structure dances with anticipation, while bringing them into a state of ecstasy. The Unni surely has a special love for their kind."

"Eparda, the feelings they share is only temporal, some day it will all pale in comparison, when compared to the pure essence of Unni's love. I need you to understand that your thoughts of physical pleasure could cause you to plunge into transgression, and potential isolation from the Unni. Eparda, you were there when a group of our fellow messengers rebelled, desiring to transform into the physical, and intermingle with females of the colonies. I can still hear them as they screamed in their torment, eternally isolated from the Unni. Rest assured Eparda, all mortals will be translated, so their soul can provide evidence of accountability, and answer for their good deeds or their injustice against the Unni."

"I am sorry Treeka, I will try to do my best to accomplish our mission, and to assist commander Ral, and hopefully lead him into the will of the Unni."

## WAKI ATTEMPTS TO KILL JEDAR

The next morning, Ral could not get Dreara off his mind, as he rode the elevator to the transporter room to wait for the arrival of Doctor Louska.

"Stand by Lieutenant Loufa to lock in and transport."

Ral then nervously commanded. "Energize! Energize!"

"I have locked in, but there is a force field preventing Dr. Louska from fully materializing."

"Renna quickly scan for my voice identification pattern."

"Captain Gornar! Have the engine room cut all secondary power boosters to concentrate the balance of the ship's power to tie into the transporter circuits."

"Negative Commander Ral." Responded Captain Gornar. "The ship's engines and all Patriska nuclear cells are working at 100 percent efficiency, but something is blocking all transfer circuits."

"Captain Gornar's explanation of the current state of affairs is illogical." Spoke Renna.

"Renna." Softly spoke the commander.

"Yes commander, I recognize your voice pattern, and by the way, thank you for not speaking so harshly." Spoke Renna.

"Renna check your memory banks for all combinations of possibilities concerning the situation at hand."

"Commander Ral, I cannot help you, because there is no logic to your request as stated. My only advice would be to request Medoa to listen to your dilemma, the answer may lie with him."

Ral turned around and Medoa was standing behind him.

"Where did you come from Medoa?"

"I just finished checking the computer data banks, which are fine, and now it is very important that you listen closely. Doctor Louska not only is in jeopardy of having every cell in his body disarranged, but it is very probable that the Tri-Star is in danger of exploding."

"Waki, the dark spirit, does not want your son to be born and has dispatched some of his strongest messengers to prevent Dr. Louska from bringing about the birth of the little one. He is holding this ship at bay and blocking the transporter mechanism, unless help arrives soon, the Waki will enjoy a great victory for evil throughout the universe."

## THE UNNI SENDS ATAR

Atar was keeping a watchful eye on his son from the spirit world. He was not permitted to impose himself in Ral's destiny but if sent by the Unni, Atar would be able to rally an equal amount of messengers to fight for the benefit of good over evil.

"I must immediately depart," exclaimed Medoa "to humble myself before the throne of the Unni." Medoa was able to transform into his spiritual form by pinching the area above the bridge of his nose and spinning at the speed of light, until he entirely disappeared. In a short span of time, Medoa had returned, it was almost as if he had never left.

"Medoa, where did you go?

"That is not important for now, you must rather concentrate your spiritual and physical energies on the matter at hand.

"Ral you might think it strange, but for the powers of Unni to be manifest, faith must be exercised, and if you will just express your belief in the Unni, all things are possible."

Ral contemplated for a brief period of time, trying hard to place Unni in his mind, and then suddenly, Ral's mind seemed to unfold like the clouds of Ceylon. His dream of the Unni instantly returned and Ral was observing it, just as if it was being shown on Ceylon's indoor visual screen.

"It was not a dream! I actually conversed with the Unni, it's all coming back to me."

"Commander Ral!" Spoke Renna. "Dr. Louska is now in the transporter room asking for you."

Ral and Dr. Louska at first never spoke, both citizens were still baffled, and the doctor appeared to be physically shaken.

"My head feels like the rocks of Ceylon have dropped on it and my aching stomach feels like it needs some of my old fashioned remedy, what happened?"

"Doctor, this mayhem resulted because of a malfunction in the transporter circuitry, I will chat with you later in the lounge, where we will have time to share refreshments. Doctor Louska, I will have Treeka accompany you to your chamber, and this evening, if you feel that you are up to it, I will arrange with Dreara to give you a stimulating massage."

"Sounds great Ral, and incidentally, the council sends you their congratulations, not only for the infant I am about to deliver, but they are also interested in your future colonizing plans."

Ral scratched his head in bewilderment as he said goodbye, departing the room. "These strange occurrences can't be happening, did the Unni really hear my prayer?"

Later that evening, Dr. Louska asked to be escorted to the recreational area, he was more interested in talking with Dreara than having a massage. Dreara entered the room and Dr. Louska gazed intently at her as she began arranging the equipment.

"Dreara you are a lovely Ceylonian female, I can understand why the commander was drawn to you. I came here to observe you, and make recommendations to the council concerning your health. I will also observe your ability to train up a child outside the auspices of the academy. We can forfeit the physical pleasures for my body tonight Dreara, I have not recovered from my bizarre arrival and I must get a good nights sleep."

Just after a brief question and answer session, Dr. Louska became further exhausted, and told Dreara that he would meet with her the next day in the Medical Lab, and there he would perform a number of tests that would be sent to the council's medical lab.

Medoa was sitting with Ral in the chamber of virtual reality enjoying the peaceful botanical gardens, by watching a variety of ocean scenes, which brought them much pleasure.

"Ral let me explain what happened today. Your father was victorious against the forces of evil, and because of his intervention, he saved not only the life of Dr. Louska, but the entire crew aboard this starship."

"Medoa is there someway I can show father my gratitude?"

"Atar is above such trivial emotions as you express, you should give thanks to the Unni, it was his power that brought us through this ordeal, but Atar was concerned and pleased to have been of service to you. The Unni also has great aspirations for you, he anticipated long ago that you would come to believe in him and to recognize him as the source of all life."

"Medoa, I have encountered many changes during my life, especially during the days, when I was a brash young captain at the academy. I have strived to investigate the troublesome questions of life, but I am beginning to realize just how limited I am. I desire to be just half the leader father was, and Medoa, I would give anything to have your spiritual nature and to share your love of the Unni."

"But please forgive me for what I am about to say. I am sorry Medoa, but until Unni confronts me face to face, in this world, then and only then, shall I fully believe in him. Excuse me, I must go to my chamber to reflect upon all these strange happenings. Why can't I believe?" Spoke Ral, as he bowed his face into his hands and cried, "why, why, why!"

Medoa was not surprised when he heard Ral's comments, he had earlier determined that the Unni was purposely sanctioning Waki, to exert his influence over Ral, in order to accomplish some great purpose in his life. Medoa also realized that things would get much worse for Ral before they would ever began to get better.

If Ral desired a cool drink of Tanger or exotic snacks from the planet of Ceysar, at his command the food was prepared and readied within seconds. The entire room was voice activated and as Ral began to relax in his chamber, he spoke "Music B-3," and the sounds of the music of Pralor began softly to play. The miniature air jets located in his bed suddenly began vibrating and seemed to hiss in time to the music. Without the addition of colorful red and green gases, Ral would not be able to find his sleeping accommodations in the dark. His sleeping chamber was free of all forms of pollution, and the temperature was set to the seasonal comfort that he had enjoyed while relaxing on Ceylon. When Ral had finished his refreshing sauna bath, every condition was perfect to speak the light to dim and go to sleep.

"Why can't I sleep?" Ral thought to himself. "Too much has happened in such a short time." But not wanting to disturb the doctor, he decided to stretch out on the couch. Ral could choose between five thousand channels, which could be tuned in throughout the Seventh Quadrant, and soon he was wrapped deeply in thought.

## RAL'S REFLECTIONS

"Why was I different from all the other Ceylonian officers? Why is my mind always drawn back to old Ceylon? No officer in the academy has wondered about such matters as these, will I ever find the truth or the answer to my existence? I enjoyed the moments that I spent with Braka at the academy, we really believed there was nothing that we could not obtain throughout the galaxies. With so much on my mind, I don't believe I'll ever sleep, unless Dr. Rhear gives me one of his knock out shots. I know one thing for certain, Dreara is real, and the child she will bear is real. I know the Feramas is alive and real, because I can touch and feel the living vegetation that grows there, but the thoughts of Medoa are filled with ideas that cannot be reasoned out logically, I can not bring myself to believe in things that are not logical."

The Ceylonians had banned many of the bad habits of old Ceylon such as smoking Strappa leaves. This was an addictive drug, which would have rendered the colonies powerless to stand before their enemies. Ral had smoked the illegal substance when he was young, and remembered the peace and euphoria he had experienced. He considered that perhaps it might control his nerves and relieve him of his exploding headache.

"I must forget these foolish thoughts and concentrate on things that are beneficial for the accomplishment of my mission. So tomorrow, I will speak with Medoa and prepare for the third patrol of my beloved gift, the Feramas."

## CHAPTER 8

### RAL RETURNS TO THE FERAMAS

Ral set pompously, high atop the crystal dome of the Tri-Star, once again looking down at the activity of the citizenship and things appeared to be in order. The prophet was observed instructing his disciples in the laws of Ceylon. Ral seemed pleased, and thought to reward the citizens for their loyalty. Soon it would be time to return Boeski to the Tri-Star, but the prophet must first finish the training program of his young apprentice.

Boeski on the day appointed, stood on top of the highest hill in that region and the one to succeed him also stood watching. The young prophet's faith was awakened, as he observed the Gyro-craft sweep down, and once again transport Boeski out of sight.

When the prophet materialized and walked into the company of the commander, it was Ral, who reached his arms out to embrace his friend.

"Welcome back prophet, I just realized that I have never called you by the name given to you at birth, what do they call you on the Feramas?"

"Ral, I never knew my father, but my mother was of royal lineage, she was the daughter of Zehon, a priest, and she was also a priestess, who struggled to grow food for our kinsmen. We were very poor and humble people, my dear mother had no more than a shroud for her body and barely food to place in her mouth, so she called me Boeski, which means, one born out of poverty."

Ral was caught off guard, quietly considering the prophet's words.

"This must be the son of Borkia, the officer that I asked to educate the citizens in regard to our law codes. Medoa's records indicated that he married a young maiden, and a male citizen was born." When Ral completed his thoughts, he placed his hands on the prophets shoulders.

"Boeski, your father was one of my finest officers and we were close friends. He would have been very proud that his son was such an honored and respected citizen. Boeski, Boeski, I must remember that name. Boeski have you ever wondered why you have attained such great age, while your fellow kinsmen live so few short years?

"Yes commander, I had always believed that my age was a special gift from the Rhadda."

"It's because your father was a Ceylonian, just as you and I, my friend, and you will live and die just like all other Ceylonians. Your first life cycle is nearly finished, and at the time of your death, you will live again, and be able to enjoy more extended life cycles. Boeski, just imagine the many things we can continue to accomplish together"

The prophet became silent, as he recalled his mother telling him that his father was a space traveler, and that he was waiting for the return of a spaceship to take them to a distant planet. Boeski was so heartbroken that he had not believed the words of his mother and responded to Ral with tears in his eyes.

"I am sorry commander," responded Boeski harshly, "but I must refuse your kindly offer, because these extended life spans are far removed from the will of the Rhadda. My natural life will end as you predict, and I appreciate having been blessed abundantly by the Rhadda. It's has been astonishing, having this extra time in order to accomplish so many great deeds in the name of my god, and now my life is drawing to a close, I desire to serve in his divine presence. There is not much I can do about being born of Ceylonian blood, but at least I am able to accept the fact, that it is a natural age, and the creator's special gift to the Ceylonians."

"Listen to me Ral, when all that exist, ends at the appointed time, the son of light, after subduing all things, will surrender totally and be transformed back into the essence of the life giver."

"Boeski, are you this son of light?"

"Ral, I know who I am, if only you would perceive of who you are, in regard to your relationship with the great Spirit."

"Boeski, will I know you when I reach the spiritual plane? What will it be like?"

"Ral these are things I am not permitted to reveal, time and season are in the hands of the Rhadda, and I am only his servant as you are."

"Boeski, since your father was a Ceylonian officer, you are entitled to his academy benefits, this includes your father's pension, exclusive rights to the Ceylonian archives, and transportation to any star-port in the galaxies, I am so sorry it has taken me this long to recognize you and to present you with your due honors."

"Commander you are a dear friend and I am honored that you think so highly of me, but I have no need of money and material things, unless you donate them for me to the poor and the needy, not just on the Feramas, but anywhere throughout the universe where there is hunger or lack of clothing. I feel that your remaining honors are in line with the plan of Rhadda, and I would like to continue my education, so that I may continue to help my people advance on the Feramas. I feel it is necessary that I spend extended periods of time with you, so that between Medoa and myself, we may help guide you into the path of your destiny."

"Well, at least for now, the citizens are reestablished on the land, and I have received good reports concerning your successor on the Feramas. I have temporarily placed officer Dadar to watch over their affairs, as I continue to establish new colonies throughout the galaxies. Boeski, it appears the Chaldocians are striving to adhere to Ceylonian laws."

"Commander, your Ceylonian laws were abolished long ago. The laws had a few great concepts, some of them reflected the benevolence of the creator, and the Chaldocians in the early years, had borrowed from your laws. But the teachings of servitude caused many problems, forcing the citizens into bondage. Ral this is why you left, because you became uncomfortable with the multitudes of injustice. The great spirit spoke with Chaldoc on the high mountain and gave his laws, which teach that we are all free to love, not only our fellowmen, but even those that lift their hand against us."

"Boeski," Ral commenced laughing loudly. "I can see me running up to Gormia, the Zecra, especially after he was responsible for my first death. Yes, I can just see me putting my arms around his stinking neck and wishing him well."

"Ral, these are the kind of laws you will need to abide by, if you are to accept your creator."

"Boeski do you mind if I call you prophet? I have called you that for so long that it just seems unnatural to call you anything else."

"Fine said Boeski, I'm ready to travel, but before I bid you goodnight, I am pleased to inform you that a wonderful blessing is about to happen, and with that thought, I will depart for my needed rest, goodnight commander."

"Prophet in the morning, I will also have some good news for you. Goodnight Boeski, I mean prophet."

Both citizens smiled as they departed.

## THE PROPHET'S SURPRISE

Ral was pacing back and forth in anticipation early the next morning.

"Medoa send for Boeski, and make sure everything is kept secret until the right moment."

"Ral I know you consider that you are right, I also realize how much you care for the prophet. But commander, I have advised you against doing this unholy act, and now you alone are the one to bear any disgrace or shame in this matter."

The prophet arrived, just as he always did, feeling very up and excited about the wonderful adventures that lay in store for him.

"Boeski, I have someone in the next room that I would like for you to meet, someone of high authority and I believe you will be pleased to meet him."

The lights were darkened and there sitting in a chair, under a colorful light, was a strong handsome citizen with very familiar features. Boeski cautiously looked deep into his eyes, but the citizen appeared to stare right through him. Boeski had the feeling that he might have known this citizen that wore the uniform of a Ceylonian officer but the silence was unnerving.

"Boeski, meet my old friend, and your father, Borkia."

The prophet stood, dumbfounded.

"Ral you can't be serious? This officer is my father?"

"Yes Boeski, this is the surprise that I promised, to honor all the great works that you have carried out in the name of Ceylon."

"Ral, do you realize you have performed sacrilege against my god? Commander this is not my father! Borkia my father lies buried on the Feramas. I can tell from observing this citizen that he is void of every mental facility. This shell of a citizen is also lacking a god given soul, commander, why have you brought such disgrace to my mother's wonderful name?"

Ral thought he was doing something wonderful for his friend, and he could not understand the prophet's way of thinking.

Borkia, had been buried under the contaminated soil of the Feramas, thus his atomic structures had been tainted. This atomic alteration could caused vast problems for the regeneration of any citizen.

"Ral, please listen to me. If I have ever asked any favor, do this one last deed for me."

"Tell me Boeski, I will do anything in my power to honor your request."

"Place this citizen's shell into the molecular field and then return his ashes to the sacred burial site next to Majia, my mother."

From that day, Boeski was never the same, and if Ral had accomplished anything, he coerced the prophet to consider his true feelings for his father. The prophet was devastated after the initial encounter with his father, and afterwards, he spent a great deal time in humble meditation.

"Mother had tried to tell me that father had claimed to be a extraterrestrial, but I mocked her words. I could not understand that others might dwell beyond the Feramas skies, and I struggled hard to wipe out father's name and his teachings from the sacred books of the Feramas. Why would I have done that? How it must have broken mother's heart."

The guilt and hurt tore into the soul of Boeski, while he thought of his mother's great love and the lost love of a father that he never knew.

"Oh great Rhadda, I realize what mother implied when she said that I would see father again."

The prophet understood for the first time in his life that he was not perfect and that he was just as sinful as all other imperfect citizens on the Feramas. But he had dishonored the memory of his mother and father, and to Boeski, this sin was unforgivable.

"Rhadda!" Boeski cried out in deep remorse. "I thought I had lived an upright and just life before you, but now I can see my blackened sin against father and mother. Did you not tell us to give special honor to those that bring up their children in righteousness? Forgive me, O' Great Spirit, for I am no longer worthy to enter into your Golden City of Light."

Tears flowed like raindrops down the prophet's face, as he tore his cloths and pulled the hair of his beard. "Oh great Rhadda, I have sinned. I was so self righteous, believing that I was worthy to be lifted higher than the Feramas skies, and loftier than my beloved citizens." Boeski caught himself when he said, "My beloved," and again, he asked his god's forgiveness. Rhadda, how could I believe that a sinner such as I, could ever deserve to sit in the very presence of your majestic throne?"

Ral walked over and tried to say something to comfort his friend, but there was nothing he could say except, "all you ask will be done."

Ral then exited the room but he knew that his relationship with the prophet had been severed. Ral would soon send the aging prophet on his final assignment, and he knew that from the day the prophet saw his father, something snapped, and Boeski would never be the same again.

## RAL & DREARA'S BLISS, THE BIRTH OF JEDAR

Ral was in a state of melancholy, as the Tri-Star soared into the regions of outer space. The Feramas was at least for the moment, safe in the hand of officer Dadar, and the Kronos had been silent for some time. It was almost like something was just waiting to happen, but Ral was willing to enjoy the tranquility and peace for as long as possible.

"Commander, commander, come quick." Spoke Lt. Loufa. "Dreara is experiencing delivery pains."

"Lt. Loufa it is for this very reason that the academy has dispatched their capable doctor to assist us, have Renna page for Dr. Louska to join us in the medical room."

Dreara appeared to be in pain, but Dr. Louska assured Ral that everything was normal, and even though Dreara was going to raise this little one, it was still to be born within the guidelines of academy rules.

Ral began feeling woozy, after all, he never experienced anything like this, because all berthing procedures took place in the secret chambers of the Academy Medical Center.

All Ceylonians, even if they were married, were forbidden to engage in sexual relations under the penalty of death. If they desired a child, the female was impregnated by veto fertilization. Only the purest sperm containing the strongest genetic chemistry from Ceylonian nobles was considered for donation.

Politicians and higher ranking officers were privileged to donate their own seed, not only to help populate the general public, but for impregnation of their wives. The nobles were forbidden to have sex under penalty of death. The Ceylonians believed this regulated child bearing, and thus continued to maintain Ceylon as the master race. After all, they reigned over the Seventh Quadrant for countless thousands of years.

While Dreara was being sedated in the delivery room, Kiah began to occupy Ral's thoughts. "Kiah was my child, but because of father's dominance, he was really raised as Atar's son, and perhaps that is why we were never close." Ral thought back to his last trip to Ceylon, when he heard that Kiah was promoted to Academy Star Base Commander. He was very proud of his son, but he wondered what the future might hold for him. Ral even considered that Kiah and his sons in the future, would join forces fighting for Ceylon's right to reign supreme throughout the Seventh Quadrant.

"It's a male citizen," shouted Dr. Louska, with a look of contentment on his face, as he held the child upside down, spanking his behind. The tiny citizen let out a loud cry and a noticeable gulp.

"Congratulations," spoke Medoa, as he watched his friend running around the room shouting, "It's a male citizen! It's a male citizen!" Medoa firmly placed his hand on Ral's shoulder, and the commander immediately slowed down and began to relax.

"Ral, Dreara will need time to be alone with the infant and I would like to take this time to speak with you in private. Ral the ways of Ceylon have never worked, and it is now necessary for you to begin judging by what's in your heart. If you feel it is important for the child to remain with Dreara, let it be so. I feel within my spirit that the Unni has great plans for the new born citizen. By the way, what will be his name?"

Ral was caught somewhat off guard, he had not given any consideration to a name. It was not so done in Ceylon, names were determined by the academy, which assigned them purposeful names that lent to their varied types of personalities and strengths.

"Ral as your personal advisor on this ship, let me give you some professional food for thought. Now that you are in a family relationship, perhaps it's time for you to begin including Dreara in the affairs of your life, and you might consider sharing with her, in this time of need."

"Yes Medoa, perhaps you may be right, I will speak with her this evening."

Dreara was sitting up in her rest chamber, while holding the little one on her lap. Ral approached her, by kneeling before her, which was strange to Dreara, because males on Ceylon never placed themselves in such compromising positions. Ral realized that this could be looked upon by his crew as a form of weakness, but Dreara placed his head in her lap and began to stroke his long flowing curly hair, pointing to the many streaks of gray. Dreara then whispered in his ear that it made him look very distinguished.

"Have you thought of a name Dreara?" Ral whispered as if he were on the verge of sleep.

"Yes, I feel that it should be a strong name, one that will be renowned and celebrated. Jedar is a name that reflects both strength and gentleness, embodying everything I see and feel in you. It is a name that for a strange reason has been fixed in my memory, I must have reiterated it over and over a hundred times or more these past few days, almost as if it were haunting me."

"You are not as the men of Ceylon, and my husband, you have never been so inclined, what you lack in knowledge, you make up in kindness and consideration. Yes, Jedar is his name."

For now, everything was going as well as expected. Ral and Dreara would be spending a great deal of time learning to care for Jedar, but in the meantime, Ragan was not idle, as he used his time to continue spreading corruption throughout the land, while Ral's interest was catered entirely to the affairs of his family.

# CHAPTER 9

## GEMAAL GREETS RAGAN ON CEYLON

Ragan had grown very desperate, especially after his last attempt to wage war against Ceylon, under the combined endeavor of the Zecra and Kronos nations, wherein he had failed miserably. This time Ragan would take his deceit and cunning into the heart of everything that Atar had stood for, Imperial Ceylon, the seat of its government.

"Gemaal this is truly an honor, you may not remember me, but we met briefly during my early years at the academy. I recollect that you had great expectations for yourself and I can see that you have fulfilled each and every dream. Gemaal, we do have one thing in common and that is our shared hatred of Atar and his family. This is the reason I have approached you in this private audience, outside of your established protocol. This is also why I have asked you not to invite Kiah, your regent of the academy fleet, it would tend to place a very dark shadow over our discussion."

"This is true Ragan, but circumstances have prevailed that Kiah, whom I by the way, recently appointed as Commander of the Academy, is currently involved in negotiations with the Peistoid Colony, which is seeking our protection from neighboring intruders. Kiah will return soon enough, and I am sure you will have a chance to meet him, he is an industrious young man, perhaps you might even enjoy conversing with him, concerning his exploits throughout the Seventh Quadrant, which by the way, are widely written about."

"Stop right there governor! For one thing, I pray that I never have to look upon the face of a man that I would cross every quadrant in the known galaxies to kill. I am apt to look at him and then plunge my knife through his superior heart, so as you see, the less I see of him, the better for our negotiations."

"That is splendid Ragan, I was just baiting you, to see your true feelings, for some strange reason you fascinate me. I have heard of your exploitation on the Feramas, just as I keep abreast of all settlements throughout our jurisdiction. Please Ragan sit, and have a strong drink of Tanger, as you know this is the most prized libation in all Ceylon. Ragan you have a natural ability to gain the influence over those you come into contact with, perhaps a citizen with your particular talents could be a valuable asset to our colonies, there is one concern, and that is the planet of your birth, Zylon, I believe?"

"Governor, my father struggled hard during his servitude to the Ceylonians, and after he achieved his freedom, he later married my mother, a citizen of Ceylon, and by pure tenacity, he was elected mayor of a major Zylonian province. I eventually left my home to offer my complete allegiance to those that conquered us, the mighty Ceylonians. I served in your academy, placing my life on the line, while campaigning in battles against the Damar and the Lekraals. The encounter with the Lekraals was the battle in which Captain Ral and myself received the academies highest accommodation for valor beyond the call of duty."

Ragan suddenly caught himself smiling, as he momentarily recalled the good times they shared together after graduating from the academy, but reality quickly sprang back into perspective and the sinister look returned to Ragan's dark countenance.

"Ragan, I have a position open in the Exploratory Division, which could benefit the both of us. Your name could be proclaimed throughout the provinces of Ceylon as my personal ambassador, and I would have the satisfaction of working with a citizen that has the power to change the destiny of the entire universe. The council will have the final say regarding your nomination, but until that time, I will appoint you as my magistrate. But before this takes place, you must be trained in the latest developments, that have taken place in Ceylon since you have been in hiatus."

Gemaal knew Ceylon would not be spinning much longer. He had concealed it from Kiah, members of the council, and at the moment, he must keep his secret hidden from Ragan. Gemaal realized, it was time to begin setting the wheels in motion, because the calamity would soon render Ceylon a void and useless planet.

## RAGAN CEYLON'S MAGISTRATE

Ragan, due to his cunning was loved by the Ceylonians and they welcomed him with parades, casting flower pedals at his feet saying, "praises to Gemaal and Ragan." The crowds roared, "live forever saviors of the land."

Ragan, began seeking favor with the citizens to appropriate all authority for himself. But in spite of his cunning, Ragan failed to consider that Gemaal had planned every event that was unfolding. For Gemaal reasoned that he could maintain his position as one of the most respected leaders of Ceylon, while placing the downfall on poor unsuspecting Ragan.

Ragan continued his pursuit for the official nomination of ambassador by making appearances throughout Ceylon in behalf of the governor. He would sit outside the large gates, at the entrance into the domed city and with insincere affections, shake the hands of each passerby that would enter in.

Gemaal suspected that Ragan's strategy would be to replace him as governor, while he set up his own rule. Gemaal realized that Ragan was a force to contend with, but for now he must maintain his honored position as governor, before the eventual demise of Ceylon. Ragan would be curtailed, but yet, permitted enough rope to hang himself. The more Ragan reflected, concerning his hate for the Ceylonians, the stronger his desire to annihilate them, for Ragan it was payback, and he was the master of evil and unmerciful revenge.

## RAGAN REJECTED AS AMBASSADOR

Once again, Ragan's plans were to be set aside, because the council decided the vote to elect the new ambassador. A few of the council members had been swayed by the smooth glib of Ragan, but this intruder disguising himself as a Ceylonian, was not of unadulterated Ceylonian lineage. When the council became aware of Ragan's revolt, Ceylon was already in a state of turmoil, fights broke out in the streets of every major province, each man began stealing from his neighbor, and disrespect for their government was widespread. Schools were closing, and the young citizens were becoming more and more defiant against their teachers and parents.

The statues of Dreeska and Atar that had stood so stately and proud, were now tumbled to the ground and left to lie in a heap for everyone to trample upon. Even the flags of Ceylon were ripped from their poles by depraved drunken citizens who slashed the old and honored black and gold colors. Many even stood urinating on the Grand O' Flag. Their laughs were that of mad men and they saluted their flag, which lay crumbled in the mud.

Kiah, after successfully completing negotiations with the Peistoid colony, had received orders to travel directly to his next assignment, which would take him deep into the Sixth Quadrant, but the commander, having not seen his family for more than a solar year, decided to temporarily defy the new order and take a few days of rest.

Gemaal recognized that Kiah was held in high esteem, not only by the academy and the citizens, but by the council itself, and if Kiah had the opportunity to observe the injustice, Gemaal knew his diabolical plans could come to an abrupt end.

After Kiah's starship landed, he walked through the Grand Pavilion, and at first things appeared fairly normal, but by the time he settled down, he was aware that something seriously was wrong.

After searching through the Media News, he began hearing concerning the saddened state of affairs taking place throughout his homeland.

"Renouna my dear wife, why didn't you let me know the seriousness of what is taking place throughout our colonies?"

"Kiah the council has been very protective of us, they have provided us with total security, and we have been issued some of the finest clothing, made by the renown tailors from Sabra. They never divulged anything to me, only that you would be gone on extended missions, and I reasoned, because you are the honored grandson of Atar, that we were being blessed."

"Renouna there is something going on and Gemaal is not letting me stay here long enough to find out why these things are happening." He pondered as he tapped his fingers against the table. "Why am I being sent on reconnaissance missions to distant areas that could be patrolled by junior academy officers?"

Kiah's children were busy in the next room, and this was the first time that Kiah heard Jemar, his first born, curse and rebel against his mother.

"Something is drastically wrong and I will somehow get to the bottom of it, I can feel it deep within every fiber of my being. Yes, ever who is responsible for this fiasco has taken Ceylon back to the conditions that existed on old Ceylon?"

## GEMAAL'S CONFESSION

Kiah arrived unannounced, as he abruptly stormed into the private chamber of Gemaal.

"Kiah what are you doing here, have you lost your mind?"

"Negative governor, it appears the destruction throughout Ceylon has been precipitated by a madman and right now, I demand some answers."

"You are right Kiah, and perhaps if these conditions can be altered, then we may be able to restore a little dignity to our beloved planet before it is blown into space dust."

Gemaal repented, regarding his injustice, and revealed to Kiah all that had been hidden from him.

## RAGAN BANISHED FROM CEYLON

"Ral, Ral!" Ragan cried out in great rage, pacing back and forth in his chamber. "You have wanted to return to the ancient days of Ceylon and fight it out man to man. I hope you soon hear of my success, when I am elected ambassador of this pathetic land. I am waiting, yes Ral, waiting for you to come and confront me man to man. By the time of your arrival, perhaps they will have proclaimed me as ambassador. And then, you pathetic piece of space crap, you will pray to your ancient god, regretting the day you were ever born and I will have my revenge upon the house of Atar."

The day passed by quickly, and Ragan was still reflecting, concerning his hatred for Ral, when suddenly he was confronted by Governor Gemaal and the Council's Enforcement Team.

"Ragan," spoke Gemaal, "you have destroyed everything that was good on our beloved planet and brought our colonies into a state of chaos. We, under the leadership of Commander Kiah, have successfully suppressed many of the uprisings, which you were able to instigate. We have just met privately with the council and have voted in complete agreement to banish you from Ceylon. With you finally out of our way, perhaps at least for the moment, our citizens may gain back some of the decency and respect that you have stolen from them."

"I first thought to have you destroyed, but the citizens may have rebelled against us. Therefore, you will be privately escorted by Commander Kiah, aboard my starship, and there transported to the Agreg Penal Colony, where you will spend the balance of your life, slaving under the cruel whip of Mondor the Agregleourite."

Ragan was stripped and led away blindfolded into the dark Ceylonian night, where the governor's starship was waiting. Gemaal hastened to have Ragan banished as quickly as possible, to prevent a potential uprising from the citizens.

"I am not finished with you Gemaal, and as for you, O' great Commander Kiah, I spit in your face, and the day will come when I Ragan, will look upon you as the worms crawl through your vile and hideous body. I will also cut off your head and permanently place it on a rock, so that your skeletal eyes will forever be looking up to me. You believe as your stupid father, that universal clown, that I am curtailed and my powers are diminished."

"Kiah you are a joke as your father and grandfather before him. When I return, you will see the greatest destruction that could ever be unleashed throughout the far reaches of the universe."

Gemaal along with members of the council, watched as the fire from the bowels of the starship faded deep into space and waned dimly out of sight.

"Keeksonn." Asked Brudda. "Do you believe that we are finally free from Ragan's treachery?"

"I don't know Brudda, I feel that his evil nature could once again surface, but my hope is that we will never hear again from this wicked citizen known throughout the galaxies as Ragan. I am elated that he is far away from our beloved Ceylon, and Brudda, I wouldn't be too offended if Kiah just dumped him off as space junk."

As the starship soared into the distant heavens, Kiah, now intoxicated on fermented Tanger, began to have thoughts about his father. It all seemed strange to Kiah, for he rarely had time for such concerns before.

"I wonder if Dreara has delivered my little half-brother or sister. Father will never know that it was my influence with Gemaal that made it possible for him to keep the little one." Kiah becoming more intoxicated, continued to rambled on. "Why am I having these thoughts of father? Perhaps I will soon meet with him face to face, and then I can explain why Gemaal chose me, the grandson of Atar, to replace him as commander of the academy. There is one thing I know." Kiah reflected, as he took another drink, "I will keep closer watch over the affairs of my family, especially the little one that is about to be born."

Kiah gazed into the distant heavens, feeling as if he must have passed by at least a trillion stars. Kiah closed his eyes and tried to remember his father's face, and all the excitement of growing up in his grandfather's home.

"Father will never realize that it was my influence with the council, that made it possible for him to keep his patrol of the Feramas, I'll probably never tell him."

Kiah was anxious to reach the penal colony of Agreg, because Ragan was unrelenting in his derogatory words against the commander, and that was something Kiah could live without, he then fell asleep from the affects of the fermented Tanger.

## CHAPTER 10

### MONDOR THE AGREGLEOURITE

Mondor's family had lived on Zerena for many generations, they had originally arrived from a small distant planet called Groga, but this was generations ago, and there was no recorded information concerning the small planet. Mondor never learned the history of his Groga ancestry, but the difference between the looks of Mondor and the typical citizen of Zerena, revealed a lot upon examination.

The citizens of Zerena were typically smaller in size than those on neighboring planets, but Mondor and his ancestors were five times larger than citizens anywhere to be found. Their physical appearance was another reason why the Groga giants were so feared among the citizenship. Mondor had facial features that were more diverse than anywhere throughout the Seventh Quadrant. Especially grotesque were the small cancerous circular pods, which encircled his head. This unique development gave the Groga on Zerena the visual advantage in combat situations by providing sight from every angle. The extended ears and immense nose, gave Mondor a bizarre appearance. Specialized molecules had evolved and combined into a resourceful organ, which was located along the side of the neck. Protruding out of this organ there was an elongated tube, which was sensitive to light, cold and heat. A foul smelling green ooze seeped from the end of the tube, it is uncertain, but it is believed to be the source of their sperm. The tube also had twenty-five senses, which could detect everything from the presence of wild game to the smell of their enemy, even if they were concealed within a distance of five miles. These organs were genetically programmed to shut down, if an odor was overbearing, especially to the point of death.

Mondor was able to drink enough fermented alcohol that in one sitting, he could drink more than all the Zerena citizens put together. Mondor had his own vineyard, which he faithfully tended, producing enough fermented juice to satisfy his horrendous thirst.

Mondor's family had lived on Zerena for a vast number of years, and due to the Groga's great size, the food supply on Zerena was becoming a rarity. In fact, the Groga had long contemplated the idea of moving once again to more productive areas.

## THE SURRENDER OF THE ZERENA

The land about Zerena was mostly comprised of volcanic ash and enormous boulders, which covered the land every few feet. The clearing for housing and business establishments was left in the hands of the strong young Groga. Mondor was a true giant by all definition of the word, and his capacity for physical energy, brought about by his life of extreme manual labor, had hardened his body to the peak of perfection.

Because of the rocky landscape on Zerena, the citizens were dependent upon imports from neighboring planets, especially needed were clothing, transportation and food. Fortunately for the Zerena, there was a remote and desolate land area called Agreg. The land was virtually uninhabitable, due to the vast abundance of sulfur and tar pits, but after the giants learned to mine the thick substance, it became a lucrative export. The tar was used as a sealant, and as fuel for homes. Only the Groga giants, like Mondor, because of their physical stamina, could withstand the rugged conditions that existed on Agreg, but in return the giants were well compensated for their labors. Zerena was virtually crime free, due to the fact, that if they broke a law, they would be sent to Agreg to die an agonizing death. Just the mention of the name, Agreg, brought fear into the hearts of the small citizens of Zerena.

When Atar was a young academy officer, Zerena fell under Ceylonian domination. The historical records of Ceylon states that when the enemy submits, protocol calls for its leaders to bow before their conqueror with head stooped in defeat.

It also reads, that the Groga failed to bow before Captain Atar, instead, Mokaz, grandfather of Mondor, reached out with his huge hands, grabbing two officers standing nearby. The Ceylonian officers were crushed by the force of Mokaz's grip, and before Atar could react, the two officers lay dead at his feet.

Captain Atar crouched low, away from the eyes of Mokaz, firing his lazier. When Mokaz fell, the ground shook, as if it were hit by a minor earthquake. With Mokaz's death, the Zerena turned their loyalty over to the Ceylonians. The son of Mokaz, Mondor's father, although very young, was required to appear before Atar to discuss the conduct of capture. Machiaz was as large and vile as his father, it was just the nature of the Groga giants to be as mean and malicious as possible.

That evening they sat down for a meal after the successful conference and it was decided that the Zerena would operate in the same manner as they always had. Trade between the planets would be conducted under Ceylonian direction and a percentage would be paid to the Ceylonian treasury.

Machiaz could care less if Atar had just killed his father, the Groga were void of any natural affection, greed was their only motivation and now Machiaz was in charge of the affairs of Zerena, which to him implied wealth.

## THE INTERPLANETARY GAMES

Machiaz was at the height of physical development, when Atar suggested that he take part in the Inter-Galactic Contest to fight as Ceylon's champion.

During the opening days of the competition, each colony throughout the quadrants would send their most fit specimens to fight for the honor of their representative planet, a sporting event of barbarity that had been observed for vast numbers of years.

The games were held on the neutral colony of Ceekra and Atar felt exhilarated, while watching the citizens engaging in life to death confrontations. After he had risen in the ranks of the academy, Atar realized he must abandon any thoughts concerning this form of entertainment, if he were to attain to higher aspirations as a military leader. But so far away from the scrutiny of the Ceylonian council, Atar felt uninhibited, while enjoying the inter galactic competition.

Atar watched as each participant engaged in their battle of death, and during intermission, he tried to reason out each life and death episode in his mind.

"On Ceylon", Atar reflected, "death is a way of life. Those that break the smallest infraction of the law are required to walk into the Molecular Field, thus, being reduced to cremated rubble. But here death is challenging, a chance to actually fight for the very existence to live, even if it implies merely surviving long enough to die in the next battle."

Atar looked somewhat bemused as the combatants from the competing planets entered the arena and Machiaz began making his entrance. Atar gazed around the stadium, and thought to himself, "I I have never beheld such ugly citizens, and I thought Mokaz and Machiaz were ugly?"

Atar knew he could not speak these words openly, because his thoughts were not protected from the telepathist, who were also in attendance, but he realized they were a peaceful people. He also considered that he was not held in high regard by those around him, and suddenly he began to grow a little apprehensive in such a hostile environment.

## THE CITIZEN FROM DA ENDEN

When the final contest began, it was not surprising to see Machiaz still standing in the victory circle. His final opponent was a citizen from one of the Da Enden colonies.

"How interesting," thought Atar, "that the citizen from Da Enden, and of such diminutive size, could have survived the many conflicts, in order to stand before the champion from Zerena." The comparison in size was so vast that Atar began to laugh quietly.

Atar, was to see the answer to his thoughts demonstrated, because the small citizen had developed his mental ability so acutely that electrical energy could shoot forth from hole-like structures in his skin. This built in defense system had worked well throughout the contest, but he had yet to face an adversary the size of Machiaz.

The bantam sized citizen believed that he had the edge to move quickly around such a large challenger, and then he cautiously began to stalk Machiaz, by turning and turning, until his opponent was facing into the sun.

When Machiaz found himself facing into the sun, he was temporarily blinded, and the citizen from Da Enden sent out shock waves that could have killed fifty normal men. Machiaz fell into the stands, killing two of the spectators from the mere weight of his fall.

The citizen from Da Enden was standing confidently in his neutral corner, waiting on his adversary to approach him, and began to ready himself for the kill.

Suddenly, Machiaz was practically on top of him. "Small one," roared Machiaz, "no one has ever gone the distance with me and lived, now prepare to die." The citizen from Da Enden puffed himself up like a horned toad and readied himself for the attack. But his efforts had drained the needed energy from his body, and before there was time to regain his strength, the large hand of Machiaz crushed the fragile bones of the tiny citizen, causing the remaining electrical impulses to go off, electrocuting him.

Machiaz held the limp frame high above his head in one hand, turning in the four directions of the stadium to receive his due honors, as the crowd cheered. "Machiaz is our champion, may his children be blessed."

Atar disliked Machiaz, but he felt a certain sense of pride that his champion had won the Intergalactic championship. For his victory, Atar offered Machiaz and his descendants an assignment, which Machiaz would not refuse.

The Ceylonian Empire long ago, established what would become known as the ultimate prison. These penal colonies were located on forsaken planets, with the purpose of punishing the vilest prisoners throughout the entire Seventh Quadrant. Machiaz accepted the assignment with one stipulation, that his prison be set up in Agreg, Zerena's remote barren land.

After the establishment of the Agreg prison, the council on Ceylon rarely sent their citizens to the penal colony, because there was little crime. The Ceylonian citizens had been so thoroughly brained washed that they voluntarily turn themselves in, and if they were found guilty, they were quickly disposed of in the Molecular Field. So if a Ceylonian was ever sent to Agreg, the sole purpose would not be to have the offender die the sweet death, but to suffer at the hands of the cruelest taskmasters in the universe, the Groga giants. Fortunately for Ceylonian criminals, only a handful of their vilest had ever ventured there.

## MONDOR TASKMASTER OF AGREG PENAL COLONY

Mondor, the son of Machiaz, grandson of Mokaz, stands unchallenged throughout the penal colony of modern day Agreg. He remains, as his father before him the people's champion, yet he is detested throughout the universe. His reputation as taskmaster has made him infamous, there has never been any tyrant that has ever surpassed his passion for the cruelty heaped upon the masses, and the name of Mondor will ever be remembered throughout planetary history.

The prisoners would look up to watch Mondor, while he purposely stood upon high mounds, which were chosen by Mondor to emphasize his enormous physique.

"I would kill him in a second, if I had him back on Pechka." Replied one of the prisoners.

"We don't have a chance against him, even if we banned together." Another cried out.

Mondor because of his heightened senses, knew those who spoke against him, and would take his spiked whip, punishing the guilty beyond recognition. He also without mercy, would take the whip to those who were standing idly by.

"This is what happens to those that dare open their mouth against Mondor." The sounds of his whip echoed in the distance.

The Groga could care less if the prisoners lived, for all they meant to Mondor was another tasty meal, for he was cannibalistic. There also was a monthly flow of new detainees, keeping Mondor's table abundant with the flesh of the galaxies most delicious citizens.

Mondor, unlike his father, held a grudge against Atar for killing his grandfather and placing the Zerena under servitude to the Ceylonians.

"If I had that Ceylonian bastard, I would squeeze the life-blood out of him." The more he thought about Atar, the more his whip would begin to crack across the backs of the prisoners.

## KIAH MEETS MONDOR ON AGREG

Little did Mondor realize that Kiah, grandson of Atar, was approaching Agreg with the most feared and dangerous prisoner of all time, Ragan.

The natural gases being emitted from beneath the surface of Agreg, fueled the fires to burn day and night, and the smoke from the burning was black as night and ascended miles into the heavens.

It was the presence of this smoke that assured Kiah that he was approaching the infamous penal colony.

When Kiah and his security officer, Rogara, began their ride from the landing zone into the prison area, it was the sounds of the screaming citizens that put a chill down the spine of Rogara.

"I have never heard such cries of torment. Kiah, please do this deed quickly, and let's get out of here."

"We will definitely be departing in the morning, Rogara." Kiah would never admit it, but the screams had also affected him.

"Kiah, what is that smell? I can barely breathe."

"Sulfur gas, and tar fumes, Rogara, place your mask over your face and you will be all-right."

Death was an extremely benevolent blessing on Agreg, but came slowly to the prisoners. The combination of suffocating gases would slowly destroy the lining of the throat and stomach of the prisoners. This along with the cruel whip of Mondor, added to a short life-span of the damned.

Mondor received word of the approaching visitors, after all, this was still a job to Mondor, and so he always made it a point to welcome each visiting party.

"I Mondor of Agreg, welcome the Ceylonian commander and his party, welcome to my home."

Rogara frowned when he heard the word home in relation to such a harsh environment.

"Perhaps I can serve you a drink." Mondor spoke, almost forgetting his hatred for the Ceylonians.

"You are very gracious," Kiah replied, "but no thank you."

The most important advice that Kiah had learned from his training was to always be aware of your enemy position, for fear of them poisoning the food, and the second consideration was that of personal contact with the enemy, which could possibly spread new diseases throughout the Seventh Quadrant.

"I am Commander of the Ceylonian Academy, and this is my security officer, Rogara."

"We have your prisoner in temporary confinement, but tell Mondor, who is this fiend that is escorted to Agreg by such high ranking officials? Many of the slime that arrive here are usually brought by the garbage detail and dropped off without ever landing. But I feel this to be something special, so tell me commander, who have you brought for Mondor to kill?"

"We have brought Ragan, a Ceylonian half-breed, born on the planet of Zylon, he is the most notorious criminal throughout the Seventh Quadrant, and has been charged by our council for breaking most rules recorded in the Ceylonian Law Codes. I am surprised that you have never heard of him." Spoke Kiah.

"Commander, you can see the conditions I live under on Agreg. There is little time to do anything but keep my mind on the task at hand. Now, your order if I read correctly, has this citizen confined to this penal colony for the duration of his existence?"

Rogara broke Mondor's thought. "If he should happen to depart this life sooner," clearing his throat, Rogara continued, "we would appreciate hearing from you."

Mondor filled the rest of their meeting by telling revolting, yet interesting tales of his victories during the Interplanetary Games. Mondor departed the room, and the stench from his breath seemed to linger.

Rogara from the affects of the wine, began mimicking the ape-like gestures of Mondor. "That giant is nasty." Stated Rogara as he began laughing uncontrollably.

"What are you laughing about Rogara?"

"For some strange reason, I was thinking about Mondor and that gross looking tube sticking out of his neck."

Mondor returned, hearing just enough of the conversation to figure out that he was the brunt of a joke.

"Look you Ceylonian dogs! Just because I am your servant does not mean that I, Mondor, am a puppet to anyone."

Mondor, realizing Rogara had mocked him, walked over and looked him directly in the eyes.

"Do you think I am ugly officer Rogara? My grandfather once snapped the bones of two of your puny Ceylonian officers, and then crushed the life from them with one single squeeze. So may I suggest that you Ceylonian officers keep your thoughts to yourself, or I will have you chained, and my puny friends, I can see from the texture of your skin that I could brew up some very tasty Ceylonian morsels, do you runts understand?"

"Sorry." Spoke Rogara, as he turned his eyes away, looking in Kiah's direction for moral support. "That was close." He spoke just above a whisper.

When Mondor stormed out of the building, Captain Rogara let out a sigh of relief, and whispered to Kiah that he believed the affect of the drinks were beginning to wear off.

"Ok, tuff guy," Kiah chuckled, "let's get some rest before our early morning departure."

The next morning after boarding the governor's craft, Kiah and Rogara were waiting for the computer to give the clearance for final countdown to lift off, and Mondor, at that very moment, began his interrogation of Ragan.

"Ragan, I haven't had a prisoner of your vast reputation to ever enter the gates of Agreg, it will provide me much enjoyment to have new blood to spill upon the rocks of Agreg. Tell me you half-breed Ceylonian, what heinous crimes have you committed to have such an illustrious escort? It must be good, so tell Mondor, before I reach in and crush your stinking throat. Tell me now! Ragan."

"It is for my hatred of the former governor of Ceylon and his son, for which I confess my crimes. If I could have put my knife through Kiah, I would have my day of revenge against Atar and his family."

Mondor immediately stopped him, and grasped Ragan by his throat.

"Tell me little man, what do you know about the Ceylonian by the name of Atar! And who is this Kiah?"

"If you don't release your grip from my throat, I will not be able to tell you anything."

Mondor realizing he could have killed Ragan, released his grip.

"The grandson of Atar was just here, talking with you."

"No! Shouted Mondor, the grandson of Atar within inches of my reach, and now he is gone, I must stop their departure, now!"

Mondor was so large that it was hard for him to swiftly move. He then boarded his shuttle and traveled at full speed to the ships departing zone. Just as Mondor was approaching the area, the governor's starship left a trail of smoke, encircling Mondor's shuttle. Kiah could not hear the words spoken so powerfully by Mondor, but from the force of his cursed screams, the words must have been felt.

.        Mondor returned, and Ragan was beginning to sense what was taking place.

"So you have let the grandson of Atar slip by you. Mondor, I can perhaps be of service to you. I have been around these bungling idiots since my days at the academy. Yes Mondor, I can tell you plenty about the family of Atar."

Mondor being of primitive mind was easily influenced by the cunning words of Ragan, after all, when it came to the family of Atar, they held a lot in common.

"Ragan I have work throughout Agreg, where you could be of great assistance to me."

Ragan thought to himself. "You are offering me a job in this garbage dump? For now Mondor," Ragan smiled to himself and thought, "it won't be long now."

# CHAPTER 11

## JEDAR GROWS UP

Ral, Dreara and Jedar, spent years living aboard the Tri-Star, which was the only home that Jedar ever knew. After Jedar was born, Boeski was there as a constant companion, telling him of his many travels throughout the galaxies. Boeski recognized that Jedar had a brilliant mind, and firmly believed that the creator had exciting plans for the young citizen. While Jedar was still a young child, the prophet was called by Ral to go on one of his extended missions and never returned. Since that time, there had been a great void in Jedar's life, especially now that he had developed into a strong and educated young citizen.

"Father." Jedar pried for the umpteenth time. "You were going to tell me concerning the conditions under which I was born. Please tell me father, you know how I enjoy hearing your wonderful stories."

"All-right Jedar, but I am sure you could enlighten us with your own account of my life. Back in the olden days of Ceylon, many social customs had been abolished, especially ones where the citizens shared a feeling called love. Jedar, after I became academy commander, I desired to experiment in this ancient love making, and your mother joined with me. We accomplished something that was wonderful, and you, my son, are the result of this forbidden liaison. The council miraculously saw fit to allow us to raise you aboard the Tri-Star. Jedar, we desire that you will also heed our example, and bear your children in this same marvelous fashion."

"Father, I could search the galaxies and never find a female citizen that has the wonderful qualities of mother, but when, and if I ever do, yes father, I would also enjoy the beautiful love making as you so vividly describe."

"Father many of the harsh laws that were administered on Ceylon are never enforced here aboard the Tri-Star, can you tell me why?"

"Jedar, It was the prophet who educated me that love was missing from my life. I was brought up under Ceylon's very harsh regulations where love was nonexistent, and because I was seeking love, I eventually had to abandoned my home. I realized this after I met your mother, she brought a spark into my life that had never existed, and by the time I learned what love was all about, I found I was able to love others."

"Jedar I also learned through love that no man is a slave to another, all men are created equal and free. There is no need to enforce Ceylonian laws, because Boeski, along with Medoa, Treeka and Simka, have converted many of those aboard the Tri-Star into conformity to the laws of the Unni. And even though your mother and I, have not been able to conform, at least we have come a long way, from the cynical Ceylonians of long ago. Jedar the older I get, the more I seem to tire, and although I need my rest, I do look forward to the enjoyable moments I share with your mother before we retire for the evening." Ral winked at Jedar as he departed.

Ral had become content with his various regenerations, but thoughts of his final death cycle was beginning to bring distress to his passive nature. But to Jedar, his father, with full length beard was the total embodiment of good in the universe. Jedar idealized that if the Unni had a face to behold, it truly would resemble that of his father.

"Well Jedar, it's getting late," Spoke Ral, "and the ways of the Unni, I leave in the capable hands of Simka."

## SIMKA TELLS FOLKLORE TO JEDAR

Simka was assigned as a guardian and tutor to Jedar, but he never spoke, unless he was first spoken to. This was ingrained in each messenger, having something to do with their nature to serve.

The next evening, Jedar said good evening to his father, walking briskly to his chamber where Simka was guarding the door. When Jedar encountered Simka, he began to chuckle as he recalled the many delightful stories told by his friend.

"Simka please tell me again, some of your wonderful stories before I retire for the evening."

"Long ago, before you were born, Ral personally ventured down to supervise the affairs of the Children of Light. When your father suddenly appeared, seemingly from out of nowhere, one of the disciples believed your father to be the great Rhadda, the god of the Feramas. Your father was in for the fight of his life. The disciple contended with him throughout the day, screaming, if you be a god, bless me?" The only means wherein Ral could get loose, was to use his lazier in the disabling position, which crippled the holy man in his thigh, and the wound remained a running sore for the duration of his life."

"The citizen became a leader of the Sons of Light, and the wounded area of his thigh, became a hallowed spot of blessings for the Chaldocians until the holy man's death."

"Ral felt terrible about hurting the disciple, but after the ordeal, he felt it best not to have further contact with the citizens, so he soon began sending Treeka or me, due to our ability to transform from the physical to the spiritual state."

"That's exciting Simka, I love to hear stories about your encounters, especially those concerning father."

"Simka I promise not to bother you again, but if you will tell me just one more story?"

"Why not? But I must be brief. The female was fair and beautiful, beyond all description, and after Ragan had relations with her, there were four significant children born unto her. Their names were Teeska, Crual, Maskra, Pluata and female offspring."

"The male was a sexual disappointment, in that he was inept, producing modest seed. He was never close to the female, spending much time in seclusion, and not much is heard concerning him. They had one son, which they called Adrada, and he realized the importance of populating the land. Sisters and brothers mated, having prominent cities named after them. The children of Adrada being: Chaldoc, Creeska. Banurk, Fraunau and Loupa."

"It was through Chaldoc that all future genealogies of the Caldocians were traced, the prophet, although unique in Ceylonian longevity, claimed this Chaldocian lineage, and kept the prophecies alive, concerning the Rhadda's son, that would someday come to dwell among them. His words of wisdom always kept the spirits of hope high in the nation of Chaldoc."

"I remember your joy, when you engage in recreation with the prophet aboard the Tri-Star, it was almost as if there was a bond between you. I know he loved you Jedar, as if you may have been his own seed."

"Yes Simka, I remember Boeski, and the Sons of Chaldoc, when they long ago, dwelt among us on the Tri-Star, but it was the many exciting stories that you told me about how father saved the prophet from his narrow escapes from the clutches of Ragan, that is what I enjoy hearing."

Simka shrugged his shoulders, as he once again explained to Jedar how Boeski had hitched a ride on a fishing vessel. "Jedar, when the captain ventured out to sea, a tempest arose and the crew accused Boeski of being a curse, throwing him overboard. Ral saved the prophet, when he sent Treeka to the rescue. When Ral saw the prophet walking toward the shore with seaweed hanging from his hair and mouth, he laughed so hard that he burst a small vessel in his neck. In fact, it was so humorous to your father that he felt the small pain was worth it, and he realized that it was an event that he would hold dear. Ral also desired to meet this extraordinary citizen and afterwards, they did become very close friends."

"What happened to the prophet Simka? Why did he not say goodbye to me?"

"Jedar, it wasn't long after you last saw the prophet that he went on his final mission for your father. Then one night in peaceful slumber, Boeski heard the Rhadda speak to him saying:

*"Boeski, it is time for your rest, you have wagged the battle over evil and you have endured the life-long test. Boeski, hear my words of comfort in this quite hour. Boeski, there is another light that will shine after you are gone, it is he, to whom all citizens shall seek. You were my special herald proclaiming to my children, my divine love. Be comforted my child, for you shall occupy a place of honor in my delightful city, where you shall see all those that came to know me through your works. Now go to sleep sweet Boeski and enter into my rest."*

"Jedar," continued Simka, "no one knew where Boeski was buried. Some say he was carried off by heavenly messengers into the Golden City, still others say he was buried in a secret place on the Feramas. There still remains a story that exist in the archives of the Chaldocians that the grave of a renown prophet was known and honored for many generations. The story is told that a citizen was buried in the prophet's grave, and that after the dead citizen came in contact with the prophet's sacred bones, he came up out of the grave, walking and prophesying concerning his god. If the story is not true, Jedar I have a feeling that Boeski expired in contentment and his spirit entered into the Golden City, shouting with triumph."

"Jedar you are full of questions, and no doubt, you are able to grasp the true meaning of all I say to you, and I would love to sit with you throughout the evening, but I have been transformed in my physical form too long, and it is tiring me in my effort to maintain it. But I will leave you with one more thought before retiring. Jedar this is of the utmost importance. Medoa is very close to the Unni, and he informs me that the Ceylonians should never have attempted to change or create life, for life is only given by the Unni, and those that attempt to alter life are doomed to fall under the wrath of the Unni."

"Jedar, closely listen to my prophecy. Ceylon, with all its transgressions, will soon be destroyed at the command of the Unni."

"Simka how can this be?"

"Jedar you know my predictions, haven't they always been true? Your father is especially loved by the Unni, he doesn't realize it, but if he would look back and take inventory of his life, he would soon realize the Unni has always been there in control, even as the Unni was also involved in the affairs of Atar, his father."

"Jedar throughout numerous generations, there comes along individuals who are so self-motivated, that after they breathe their final breath, their impression is woven into the fabric of space, and into the minds of every citizen they ever encountered."

"You mean those like grandfather, and father?"

"Yes Jedar, they will be remembered, but it is to you that I prophesy. Your life was not by chance but was divinely directed by the Unni. Soon your name, along with that of Kiah your brother, will be echoed throughout the universe. I have also seen visions of you fighting the forces of evil. I can tell you Jedar the last part of this prophecy will happen after you enter the spirit world. In my vision, I see you, not being assigned the position of a messenger, but I see you at the head of the Unni's armies, fighting side by side with your grandfather."

"Simka, where will father be, you never mentioned him?

"Your father will receive his blessing in the Golden City, where he shall dwell in unlimited peace and happiness, but he is of a dissimilar spiritual nature, he is not of the warrior essence, these qualities were preordained by the Unni before the original creation. Perhaps you can understand it, if you compare the voracious nature of the infamous dragon, to the peaceful nature of the white doves, they are created to be what they are, and their innate nature can not be altered. Jedar if you will, just have faith in the Unni, he will become real forever in your mind. The vision is not far off, soon the Unni will have great need of you and your brother to bring about the ending and beginning of all life. This will all be revealed to you, so for now, just concentrate on the Unni and his unending love."

"Tell me Simka, how do I thank the Unni for all he has done for me and my family?"

"Before you ever spoke Jedar, your gratitude was heard by Unni, because he knows your every thought. Jedar, your father has had many opportunities to accept the creator, and now, because of the hardness of his heart, he has condemned himself to patrol the universe. Can't you see that you are imprisoned in this starship? You have not set foot on Ceylon, or the Feramas, you have never been out of the confines of the Tri-Star. What kind of life is that for a young citizen, who is full of visions to explore other worlds? The greatest benefit that I can draw from this, is that you have been educated and better trained in all aspects of space travel, than any officer in the entire academy fleet. You probably know more than anyone in the annals of Ceylonian history, and no doubt, you have the greatest wisdom, knowledge and ability to come to all logical decisions."

"Jedar, what I am trying to say is this. The Unni has better plans for you, than to have you roaming aimlessly around in space. What ever happens of interest? Are there adventurous space battles with the Kronos nation? Do you jettison down and fancy yourself to females of the exotic planets, with all the allure? No Jedar, the Unni will soon alter time and space, and you my friend, will be part of this great plan of the Unni. Jedar, I feel honored to have called you friend these many years, I have also been waiting for this day to arrive, as I watch you take your place in the divine order of things. Jedar you can accomplish all things, if you will just place your trust in the Unni, call upon his name and adhere to his laws of good."

"You will notice I did not say that you must hold fast to the man made laws of Ceylon, or even to the commandments given to Chaldoc on the holy mountain. These laws were merely guidelines, foreshadowing the coming of the Unni's son. With the arrival of the prophesied redeemer, a new law was instituted, which would free all citizens from their bondage and offer them life eternal in the Golden City."

"Simka don't play games with me, tell me what this new law is?"

"This new law is love, it has replaced the old existing laws which merely foreshadowed the arrival of the Unni's son, who is the embodiment of love."

"Simka, I feel Boeski the prophet truly believed he was the Unni's promised son, written about in the sacred writings, when do you think he realized there was another one to follow?"

"Just before he died Jedar, when he surmised, he was not perfect, and had sinned against his mother and father."

"Simka you alone are responsible for the knowledge that I have acquired, you have been my tutor, teaching me the proper course of study, in not only ancient Ceylonian history, but you have also enlightened me with the accumulated knowledge of planets and galaxies."

"Jedar you say you have been enlightened by me, but if you truly desire to be enlightened, except the Unni now. Just ask Jedar, just like you would inquire of your father, when asking for the finest clothing from far off places. If you will just invite the Unni's son into your heart and ask forgiveness for your sins, he will welcome you with open arms. He will provide you knowledge and wealth, more abundant than anything you could ever imagine in this life. Jedar there is nothing else you have to do, the Unni has always been with you and loved you, now it is up to you to just accept his love, and then you and your creator shall be as one."

After Simka departed, Jedar needed to be alone in order to consider Simka's words of wisdom. He yearned to transport down and meet the citizens, but Ral had forbidden such encounters, except for the messengers such as Medoa, Treeka and Simka.

"If Simka just realized how much I yearn to visit the many intriguing planets throughout the cosmos. I wish to look upon the faces of citizens that look as strange to me as I do to them, such as the Pluma, who have three faces, one body, and two sets of arms. Which hand would I grasp in meeting, would they be a friendly colony? There is much I need to learn."

After Jedar fell asleep, the young space traveler drifted off too far off places, and he envisioned the many wonderful citizens he would encounter in his travels. Jedar suddenly awoke with the name of his brother on his lips.

"Why is my brother haunting my mind, father never told me much concerning him, and I recall they were never close, but Kiah is seed of my father, he is also my half brother, and I would enjoy meeting him. He is also one of the highest ranking officers in the academy, perhaps we will meet someday in our travels, I may ask father to return to Ceylon?"

The young captain received a superior education and was able to read the stars, and self navigate the Tri-Star, long before he was legally permitted to do so. And the academy, which still held a special pride in the young and somewhat cocky grandson of one of their greatest citizens, was considering giving him a command of his own. After all, they were the ones that broke with their sacred rules, and let Dreara and Ral raise Jedar outside the academy's established protocol.

## THE FERAMAS LEFT TO GOVERN ALONE

The Feramas had grown into a modern civilization, while evil leaders were ruthlessly ruling various strategic sectors of its colonies. Many thousands of their citizens were being murdered and the Chaldocians were on the threshold of becoming only a memory.

Ral had been active for many years, colonizing new planets for Ceylon, and during his absence the citizens had long forgotten about the protective starship that once hovered high above them for protection. The armed forces throughout the Feramas disclaimed all documentation in regard to past alien intervention, casting off such reports as events, which could be explained away logically.

Ral took full advantage of his extended times away from the Feramas to investigate new territories. The excitement of space travel had waned, and Ral had now become disheartened because he was no longer recognized by the academy for his colonizing ability. But in spite of his continued rejection, he found some satisfaction living the life of a devoted family man.

"Dreara." Spoke Ral in a state of depression. "I feel like I am stuck in orbit, spinning but going nowhere, what's wrong with me? I have power and authority over the hundreds of crew members living aboard the Tri-Star. I have you and Jedar, no citizen could ask for a better family, but I feel lost, and I feel like I might just give it all up. Medoa says it comes from my rejection of the Unni, what do you feel Dreara?"

"Ridiculous." Shouted Dreara. "I believe that you are the victim of unethical citizens such as Gemaal and Ragan. If it had not been for the likes of them, you my husband, may have been one of Ceylon's greatest citizens, equal to the likes of Dreeska and Ral, if you just had not involved yourself with the Feramas, devoting so much of your life to its success, where would you be today? Just think about it, where would you have been today? Ral I have told you over and over again to conform to the laws of the council, but you continually choose to do things that are contrary to the great law code. Ral, please consider this, without your commission from the academy, we could be left homeless, even this fancy starship that has served so long as our home could be taken away."

"Dreara, you are right, and even though there has never been a time when we've had to experience such severe conditions, I am sure things would work out, and what about the Unni Dreara?"

"Oh stop it Ral! That is exactly how you got yourself into this mess. Forsake these thoughts about a distant god and perhaps we will be able to return to the benevolent mercy of the council, and maybe you will regain favor, even if it is picking up space junk."

"Commander Ral." Spoke Renna. "The council has issued a top priority message for your immediate return to Ceylon."

"Yes Renna, tell them we are on our way."

The Tri-Star soared past the planets on its way to Ceylon, and after their arrival, Ral was escorted to Ceylon's Governmental Headquarters, while the crew anxiously waited.

## CHAPTER 12

### RAL FIRED

Ral strolled nervously back and forth while waiting in the office of the commissioner. His thoughts were filled with questions concerning the possible ramifications of the meeting, but there was no way he could imagine the terrible events that he would have to endure because of his rejection of the Unni.

"Commissioner Keeksonn, good to see you again my old friend."

It is wonderful to see you, but Ral, Governor Gemaal has issued a decree against you, because of your refusal to abandon the Feramas. He also has documentation of your sedition, showing that you have been resurrecting the ancient religion, which was banned by Governor Dreeska. Ral, there has been talk of shipping you to Agreg to be imprisoned, but your friends on the council and those that remembered your father, voted against it. Ral if it hadn't been for the strong influence held over Gemaal by Kiah, you would have been brought before the council long ago."

Ral contemplated upon Keeksonn's words. "Kiah defended me before the council? Perhaps he doesn't hate me, I wish we could have worked things out, all those wasted years we could have shared together.".

"What did you say Ral?"

"Oh, it was nothing Keeksonn, it has been so long since I last saw my son that my mind drifted off."

"Ral, Gemaal has issued an order, that you and your family are to be exiled here on Ceylon, in isolation away from the general population. Gemaal has taken away your pension, it will be up to you to survive off the land."

Outside of Ceylon's protective dome, the food was dried for distribution during the winter months. It was then dehydrated and chemically broken down into its nutritional value. This mixture was then distributed as pills throughout the Seventh Quadrant at excessive prices. The pyramid domed city in contrast was 1500 miles long in every direction, containing perfect climate, adjusted to the comfort level of each citizen. The climate, whether in summer or winter, was nearly unbearable outside the enormous dome.

# Ral, Space Colonizer

Ral and Jedar felt they could survive almost anything as long as they were all together, but Dreara still spent most of her time cursing the thought of a divine presence that had brought them to such a god forsaken land. Ral and his family survived the first year because some of their loyal friends were able to smuggle food, clothing and supplies. This devotion was truly heroic, if perchance the traitors were caught, their lives would be forfeited in the Molecular Field. It was an act of fate that caused Ral, one day to stumble upon the brilliant piece of rock that glittered from within a cave nearby where they were living. At first Ral past it off as another pretty stone, until upon further investigation.

"It's Patriska!" Ral shouted. "It's Patriska! Jedar, bring your mother and look."

Jedar had studied enough geology to know that Ral indeed had stumbled upon the primary source of Ceylon's energy, which also supplied power throughout the Seventh Quadrant. When word got out about Ral's discovery, the citizens all hailed him as Ceylon's hero, and remarkably the council members were able to overturn the decision, reestablishing Ral's former status in the academy. But due to his insurrections, he was demoted, which was to be expected. Ral retained his position as commander, but it was an honorary title, no one dared to tell him that Kiah had previously replaced him as the Academy Commander.

Gemaal cursed in his chamber, as he watched the accolades being heaped upon Ral by the citizenship.

"For now Ral, fill yourself with the sweet taste of victory, when you leave, I shall cause them to soon forget you, and I will let you rot while idly patrolling your precious Feramas."

"Medoa." Spoke Ral. "It feels good being back aboard the Tri-Star, I sure missed you and the crew."

"Ral nothing happens without a reason, and the Unni must have some great need of your services to have put you through such horrific tribulation."

"What reason Medoa? My family suffered, and could have died there, so tell me, what good was brought about?"

"The answer my friend may possibly lie in the Patriska you discovered on Ceylon. The Unni may have need of it to further his will throughout the cosmos."

"Thank you Medoa, I know I can always count on you for your excellence guidance."

"Someday you will come to know the Unni on a personal level and he will then become the source of all your knowledge and strength. But as the Unni daily provides your spiritual strength, then I must decrease, until you become totally dependent upon him."

## WAKI ATTACKS RAL

Ral found himself in a severe state of depression, and soon he slipped into a state of mind, where he failed to provide for his personal needs. Dreara was startled when Ral awoke from his rest, looking at her through eyes that were not his own.

Ral what is wrong?"

Ral sat up, looking around the room in a dazed manner, and then suddenly Dreara was lying on the floor.

"Why have you hit me my husband? What have I done to bring on so much reproach?"

Ral, failed to respond, and Dreara became frightened, when he suddenly dash toward the engine room as if there was an extreme emergency, or conceivably, there was someone chasing him. Dreara stumbled upon Simka, pleading for his help to unravel Ral's bizarre nature.

"Dreara, go to your room and wait, I will summon Medoa and Dr. Rhear."

Captain Katrane stood to greet Ral as he entered the room, and he was also knocked to the floor, but by natural reflex due to his military training, he began fighting back. Commander Ral, suddenly endowed with the strength of ten men, picked up the captain, as if he was lighter than a feather and threw him against the metal table, knocking him out.

The five member security team arrived at that moment, and never experiencing such an ordeal, stood motionless, as Ral looked with rage in his eyes. Ral started to make his advance toward them, when suddenly, just as his evil had come to mind, it departed. The security team began placing the invisible restraint field around the commander for his own protection.

"Release him!" Spoke Medoa, as he entered the room with Simka and Dr. Rhear. "Take him to the medical lab doctor, and keep me informed of the commander's condition."

Medical technology had advanced tremendously during the glory days of Ceylon and Dr. Rhear felt privileged to have access to such scientific equipment.

"Medoa can you hear me?"

"Yes, loud and clear doctor, go ahead."

"All reports are negative, and except for the commander's age, he is in excellent health. It appears if there is a problem at all, it may be the result of a mental aberration. Perhaps it is time for the commander to take a well deserved vacation, do you agree Medoa?"

"Yes, Dr. Rhear, I believe I have the perfect place for his recuperation, it is a quiet and peaceful place in a remote area of the Feramas, away from the populace. It's a place where the commander might perchance, rediscover his inner self."

Ral, and Captain Katrane were transported to the Feramas, and as he gazed upon his new environment, his mind kept playing back the accounts of the previous day.

"What's happening to me? I have never acted in such a manner, will Dreara ever forgive me for hitting her? In the name of Unni, what have I done? Perhaps a brief vacation away from the confines of the Tri-Star would be just what I need."

"What is this ringing in my ears? It sounds like there are voices singing in unison by the thousands. Now it's gone. That was strange." He considered, as he rolled some forbidden leaf which was known to grow wild on the Feramas.

"Commander," Captain Katrane politely asked, "when did you take up the habit?"

"I don't know," Ral angrily answered, "and really it's none of your damned business."

"Sorry commander." Spoke the captain.

This was the same officer that Ral had viciously attacked the previous day. Captain Katrane began logging his routine notes, Ral then walked over and observed the captain as he was writing.

"What is this?" Screamed Ral. "You have the gull to write a letter against me? I hired you on this piece of garbage and you will pay severely, you insubordinate ass."

Suddenly, Captain Katrane, once again, found that he was knocked to the ground, as his computerized log book went soaring, crashing against a rock. Ral had planted a perfect kick with his shoe, and was just about to continue his attack when he suddenly stopped.

"Captain, let me help you up." Ral stated apologetically.

"Ral I believe you have done enough damage for one day, I need to be transported to the Tri-Star for medical attention."

Katrane did file charges against Ral, as was to be expected, although everyone anticipated that all legalities would be tied up for months in complex bureaucratic channels.

"Katrane deserved everything I did to him," screamed Ral, "he was plotting against me, they are all out to get me. Is there no place where I can be alone? I can feel their eyes upon me, watching every move I make, yes, Katrane must be the leader of this mutiny. I can hear their insurrection, the cries of my enemy ring loudly in my ears, if I could lay my hands on Katrane, I would ring his skinny neck."

That evening, Ral's hands began trembling, and his body shivered as he contemplated his next move. Periodically these spells came over Ral, and the only way he was able to get over them was to have Zareen, the starship's telepathist, come before him and play music on stringed instruments. Zareen's voice was as melodious as any to be heard throughout the galaxies.

"What song do you wish to hear?" Asked Zareen?

"You are my music tonight," shouted Ral.

Ral, full of animal lust, wrestled Zareen to the floor, and engaged in every kind of sexual perversion that he could imagine. Zareen, being a telepath, knew what would happen, but she never spoke a word, because her father was emperor of Phalor, and had sworn her to an oath of servitude to the mighty Ceylonians.

When she departed the room, Simka conjectured, why she was walking in such a strange fashion, at least until he saw Ral open the door, then he understood. When Ral began cursing at Simka, it was taken in stride, the messenger's feelings were too evolved to be hurt.

"The citizens of the Feramas need a real leader, why am I confined to sit up here in this forsaken piece of shit and waste my valuable time. I have at my disposal everything I need to establish myself as the greatest leader ever to walk upon the Feramas."

"Simka in the morning, be ready to transport me into the heart of the Feramas, so that I may rule among my subjects."

"As you wish." Spoke Simka.

The next morning Ral was transported to the Feramas. He chose this time the area of the Feramas where the prophet had long ago helped establish a national library. The first event of order was to murder the existing leader and his cabinet.

"Build me a tower that will reach into the heavens." Cried out Ral to his people. "I am your god and your provider, you will bow down and worship me only. You will also bring your gold and silver to be placed in the treasury, where I will have it melted down to line the walls of my temple."

During some of the few quite nights on the Feramas, Ral's mind would become more settled, and occasionally he would hear the Unni's faint voice, whispering over and over, "Ral, I am here." Ral had heard the voice so often that he more or less cast it aside as meaningless.

"Treeka, I am going to appear before the Unni." Spoke Medoa. "So I am temporarily placing you in charge of the Tri-Star, so make every effort to keep track of the commander." Medoa then placed his fingers near the bridge of his nose, while twirling at the speed of light. When he stopped spinning, he prostrated himself in reverence, before the Unni's throne.

"Medoa," spoke the Unni. "Ral has had many opportunities to recognize my sovereignty, therefore, I have not only turned him over to my universal negative force, but I have also brought him to his time and place of testing. It will be up to Ral to recognize me as his creator, or to fall away to his own destruction. I will always have great love for him, no matter what his decision."

"If he turns to me, I will forgive him, but he will have to pay for his transgressions against his fellow citizens. He will never have the honored place that he once held in my heart, because his inner loathing has been keeping with idolatry, rape, murder, and plunder. I will not permit him to see the glory of my last days, but through the eyes of Kiah and Jedar, if they will only believe on me, they shall be blessed instead of him, but nothing will be spared my judgment that shall be unleashed throughout my unlimited heavens."

"Yes Medoa, I will pull Ral down from his high throne and cause him to lick at the dust of the Feramas, in order to humble him. But Medoa, he must truly believe in me, and that remains to be seen, for I have created all my children with a free will."

The next morning, the citizens looked bewildered at their king. The warring tribes came from miles to behold the spectacle of a naked old man, walking aimlessly through the streets, looking and acting more like a wild animal than a citizen of nobility.

"I will cast lots to see who gets the honor of killing this idiot, where did he ever come from." Cried out one of the citizen.

The rival groups were closing in on Ral from all sides, but he could not comprehend their actions, his mind was a fog, so thick that it could not be penetrated. The citizens lunged at Ral with their daggers, but before they found their mark, Ral had disappeared from their midst.

"Rogara that was an amazing job and you are to be highly commended. Please give my compliments to the transporter room, that was great timing, but the commander is not out of danger yet." Medoa continued speaking, "In the morning we will once again take him to a remote area of the Feramas where he will be left alone until he comes to his reasoning, if this fails to happen, he will live out the rest of his days in protective isolation."

It was a cool Feramas morning and seven years had passed. The morning rains were gently falling, as vapor was rising from the volcanic springs, warming the hands of the lonely traveler.

"Loose me from these chains!" Screamed Ral. "Someone help me!" Ral cried even louder, but there was no one to come to his rescue. And for the first time in his life, he felt fear as he looked around his environment. The animals began running, as he stridently approached in their path. There was a cool pond of water nearby and Ral fumble about, ape like, in the direction of his refreshing. As Ral lightly touched the water his reflection startled him, for there before his eyes, appearing out of the water's broken circles, was the face of a primitive. Long hair hung from his head and a straggly beard filled with tangles covered his face.

"Who am I?" Ral wondered. "Where am I?" He scratched at his mud caked skin with fingernails that resembled long talon like claws, and from deep within his inner spirit, Ral began to speak.

"Unni, help me." For some strange reason the Unni's name sounded pleasing to Ral as he repeatedly spoke the name.

Suddenly there came a streak of light through the skies and a gentle voice began to inwardly speak. "Ral, Ral."

Ral looked up and saw the feathered creatures flying across the heavens, and this time, he boldly spoke the Unni's name.

## RAL'S DESTINY

"Ral welcome home." Spoke Medoa.

"What happened Medoa, Where have I been?" Ral asked in bewilderment.

"Ral, citizens that have faith, and the desire to be identified with god, must prove themselves by having their faith tested, even if the result of that faith is death. I realize you have suffered, but Ral, if you had only called upon the Unni's name long ago, then you may have avoided your walk, through the proverbial wilderness. Ral, you are the only one to blame, because it was your hardened heart that brought you down into great tribulation."

"It is all coming back to me Medoa, and I have this gut feeling that everything will be all-right, how are Dreara and Jedar?"

"They are fine Ral, they have stood beside you throughout this entire ordeal, offering their undying love and support."

"I must go to them Medoa, but first, I need to shave this stinking beard and try to look presentable to my family."

"Ral, listen to what I have to say. The Unni has expressed, the days of colonization are near at hand. Vast changes are already being felt throughout the quadrants. Ral, life is coming to an end, and the light that powers every galaxy throughout the cosmos will be commanded to burn out, until it is extinguish and is no more. Ral your sons will be privileged to be used by the Unni during this time of unfolding events. And then, after your grandsons have lived out their natural life span, time and space will ultimately end."

"Tell me Medoa, what is the reason of it all?"

"Ral there is no reason, there is only the creator, who is the beginning and the end of all things, and this phase of his universal destruction is destined to bring about the rebirth of all cosmological truth."

"Yes Medoa, I have also felt this unrest, as if something unprecedented is about to occur, and I thank you for at least trying to explain the complexity of your good judgment. I would like to speak with you again tomorrow evening concerning the Unni, so for now, I will bid you goodnight."

"Ral, get plenty of rest, for you will need it in the morning when you show to your officers that you are once again competent to lead."

The following night, Ral approached the private chamber of Medoa. "Medoa, I have felt the Unni's presence throughout my life, and now I desire to secure my relationship with him. Tell me, what do I need to do?"

"Ral, you have always belonged to the Unni, he never left you, you left him. The Unni was with you from the day of your birth and he continually guided you to bring you to this time and place. Now that you have accepted him, the universal plan of the Unni can begin to unfold."

"Medoa, this is above the scope of my understanding, you're telling me that I am the last link in the final plan of the Unni? I am just a Ceylonian of noble birth, the son of Atar, a citizen of renown. If anyone, the Unni should have selected him to carry out his great plan."

"Ral prepare yourself, for now that you have accepted the Unni the dark forces knowing their days are short, will be constantly attacking you. The only way to stand against them is by trusting in the Unni. Ral talk to the Unni, just like you do with me. I must now go and receive my instructions, I will speak to you later concerning this matter."

# CHAPTER 13

## RAL REVEALS THE UNNI TO DREARA

"Ral, what is wrong,?" Dreara spoke in a concerned tone of voice.

"Oh, nothing Dreara, Medoa and I were just talking and I feel so inadequate in my effort to phantom the meaning of it all."

"Ral, you have always been open and frank with me, but I know something is wrong, and I will haunt you until you reveal all that is troubling you."

"Not tonight Dreara. Tell me, how is Jedar?"

"He looked fine the last time I saw him, I believe he was caught up in some philosophical discussion with Simka. I believe I heard them speaking concerning Atar, but I could not understand the gist of their conversation. Ral, do you think Simka exerts too much influence over our son?"

"No, I do not believe so Dreara, because Jedar is under the Unni's protection now."

"What did you say? Ral no! Tell me that you do not want to accept the ways of old Ceylon, of beliefs and ideas that have been banned under the orders of Governor Dreeska. Ral don't you care that we could lose everything? Look what we went through back on Ceylon. Ral they fired you! It was very fortunate that you found the Patriska. Once again you could jeopardize your entire career just for thinking such foolish thoughts. Gemaal is looking for the slightest infringement against you for humiliating him. Please Ral, don't."

When Ral spoke it was in a humble fashion, akin to that of a mischievous lad getting his finger caught in the cookie jar.

"Dreara I never told you, but I once had an encounter with the Unni, I recall it was just before waking from my sleep. Much to my surprise, I was carried through time to the most magnificent city, the beauty, which cannot be told. There the Unni spoke with me for a long period of time telling me that he had a plan for my life, if I would follow him and adhere to his laws. Dreara I saw a messenger with a large book standing beside his throne. The book was opened, and I was permitted to read the laws of good, that were completely contrary to the laws of Ceylon."

"Ral, read my lips! You were dreaming! And tell me, my husband, what laws exist other than the great laws of Ceylon? There is only one law and that is complete allegiance to our supreme and royal homeland."

"Yes, Dreara, I have always felt the same, but after talking with the Unni, my mind was enlightened. I knew from that moment Ceylon's laws were wrong, and that they had been incorporated by a evil and corrupt government, which was structured to bring citizens into bondage. Dreara, we were not created to be prisoners, Ceylon enslaves us all. It sets harsh and stringent rules that are virtually impossible to follow. For those that refuse to adhere to the council's rules, their lives are forfeited in the molecular field."

"Can't you see Dreara, this injustice is not right? We were born free to choose between right and wrong, free to serve a god or a country. After I awakened from my troubled sleep, I felt myself day after day, and month after month, becoming more attuned to my surroundings. I soon became aware of things before they actually happened. I knew thoughts of others before they spoke, and feared these feelings were coming from a mind needing professional help. But when I became more accustomed to this phenomenon, I began to feel privileged to be part of the Unni's plan for my life."

"Until this day Dreara, I have never acknowledged this to anyone, with the exception of Medoa. Will the Unni ever forgive me for my foolish rebellion? Dreara my injustices are horrendous, but it is because of my transgression against you, that I humbly beg your forgiveness."

"Simka have the maintenance officer find a suitable room where I can retire to speak with the Unni. I also request that Dreara and Jedar join me there."

## THE FAMILY CONVERSATION

The room that was prepared for the family's mediation was crude, and the maintenance officer had nothing to compare with, except photos of old Ceylon's religious era. Ral, Dreara and Jedar looked silently at each other for lack of what to say.

"Dreara will you join our silent mediation in reverence to the Unni?"

"Ral, I will never bow down and pray to your ancient god." Dreara began to regain her composure, as she wiped the bitter tears from her eyes.

"Your Unni does not speak to me, nor has he ever revealed himself to me, Dreeska was right to put a stop to this foolish folly.

Ral each of us has the power within to accomplish great things, if only we will exorcize our innate abilities, and it does not come from a distant fictitious god. Ral, do not the Ceylonian books speak to us, telling that life has evolved over billions of years? See this writing instrument, is it tangible, I can see it, I can feel it, here my husband, feel this pen, does it not feel real to you?"

"Yes Dreara, I have always believed as you but now I have changed. Everything about me is somehow unique and different, I am not the citizen I was. If you would ask Jedar, I am sure he would tell you the same. I am sorry that you feel this way Dreara, but there is no turning back, there's nothing behind us but destruction."

"The solar energy that runs this dynamo of a spaceship is invisible to us, yet its atomic power can be unleashed, destroying everything that stands in our way. Does it exist? Do you believe in its power, even though it's atomic structure cannot be seen? How strange, I assembled to be in the Unni's presence, but it has led to embitterment and added conflicts. I am sorry, but perhaps we should assemble at different times. Jedar take your mother to her room, but before you leave, I have something to say that has been on my mind for quite some time."

"Yes father, by all means, speak freely."

"Jedar, Simka has spoken with me and has told me of your desire to journey to the Feramas. I have given it much thought and feel it is now time, do you still want to go?"

"Father you know I do, when will this happen?"

"Jedar I will place you in command of the Reserve Fleet, to visit, not just the Feramas, but you will travel to the outer galaxies to intervene in the affairs of the citizens, and boldly lead them into a life of righteousness. When Medoa returns from appearing before the Unni, I will be more able to inform you of all the details. Don't worry about your mother Jedar, I have enough faith in our creator for the three of us, and the Unni will not let any harm come to the mother of Jedar."

## JEDAR AMBASSODORE TO THE STARS

With the blessings of the council, star fleet officer Jedar, traveled throughout the Seventh Quadrant, personally supervising the operations of each colony that fell under Ceylonian servitude. The enemy had always looked upon their captors with a great deal of despicable disdain, but due to Jedar's down to earth personality, he had tremendous appeal and the citizens were often heard to cry out, "General Jedar, stay and rule over us."

The Unni sent spiritual blindness to fall throughout Ceylon, causing Jedar's insurrection to be overlooked by the council. Due to this divine intervention, the Ceylonians could only see the good, as they continued to look with favor upon Jedar's every action. They were even contemplating, which further honors to bestow upon their young general.

"The Unni," Ral contemplated, "never instilled in me the thrill that Jedar exhibits for space travel, and why was I not given his great love for the citizenship? I would have loved the fight, the challenge, just as in the days when I dreamed of the conflicts, which took place in old Ceylon. But except for my encounter with Gormia and the United alliance, along with the revolts that occurred in the Ventura colonies, I have little experience in actual combat missions, when compared to the successful campaigns of Jedar. Yes Jedar's name will be written in the pages of Ceylonian history, it will be to my glory that he shall increase while I must decrease, and with all humility, I will live through him."

Jedar began feeling somewhat cocky, because the council placed their seal of approval upon his performance, by promoting him to General of the Fleet. They also approved his first request, to have his trusted confident, Simka, to serve as his advisor and second in command. Treeka would have been offered the assignment, but he was too involved in his newly assigned capacity as advisor to the international regents. Several of the officers that had originally been commissioned to the Tri-Star were reassigned to serve under the command of General Jedar aboard his starship, the Comatra.

# CHAPTER 14

## LIFE ON CEYLON IS ENDING

While Ral was contemplating his future and that of his family, life was becoming very chaotic throughout the colonies on Ceylon. The council was meeting under closed door sessions, and it appeared from their tone of conversation that the planet was in dire jeopardy of collapsing and the total consensus indicated the days of Ceylon's glory were abruptly coming to an end.

Governor Gemaal stood up. "Members of the council and my beloved citizens, may I address you? I Gemaal will not give credence to the idea that these troubles befalling us are the result of some great intercession of the resurrected god of old Ceylon. The travesty that is soon to befall Ceylon is the result of a predictable natural event, just as the asteroid that destroyed old Ceylon was of the natural."

"I'll answer the prognosticators by saying that astrologers have made these predictions throughout the ages. Yes, my fellow citizens, if this great and honored planet falls, it will be the result of a natural occurrence, and not because of some divine curse. I stand upon Dreeska's memorial words, which he spoke concerning our homeland, *Live Forever, In the Hearts of Our Citizens*."

"My esteemed citizens, celebrate the name of Dreeska, the great patriot who disembarked our fellow citizens from old Ceylon, took them to the recreational planet, and then reestablished them on this glorious planet. No wonder his name has been perpetuated and honored these many years. Is his statue still among us, standing in the capital of Sair-Dreeska? We only have days for this destruction to take place. The colonies throughout our sister planet of Durran, has been prepared, and is ready and waiting for our starships to make their departure. Our Scientific Department has miscalculated the asteroids speed and its destruction will take place to soon for a mass evacuation."

Gemaal carefully read his prepared notes, causing a hush to fall upon the crowd. "Only essential governmental personnel, and all citizens that have been selected, will depart the planet to work with the Durranians in the rebuilding of our colonies. But rest assured, I will remain behind to share in this glorious destruction. When the asteroid arrives, we will look up, and as proud Ceylonians, we will stand firm, with our hands out stretched toward the four directions of the Ceylonian skies. There we will gaze into the same beautiful destruction that long ago silenced old Ceylon, and we will say our goodbyes to the colonies of the north, south, east and west."

It was difficult to look into the eyes of Gemaal and witness his tears of remorse, but everyone knew, these were not the tears of a coward awaiting death, but the honest love of a citizen for his homeland.

The citizens that were watching Gemaal's address began to chant, "we will die proudly with our beloved colonies. Ceylon!" They began shouting, louder and louder, as the wind echoed their words, "Ceylon! Ceylon! Ceylon!"

## GEMAAL'S CONFESSION

"My son," Gemaal began stumbling with his words, "that is Kiah, you heard me speaking to the citizens concerning the state of our beloved Ceylon?"

"Yes governor I was there."

" Kiah, you must immediately coordinate all the essential human resources such as masonry workers, government employees etc., I have selected you to be the sole leader of Durran, it will be your assignment to quickly establish military dominance, and thus establish yourself as governor, not only on Durran but throughout all provinces that lie under Ceylonian jurisdiction. I have a detailed list prepared for you, and as soon as you have landed, you will begin absorbing the Durranians into the Ceylonian culture, until they are one in agreement with us."

"I admit to you now, before I perish on this glorious planet, the secret that I have kept hidden from you. Yes Kiah, it was all due to my jealously, if you can believe that possible from a member of the honored council, a citizen that is presumed to be above such trivial emotions. When Atar was elected to the council, I felt that I, Gemaal, had all rights to that privileged position, but the council elected your grandfather. Because of my hatred for Atar, I cursed the miserable, rotten day, he was born. I also limited your father's colonization endeavors, causing Ral to be restricted to the regions of the Feramas. If all the words Kiah was hearing were spoken in such a manner, in another time and place, he would have destroyed this insolent citizen standing before him, but in spite of all the hurting and cruel words being spit out by the governor, Kiah felt not anger for Gemaal, but pity.

"Gemaal has at all times treated me as a son," he thought to himself, "and I have always been aware of his hatred for my family, but I selfishly tolerated it to further secure my military position in the academy. It appears that I needed and used Gemaal as much as he desired to exploit me. I knew he hated father, and would have exterminated him, but Gemaal employed great restraint, due to my interventions."

The seconds ticked by slowly, as Ceylon's top two leaders lingered in silent complex thought. Kiah by now had figured out that Gemaal was lying about not knowing the time frame of Ceylon's destruction and Gemaal unexpectedly raised his voice to break the commander's silence.

"So you can see Kiah, I need to cleanse my mind before I perish, but I repent to you only for my wrong, and not to a god. It is time to instruct you in regard to my evacuation plans and Kiah, time is almost upon us."

Gemaal's harsh words had greatly affected Kiah, but he felt assured that Gemaal would have set in motion all things necessary to make way for an orderly transition. Kiah also determined that he would not encourage the governor to change his mind, he felt it best to let the old citizen die in his guilt on Ceylon, the planet he loved.

## KIAH DEPARTS FOR DURRAN

In the red and purple light of Ceylon's morning sun, Kiah prepared to depart with the academy's finest squadrons. The cargo crafts were filled with military personnel, supplies, records and the academies top scientist, plus multitudes of citizens. If for no other reason, the Ceylonians sought to remind the citizens throughout the Seventh Quadrant that their great and honored planet had occupied a place of prominence in the eastern portion of the Seventh Quadrant.

"Why me." Kiah reasoned. "Why have I been given this honored position? There are far wiser and brighter academy officers that would be better qualified to accomplish this great feat."

Kiah descended with massive amounts of spacecraft to the red sands of Durran, the citizens below stirred about in anticipation of his arrival.

"What do our masters mean to imply by such an arrival? We have never observed them in such awesome fashion, something exciting is in the air." The Durranians had time after time, witnessed the barrage of supply ships, this time however, the sky was packed with the constant barrage of unending space vessels, landing and unloading tons of supplies and personnel. Throughout the years, Ceylon had infused Durran with high ranking Ceylonian officials to rule throughout the colonies. Kiah was met by Rokak, mayor of the province.

"Greetings commander, for what do we owe this unexpected honor?"

"In just a few hours my friend, "spoke Kiah, "you will see the question answered to your satisfaction. In the meantime, prepare your work crews to assist us for we must act quickly."

The following month the citizens watched intently through Durranian telescopes, as another distant planet faded away without a whimper. One moment there was a beautiful glowing circle in the sky, and the next, it was like the lights were instantly turned off on distant Ceylon, and the planet silently went to sleep.

## KIAH GOVERNOR OF DURRAN

Kiah and Renouna began holding hands as they looked into the Durranian sunset, and silently Kiah began to wonder, "where is father? He must have heard of the destruction? Will I ever meet with him again?" Kiah knew for certain, he was committed to this planet for the duration of his life, and he reasoned with a sense of pride that perhaps one of his sons would be the next Atar.

Long before Ceylon was the supreme ruler of the Seventh Quadrant, Durran was well-known for its peaceful nature. This was the reason the council had selected it from among the large numbers of planets that lay within this distant sector of the Seventh Quadrant.

It would be years before the Durranians would attain to Ceylon's former state of exalted supremacy, but Kiah knew he had brought with him enough scientific knowledge and military might to accomplish his purpose. Much of the technical equipment had long ago been brought to Durran and stored in vast caverns to be used for this purpose. The workers and military personnel working in secret chambers below the ground were never permitted to leave, this was mandated to protect Ceylon's military secrets.

Durran made great advancements, and Kiah was more than able to train the citizens into a formidable army, his past position as commander provided him with enough knowledge to conquer all obstacles. The name of Kiah was by this time, widely honored and proclaimed throughout Durran. His statues stood throughout many of Durran's colonies, just as Dreeska had attained such notoriety in old Ceylon.

## THE ZORBER

Light years away from the outer boundary of the Seventh Quadrant, the Zorber confederations were experiencing devastating problems. Their land was engulfed in great pandemic, and adding to their adversity, water was contaminated and drying up. It was also reported throughout the outer regions of the Seventh Quadrant that due to their advanced state of evolution, the Zorber were mentally superior to their rivals planets. Probability of Zorber intrusion was troublesome for Kiah, because none of the Ceylonian alliances had encountered one dreaded Zorber. Kiah would be compelled to look upon the Zorber insurrection as a legitimate threat, but his decision would be held in reserve until more concrete evidence was reported

Even as Kiah was contemplating his course of action, the Ventura Alliance began adding fuel to the fire by reporting possible Zorber intrusion outside the borders of the Eighth Quadrant, they also reported that the Zorber had kidnapped citizens, to study them for medical investigation. These examinations were purported to be so brutal, that many of the abducted citizens, died shortly after the medical probes were administered, the pain and torture was just to excruciating.

Kiah received the Ventura report cautiously, he presumed that if the Zorber were in fact encroaching into Ceylonian territories, they would initially concentrate their efforts to that of fact finding missions. The uncertainties of the Ventura exaggerated the galactic phobia, causing even greater fear to spread, and Kiah knew in spite of his doubts, that Durran could be in danger, if the Zorber decided to actually challenge Durran's outer, and less protected territories.

The computers transmitted the piercing sounds of alert, all essential starships patrolling the outer sectors had been notified. But due to confusion concerning Ral's status as commander, the Tri-Star did not receive notice concerning the Zorber incursion, because it had incorrectly been passed over by academy intelligence.

Ral, because of his advanced age was beginning to look the part of a patriarch, with his long hair and snow white beard, and Dreara and Ral still in love. were approaching the beginning of their final life cycle.

Jedar, General of the Academy Fleet, was spending much of his time out of the academy's communication range, overseeing newly established colonies. Jedar enjoyed these assignments, but by now he had accomplished all that he had set out to do, and he knew it would have never been possible, if he had never left the confines of the Tri-Star, and he felt, he owed it all to Simka.

Jedar made the decision before returning to Ceylon's port, to stop by and visit his family and friends aboard the Tri-Star for a little rest & recuperation.

Jedar's great disappointment was that he never encountered his half brother Kiah. Just as Ral had so often dreamed of returning to Ceylon's days of old, Jedar longed for the excitement of fighting beside his famous brother in combat. Simka had been informed by Medoa that this encounter was soon to take place but it would not be reveled to Jedar until the opportune time was at hand.

## KIAH SIGNALS RAL FOR HELP

"Commander Ral, Commander Ral, report to the bridge."

"Yes Renna." Spoke Ral in a softer tone, that he knew the computer expected to hear from him.

"Kiah, Durran's governor request an audience with you and is now awaiting your response. The governor is on route aboard the Galuppa, his private starship, and will arrive this evening.

Ral was unexpectedly taken aback. "Renna, before I speak with Kiah would you please provide a brief synopsis of his current standing in the academy?"

Renna without delay, described in limited detail, Ceylon's destruction, as well as, Kiah's new position as Governor of Durran. Ral's heart became troubled, because he realized that his family and friends were gone, and he silently mourned for his beloved Ceylon.

"Renna, I will now speak with my son, and Renna, switch off the ship's monitoring system but continue maintaining standard security measures."

"Yes commander." Replied Renna.

"Kiah, Kiah my son, I deeply apologize for my delay, is it really you?"

"Yes father, and I hope that all is well with you and your family. Father, I urgently request that you transport me to the Tri-Star when I arrive this evening, there is news of great importance that I must share. I also request that Jedar rendezvous with us at the appointed hour, I also have some good news for him."

"Yes Kiah, he recently stopped by for a short visit, but he is scheduled to depart early in the morning, but rest assured, General Jedar will surely be honored to attend."

"Kiah I have a million questions to ask you, and my son, it will be wonderful to see you again, I know it must be the Unni that has brought us together."

"Careful father, you speak of forbidden ancient beliefs, and you know the consequences of those that speak heresy against our sacred laws."

"Please accept my humble apology Kiah, I look forward to our meeting and I will notify you at the appointed time."

"Commander it is protocol that when high ranking officers come aboard the Tri-Star, that I am required to scan the systems for any mechanical deficiencies, but everything will be back in standard operation before you can blink an eye."

Ral feeling elated after his conversation with Kiah began to interact with Renna. "If you were real Renna, perhaps I'd give you a big kiss but I have to admit, you undeniably have the neatest vocal expressions, where did you learn to speak in such a fashion?"

"Have you forgotten commander that long ago you asked me to process detailed information relating to old Ceylon, your request included total physical descriptions of the female citizens? I logically also construe by your request that you desire to see what I would look like, if I were transformed into the life form of a citizen, one moment commander and I will work my magic."

Ral watched the monitor as hair darkened in, and Renna began to take on physical form. Her physical appearance was more akin to some of the females that may have worked in the Ceylonian iron yards, appearing calloused, and not at all pleasing to look upon.

"Renna." Ral spoke pryingly. "How can such a sweet voice come out of the likes of such a homely projection?"

"Commander my voice pattern was selected because you were known to have a history of flirtation with the ladies, and the council programmed me to match the sounds of female citizens that were appeasing to your particular standards. Is my voice pattern to your satisfaction commander?"

"Yes Renna, at this moment, I'll agree to anything, but there is one thing I ask of you."

"What is that?"

"Just forget about the kiss."

"Commander Ral, here comes my big Ceylonian lips, you cute little son of Waki."

Ral couldn't stop laughing at Renna's humor. It appeared that Kiah's visit had brought back the missing spark that had long grown dim in Ral's heart.

## JEDAR MEETS KIAH

It was providential that Jedar happened to be home aboard the Tri-Star, and Ral was very excited to see his son, especially in his decorated general's uniform. Ral had desired to see his family together again, especially now during his golden years.

"Thank you Unni," Spoke Ral, as he looked up prayerfully, humbling himself before the Great Spirit, which he believed made this all possible.

"Father, is my half brother, I mean Governor Kiah, coming to meet with you this evening? It's being spoken of throughout the entire ship."

"Settle down young man," laughed Ral, "you are Jedar, a general in the Ceylonian academy, not a bumbling school boy who is wondering aimlessly in circles, and by the way, thank the crew for spoiling my surprise."

Ral was just as nervous as Jedar, but not wanting to reveal his moment of weakness, sheepishly summoned Simka.

"Simka, make sure all the proper arrangements are made, and Simka, do me one favor."

"What is that commander?"

"Make provision for Kiah and Jedar to room together while he makes his stay with us."

"I understand Commander Ral." Simka smiled in response, for he had already made the arrangements.

Jedar was all nerves as he stood near the transporter.

"It's almost time father, is it ok if I transfer Kiah aboard?"

"By all means Jedar, just don't lose your brother, he might get a little upset." Spoke Ral in jest.

Dreara had a look of joy on her face, feeling the excitement that was going through her son. Dreara had never met Kiah and was also a little reserved as she waited.

Suddenly, he was materializing before their eyes, as Kiah's atomic structure spun, encircling his indistinct form. Kiah swiftly stepped off the transporter pad and glanced in the direction of his father. Ral hurried to greet his son, and suddenly the vision of their previous encounter flashed in his mind. There was no embrace at that time and Ral felt very uncomfortable at the thought of finding himself involved in another awkward situation.

Kiah saved the moment by reaching his strong arms in the direction of his father, and he briskly pulled his frail father forward, embracing him for quite some time. Tears began to well up in the eyes of Ral, but being ever mindful that he was being watched, was capable to somewhat suppress his emotions. But those close to Ral realized what was happening, and no one in the room could suppress their inner emotions for their commander and friend.

"Hello father, it is wonderful to see you, and is this your Ceylonian wife, Dreara?" Kiah surprised her as he lifted her above his head, giving her an unexpected kiss on the cheek. "And let me guess, by all these shinny medals pinned on his chest this must be Jedar, my little brother. It is indeed a pleasure to be here aboard the Tri-Star. Father, I have kept abreast of your accomplishments and your many acts of great courage are recorded, as an example to our young Durranian students."

"Jedar," Kiah continued, "before Ceylon was destroyed the council was in the process of cutting orders for your next promotion for services rendered to the academy, and now that Ceylon has been reestablished on Durran, I now have the honor of carrying out this long and overdue presentation."

Kiah walked proudly toward Jedar, firmly affixing several metals on his uniform, but the smallest and most decorative was the one that brought tears to all that observed this historic moment. And to everyone's amazement, Kiah, after shaking Jedar's hand, pulled him to his chest, embracing him.

"Jedar, I used to sit under the Ceylonian heavens trying to envision what you looked like, or what kind of personality you may have. I wondered if you had the strength and fortitude of Atar, our grandfather, or the gentle nature of father, who has taken on quite a look of distinction." (Referring to his silver hair) "Jedar, if you only knew how much I have longed to see you. Until I heard about your heroic accomplishments, I wondered," (chuckling to himself) "if perhaps, you were an interstellar galactic wimp."

Jedar became rather amused, because it appeared he shared some magnetic bond with his brother, and even though he desired to know everything possible about his brother, he decided to keep his thoughts to himself, at least for the moment.

"Father," Kiah interrupted, "I have traveled here to discuss some important issues with you, but at the moment I must retire to my chamber to take my rest."

"Simka please walk my son to his chamber, and escort him to the banquet room at the appointed time."

As Simka escorted Kiah down the long hall to his chamber, the echo of Jedar's voice rang out in excitement as he continued to speak with Ral concerning Kiah's visit.

### THE BANQUET TABLE

Ral and Jedar were anxiously sitting in the room, dressed in their finest and recently pressed uniforms.

Ral looked pleased, when Kiah entered the room and sat down at the table, which was prepared for this special occasion.

"Father, I know you are disheartened over the destruction of our beloved homeland, and when the historians look back seeking answers, they will record that the devastation was brought about by the predicted asteroid. But as they begin to piece the facts together, they will figure out that the citizenship was needlessly destroyed, and the blame must fall entirely on Gemaal's inexcusable folly."

"I have never told the true story of the conditions that took place on Ceylon, but I thought it best that you know. Ragan tried to become ambassador of the Ceylonian colonies, under the auspices of Gemaal's badge. Ragan convinced our citizens to rebel, causing civil unrest to plummet throughout our fatherland. I will get right to the point father. I was instructed to restore harmony, and bring law back to the land, I was then instrumental in banishing Ragan, this I was able accomplish by sending him to the penal colony on Agreg, which was under the judgment of Mondor, the Agregleourite, there to live out the duration of his life."

"Father, Ceylon never regretted their disloyalty against the council, and if the asteroid had not swiftly accomplished its purpose, it would have expired just as abruptly. Gemaal confessed to me, his hatred for you and the family of Atar, and yet, he chose me of all the leaders on Ceylon to continue the Ceylonian way of life on Durran. Gemaal, although he cared so little for you and our family, loved Ceylon and chose to die along with the citizens that he loved and respected. Father, I know this may be hard for you to understand, but I believe Gemaal was a decent citizen, and even if he appointed Ragan as his ambassador, he believed in his deranged mind, that his decision was in the best interest of the citizenship."

"Gemaal knew far in advance that the asteroid was coming, but as a result of his indecision, multitudes of our comrades were unnecessarily slaughtered. Father I need to inform you that Gemaal repented to me of his injustices, especially those that concerned you and grandfather and I hope you will somehow not hold it against him."

"Kiah, I have known for many years of the calloused heart of Gemaal and the hidden feelings he held against our family. I also hated him for his strong armed rule of Ceylon, but long ago I found room in my heart to forgive him. He will pay in the spirit world for his deeds, whether good or bad."

"Please father! Stop there. This is the second time I have heard you speak in regard to forbidden matters, so please spare me your religious glib. Ragan has murdered Mondor, and released the prisoners, then they forcefully commandeered Mondor's spacecraft, and escaped to the outer regions of the Seventh Quadrant, and it is rumored that he is conferring with the ruthless Zorber."

"Father, if the Zorber are permitted to begin unchallenged colonization within the Seventh Quadrant, Durran, the Feramas, and massive amounts of our established colonies could be in jeopardy of extinction. Perhaps you haven't heard, but the Zorber, are alleged to be colonizers of paramount cruelty. Father, I will brief you later concerning the Zorber's unorthodox behaviors, but now, I require your help and especially the assistance of this young commander."

"Jedar, if you choose not to fight with me in this battle, I will understand, but if you say yes, we will need to gather your most experienced officers, quickly organize our master plan and then set a rendezvous date."

Kiah did not need Ral's intervention in the conflict with the Zorber, he had merely found an ideal situation to see his father and meet his half brother. Because Jedar had been waiting his entire life for this moment, there was no delay in his response.

"Yes brother, I am honored to serve by your side."

Jedar all of a sudden had a blank look on his face and those around him wondered what he was thinking.

Jedar whispered to himself. "If only grandfather was here, I know he would approve of my decision to serve with Kiah."

"Renna to Governor Kiah, please respond."

"Yes Renna?"

"Governor, Rogara, your security officer on the Galuppa, reports that Zorber have been sighted in Feramas airspace, and that their citizens are being abducted and medically experimented on."

"Jedar, we must act swiftly," shouted Kiah, "it appears that the Zorber are not prepared to reveal their plan of attack. We need to post security patrols in five strategic locations of the outer quadrants and I highly suggest that you also assign five of your top officers to fill these important posts. If the Zorber are observed intruding into Durranian airspace, we will be able to triangulate, mapping out their positions, and consequently allowing for a swift response from our academy fighters."

"Governor Kiah." Renna softly but hurriedly spoke. "It has just been reported that an explosion has occurred on the Feramas."

"Renna, monitor all the pertinent information and quickly transmit all reports to this location. Renna also keep us informed of continuing developments taking place on the Feramas."

"Governor the council on the Feramas has confirmed that it has captured an alien spacecraft of unknown origin, and the military has classified the project as top secret. They also indicate they will be concealing the only survivor in a remote military base to prevent panic."

"Jedar," Ral cried out, "we must save the Feramas citizens. We have not been in contact with the Feramas since the prophet last returned there to accomplish his final mission."

"Father, you speak of strange and alien ideas, who is this prophet you speak of?"

"The prophet was indirectly of our Ceylonian kinship and possibly the most venerated citizen that ever lived on the Feramas.

Because of his position as high priest and prophet, there was even suspicion that he was a god, Medoa, my second in command can explain it much better."

"Father you scare me, and I wonder if your mind has been turned into space dust from all your isolated years dealings with this brown planet. Simka remove father to his chamber for some needed rest."

"Renna continue."

Governor, all Zorber, except for their leader has perished in the initial crash. He is critically wounded and is being interrogated on the military base."

"Jedar, my data concerning the Zorber colonies appears to be grossly exaggerated. The military on the Feramas has diligently questioned their commander, and are inclined to believe that the aliens have never been inclined to aggression and war. The Zorber revealed that his fellow citizens had been annihilated by pandemic of unknown origin, and their travels into the Seventh Quadrant was exploratory, in order to seek out land for possible colonization."

The military reports that the Zorber was a superior race that had accomplished a great deal, both scientifically and medically. It is also reported that they successfully cured many health conditions throughout the quadrants. The Zorber in truth, was waiting for an opportune time to make their presence known, they suspected that the citizens would become hostile, if they revealed themselves to soon.

"Governor Kiah, the Zorber recently died, and the military doctors has performed a post-mortem examination."

"Renna, cease all further reports regarding the Zorber, and classify all previous communication as top secret."

"Kiah, there was no report of contact with Ragan, if that is true, then our biggest challenge now lies with him, and his current alliance with the escaped prisoners from Agreg."

"Perhaps you are right little brother, so tell me, can I be honored with your presence commanding the Galuppa in the search for this buffoon called Ragan?"

"My answer is the same, but before we depart, we need to discuss our relationship concerning the Unni, and perhaps Medoa will honor us with his presence. Kiah, father as you suspicion is a follower of the Unni, just as I am."

"Jedar, this conference is of the most importance, and I can't believe you would tell me of these forbidden ancient folklores.

Father I'm beside myself, if this foolishness would have taken place at a different time, I don't know what I would have done with you."

"Kiah, father and I share something that is of a spiritual nature, it cannot be taught in the academy, because it is something that fills our very being with love. Kiah, if you in all your high and superior position as governor cannot respect our belief, then I, Jedar, son of Ral, must distant myself from you. Kiah we have broken with the traditions of Ceylon, with the intention of having the freedom to choose our own destiny, and it is this same freedom that helps us believe something that is contrary to your Ceylonian laws. So you, my puffed up brother, can take your haughty attitude back to Durran and play god, but for me and my house, we know whom we serve, and if you in your diffidence can not honor our belief, then we share nothing in common."

"Jedar, I vividly remember when father and I last spoke on Ceylon, I knew he wished to depart from our ways at that time, and it hurts that he cared so little for mother and me. And then to watch him leave so hurriedly, barely without a proper adieu. Jedar I know you have great feelings for father, but he is the same citizen that left his wife and family alone to colonize planets, thus assuring his name would be perpetuated as a space colonizer."

"My mother died in a mental hospital from loneliness after father left Ceylon, and to prove to myself that I could not hate him, I worked hard to make myself one of the finest military officer since Atar. Tell me Jedar, where is the love you speak about? Where was the love for mother and myself? And how about the love for the millions of Ceylonian citizens that perished, where is the evidence of his love for them?"

"Even now Jedar, I can look into his eyes and tell how little he cared for our departed comrades. You speak about a god, so tell me young brother, who would want a god like that? I have made it on my own, and I have never called upon a dead god. You shame our way of life by giving credence to such folly. Jedar if you are still contemplating joining with me in battle we need to resolve these issues now."

"You are correct Kiah, father did the things that you accuse him of, and he has never denied any of your harsh accusations. My god Kiah, you are talking about your father, and I am honored to be called his son. Are you really so hardened and bias that someone has to believe the same as you? I am beginning to wonder if the great Kiah, governor of Durran, is jealous because I was permitted to be raised by my father, without the intervention of the council? Perhaps you would like to fight it out until the best man attains the victory. If so Kiah, then let's get it on, but even if you prevail against me, you will have gained nothing because the Unni will still live in the hearts of his people, just as he can live in yours."

"Jedar, not much is going to be resolved by this tongue-lashing. Perhaps, I may have been harsh and hasty in my judgments, and I truly admire your fortitude for defending that in which you believe, but I will need time to consider this matter."

"Thank you Kiah, I knew a citizen of your stature could not be subject to such prejudices. Could it be that the Unni has his hand on the great Governor of Durran?"

"Jedar I believe that your mind is deranged, but I have stronger feelings for you and father than I ever imagined, so in spite of yourself, I will make arrangements to depart on the Galuppa, and if you are agreeable, I will be ready by morning light. While we're on the subject, little brother, who will the crew aboard the Galuppa answer to, me or you?"

"Are you ready for that wrestling match you little wimp." Kiah laughed lovingly.

"You are beautiful Kiah, the Unni loves you, and I love you, so let's go kick some space but."

"Jedar, now that the Zorber problem has been settled, in the morning we must concentrate on the true issue at hand, Ragan. This enemy is just a citizen as you and I, and possesses the same strength and points of weakness as we, do you have any ideas where to begin our search for this extraordinary terror of the universe?"

"Kiah an adversary that displays passion for murder, and incites entire nations to do their vilest deeds, is truly possessed with an evil and unmitigated power that can only come from an outside force. With these kinds of credentials, he can't be hard to find. Kiah, please understand, yes, he is a citizen, but our battle is not against flesh and blood but against evil spirit forces. Just before I was born, there was a spiritual battle taking place on the Tri-Star against good and evil. During that battle, grandfather intervened and fought off Waki's evil messengers saving Dr. Louska, and this entire starship from destruction. Simka, my second in command has told us, there is coming a time when great conflict will take place throughout the cosmos, just before the end of all physical existence and life as we know it will end."

"Jedar I am going to let you ramble, I know that if I start to take you seriously, I will just become more upset. I never realized I had harbored such a close affinity for my family, which appears to be one of the few things that we share in common."

"Jedar, for now just go, I will see you soon enough aboard the Galuppa. Is this what I must endure until we find Ragan? If so, god help me?"

"Kiah, did I just hear a prayer to the Unni?"

"Just go young brother, just go."

## CHAPTER 15

## THE SEARCH FOR RAGAN

"Kiah, I never dreamed that Durran had such an advanced starship as the Galuppa. Father always told me that the Tri-Star was the finest in all the fleet, but it is just a junk heap in comparison to this jewel of a ship."

"Jedar, I know that you have been trained to command the most updated star fleet vessels, and I am confident that you are more than capable to command them all. The Galuppa is not listed in the training manuals, it along with its sister ships are classified top secret, and only available to Durran's highest ranking officers. I am sorry that I do not have one of your superior messengers to assist in your training, but I do have some of the finest navigators that have survived the destruction of my planet. To start with, I would like to introduce Rogara my top security officer, he will coach you in the starship's essential operation. Yes Jedar, I trust that you will quickly rise to the challenge, not only in the operations of this ship but also with the new fleet of starships assigned to you in your new position as Academy Commander."

Jedar suddenly had a blank look on his face, for it truly just dawned on him what Kiah had inferred.

"Kiah when you say Commander of the Academy, are you implying that I received this shinny little medal because I have been promoted to commander of the entire Durranian military fleet?"

"Little brother that is affirmative, does that sound like too big of a task? If so, perhaps I should give the position to Rogara."

"No! No! Kiah," Jedar came back laughing. "Commander of the academy, grandfather, father, you, and now me, I just cannot believe it."

"What about father? You have taken away his command, Kiah this will break his heart."

"Little brother you must truly believe that I am extremely unkind and just as uncaring. Just before my arrival, I conversed with father aboard the Galuppa, informing him that I had replaced him as academy commander. Father did confess to me that his age hindered him from commanding with authority, and he fully understood his commandership was only an honorary title. But he was delighted for you, and asked me to postpone the award ceremony, until the proper moment. Don't worry, father will still preside over the Feramas as long as he is able."

"Now," Kiah spoke harshly, "it's time to get your head out of your ass, for we have important work to do."

"All-right!" Jedar shouted. "Let's get ready to rumble!"

Kiah was suddenly interrupted by Rogara. "Governor Kiah, you asked me to report any unrest taking place throughout the outer star system, and I have just been informed by stellar intelligence that there is a citizen from a distant planet who is brewing up trouble, it is also reported that he is seeking an alliance with the magistrate of the Boravian Alliance."

"Rogara, is this Ragan?"

"Commander, intelligence has definitely confirmed that it is indeed Ragan, and he has with him men of the vilest nature who has escaped from the penal colony on Agreg. There are also reports that Agregleourite bounty hunters are in pursuit of this known liar and thief who murdered Mondor."

"Jedar, it appears that we are about to put an end to the long reign of this evil citizen that has so long troubled us."

"Kiah please! I must have this honor for myself, because I want to tear out his evil heart. After I smite him once I will say, this slash is for father, and the way you troubled him on the Feramas. My second smite will be for putting a knife through father's friend the prophet, and the third smite will be for destroying the moral fiber of our great planet, Ceylon."

"Save some justice for me little brother, I also have an axe to grind against this well-known tyrant, so let's depart immediately before the confederation of bounty hunters beat us to him."

## THE BORAVIAN MAGISTRATE

Ragan was putting on a show, displaying his great charm to the Boravian Magistrate, while sipping strong alcoholic drink. The magistrate grew weary listening to Ragan's continual boasting of how he was the first to escape the infamous Agreg penal colony, he also gloated how he was the only one to ever kill an Agregleourite, especially one of the stature of Mondor. The magistrate was aware of Ragan's reputation and wanted nothing to do with him, especially after learning about the chaos he instigated on Ceylon, just before its destruction.

The Boravians were acknowledged as a peace-loving world while living under Ceylonian servitude. The tyrants that Ragan had brought with him were of no use to his cause, and he looked down upon them as ignominious and beneath him. He realized they could not be taught difficult instruction, which would be necessary for any kind of a take over. Many of the Boravian women had been defiled by these citizens, and the only way the magistrate could muster up a plan, was by supplying his guest with alcohol and tranquilizer pills, which was used to sedate the fearsome creatures that occasioned to infiltrate their land.

When the Galuppa approached into Boravian airspace, the magistrate began sending distress calls, until Kiah finally responded. "Governor, I am Zepna, the magistrate of Boravia, the rebel that you seek is here, at coordinates to follow, Ragan and his men are fully sedated and they should present no problem in their apprehension."

Ragan greatly intoxicated, did not sense the invisible force field encircling him when he awoke.

"Kiah," spoke Ragan smugly, "who is this young buck that you have brought along to capture the infamous Ragan? He looks a little green behind the ears."

Jedar reacting in disgust, pointed his lazier at Ragan, firing repeatedly, the impact of the reverberations bouncing off the force field, caused Jedar and Kiah to collapse on the floor.

"Jedar are you okay?"

"Yes Kiah, I am fine."

"So this is Jedar, the son of the Feramas buffoon, and now an inept son, perfect to fill his shoes."

"Let me at him, I will rip his eyes out." Screamed Jedar.

## THE VIGILANTES CHALLENGE

Loud voices roared from the direction of the door. "He is ours, hand him over, for he must pay for the murder of Mondor." Cried out the bounty hunters. "You cannot deny us of our revenge and we will not leave without him."

"Galuppa." Kiah whispered unobserved. "Code B-Z, lock in on assigned DNA selection including prisoner Ragan."

"Roger," quietly responded Rogara, "three entities to be immediately transported."

The bounty hunter's quickly fired their weapons and lit up the space, where the three had been standing. The primitive bounty hunters were left alone dumbfounded, with their mouth agape.

"Have you calmed down Jedar?"

"Yes Kiah that was close and it's great to be back on board the Galuppa."

"Jedar we must decide what to do with Ragan, remember he is extremely intelligent and we need to incarcerate him so that we can finally put a stop to his folly forever."

"Jedar, there is an urgent message from Medoa on the Tri-Star, I will now transmit." Spoke Rogara

"Jedar take Ragan to the outer edge of our star system and there you will encounter a large black hole. This is the place where Ragan shall spend his eternity in torment, paying for his rebellious acts. Jedar tell your brother that there is a passageway, which will lead the Galuppa deep inside the vortex of the black hole, and if you trust in the Unni, he will safely guide you on your mission."

"Are you out of your mind Jedar? You here a voice and you decide to put the lives of this crew in danger. Little brother, no starship has endured an encounter with a black hole, it devours stars, planets, light, and whatever else happens to be passing near its insatiable mouth. Black holes beguilingly pulls in their prey, it then gobbles up, and spits everything out into another dimension in time. But Jedar, for some bizarre reason, I have a feeling that Medoa is right. Little brother, there is something I have never told anyone, not even the council."

"I have to hear this, it must be good, the great Kiah holding back secrets, this sounds like treason to me." Jedar rolled back in his seat and laughed.

"Jedar this is serious and if you ever gain your composure, I will fill you in on the details."

"I am sorry Kiah, but you are so legalistic that I just can't conceive of you ever deceiving the council or anyone, it just doesn't seem to be part of your high and mighty Durranian nature."

"Jedar listen closely to me. I once encountered a black hole and Medoa's information is truthful, there is a passageway through time. I recognized you were in contact with a higher power, because no one has had access to such classified information. I learned that each black hole has a parallel world, brought about by dimensions in time. I am the only officer to ever accomplished this feat, and I have never revealed it to anyone. Jedar I have this inner feeling that I can do it again."

"Kiah, I believe you, but from what I understand the black hole is more immense than any that has ever been cataloged in the academy's files, there will be too many unexplained variables. Kiah the Unni does seem to have plans for you, I trust he has brought you to this place in time to further fulfill his purpose."

"Jedar, just because I see one small beam of logic, does not constitute enough evidence to make me a believer in the ways of your Unni. Perhaps Medoa just made a calculated guess or he may have previously learned that I had traversed a black hole, there are many possibilities to consider."

"Kiah, Kiah, didn't you just tell me that you never told a living soul. Kiah the journey to our star system is at least one third of a solar year journey, so big brother it looks like we have lots of time, and I yearn to hear about the many interesting citizens that you have encountered on your travels."

"Jedar I do have information that you may find interesting. A number of years ago, just before Ceylon's destruction, the council permitted conferences where philosophical ideas were liberally interchanged between the planets. The citizens arrived on Ceylon in large numbers, but their quest for truth seeking quickly gave way to religious idealism. The council realized that their good intention had become a national disaster. Then these cults spread like wildfire and the beliefs of old Ceylon was once again resurrected. I secretly spied upon them to learn of their sedition. I then began arresting hundreds, torturing them to discourage their cause, and when they continued to resist, I compelled them to forfeit their lives by walking into the molecular field, and commanding that their ashes be cast into the Ceylonian River."

"Jedar one of the citizens that I exterminated was my old friend from the academy, I recall just before I turned on the switch, he looked serenely into my eyes and said that he had forgiven me. And you, my dear brother, although the cult leaders tried to keep it a secret, I eventually found out through my informants that the source of this insurgence was instigated at the hand of Atar's, grandson. Because of my injustice against these misguided Ceylonian citizens, I have suffered many haunting, sleepless nights living in my guilt."

"Kiah, father and I had to learn the hard way, and I believe enough unusual undertakings have occurred for you to believe in the Unni. I have been observing you and I have become aware  that you are not the calloused officer that father spoke of after he left Ceylon. Your ways are gentle and your heart is forgiving, these are not the ways of my father's people, so yes Kiah, I knew you had undergone a spiritual change. I can have Simka sit with you and educate you in the ways of the Unni."

"Jedar I confess that there has been changes in my ways of thinking, and perhaps my disturbing experience with the religious revolt gave me much to think about, but for the moment I have to pay heed to the hundreds of crew members aboard the Galuppa, so if you must try to proselytize me, at least wait till our mission is accomplished."

Kiah expressed his great concern regarding the welfare of the Durranian citizens, wondering how they would get by without his leadership during the extensive space journey, and Jedar talked at length about their father and his great love for the Feramas.

## THE BLACK HOLE

The Gallupa's computer began blasting emergency alarms. "Governor there is extreme heat, affecting the internal operations of the Galuppa."

"Computer, provide for me an analytical report concerning the present situation?"

"Governor, gravity is pulling the ship into the vortex of an immense black hole. Danger! Danger! Governor, my data banks are not programmed for emergencies of this magnitude, all systems are indicating it is imperative that you turn back now!"

"Negative computer, cool the ship with strong hydro sprays and prepare to set all controls to manual. My mission is to navigate this starship straight into the lower entranceway of the black hole, where there is hopefully a locking jet stream, which will hurl us into its inner core, and if this ship holds up, we should find ourselves in another dimension of time."

"Rogara maintain course, we are just beginning to enter into the strong currents of the jet stream."

"I am having enough problems Kiah, the Galuppa feels like it's about to break apart, it can't hold up too much longer with all this pressure being exerted on its hulls."

"You're doing fine Rogara. You can commence cutting all engines and placing all controls on automatic, and just sit back and enjoy the free ride."

"Kiah," screamed Jedar, "the heat is overbearing!"

"Rogara, Jedar, listen closely. No matter what happens, it is imperative that you stay awake, we must resist the gravitational pull, no matter how terrifying it may be."

The extreme pressures being exerted on the fearless space travelers, filled their mind with bizarre images of departed souls. As a few of the faces appeared, smiling and loving, there would appear others that was grotesque and tortured, screaming inside their hell.

It seemed like time rolled back, as Kiah and Jedar relived past event of their lives. Jedar furthermore, watched in horror as the citizens of Ceylon, fixed their eyes intently upon the heavens, as the asteroid descended so quickly upon them. The scene was so intense, that Jedar's primordial scream, became so piercing that he thought his brain would burst asunder if it didn't stop.

Kiah relived scenes from his childhood, when Ral held him in his arms, telling him secret thoughts of his heart, and for the first time, Kiah was able to look into his father's eyes and see the love that had been denied, due to the ill feelings he had harbored toward his father.

Ragan physically displayed the evil presence, which was in control of his tortured mind. Ragan's face became distorted due to the tremendous forces that were exerted, as the evil entity would try to exit from Ragan's tortured body to the freedom of the spaceship. But for unknown reasons, the evil one was forced to remain inside.

The colors were so vivid that it was impossible to describe the stunning heavenly hues, the stronger the pain, the more vibrant and beautiful the colors. The screams of Ragan could be heard from his confinement in the lower regions of the Galuppa, but there was not one that was concerned, for each of the tortured space travelers was living in their own personal hell.

"Kiah," spoke Jedar, "this is not only the prison for Ragan but also for the multitudes of Waki's evil messengers, no mortal can survive if we penetrate any deeper into the purity of the darkness. It's in this place of safety that we must leave Ragan. Have security remove Ragan to the transport capsule and jettison him toward the screams of torment, which are coming from the great abyss. I am confident he will be provided for, I only know one thing for certain, this is a place I never want to encounter again."

"Kiah, I can barely see the messengers, but it appears they are releasing Ragan from his encapsulation. The messengers looked toward the Galuppa, crying out, "here In this impasse, Ragan will be held in isolation until the day of final judgment, when his soul will be tormented and held imprisoned for eternity."

Suddenly the Galuppa was projected into a new dimension, similar to going from one room to another, and it seemed, they were still moving. Jedar began to hold his hands to his ears. "It hurts! It hurts! It sounds like the voices of millions of singers, all singing in accord, it is wonderful, but these mortal ears can not bear the pain." Suddenly the music stopped, and it seemed they were in a dead zone between the two gulfs.

"Kiah, do you think this is the abode of the Unni?"

"Well Jedar, from everything that I have seen and heard, it certainly is a distinct possibility."

"Kiah, ever since time began, Waki's dark messengers has been influencing citizens to do their bidding, but there are a few that the Waki personally chooses, controlling their mind, body and soul. This happened when Ragan started rebelling against father on the

Feramas. His continual jealously of father's position allowed hate to fester, this was all that Waki needed to take possession of Ragan's mind. This force for unbridled evil has been around since creation, and continues to wage war against the Unni's children, but Waki will in due course of time be defeated."

"Jedar, I recall you telling me that Ragan and father were close friends in the academy, how strange," Kiah rubbed his chin in contemplation, "that he could have gone so far astray."

"Kiah we must return to our homes, so that we can begin preparing the citizens of the universe to accept Unni or be destroyed in this eternal damnation. With Ragan out of the picture, perhaps the Feramas and Durran can find eternal salvation, and be brought into the express will of the Unni."

The journey through the black hole was slow and dangerous, and Kiah suddenly became aware that they were still not in control of the Galuppa, which appeared to be steered by unseen hands. The ship stopped unexpectedly, and Jedar watched in awe as the heavens rolled back, revealing someone with the appearance of a king, sitting high upon a magnificent throne.

"It's the Golden City!" Shouted Jedar, "And look Kiah! Boeski the prophet is standing near the Unni and his son. Kiah, can't you see him, he's smiling and waving at us."

"Wake up Jedar! Jedar wake up!" Shouted Kiah.

"Kiah, tell me, where am I? I saw Boeski the prophet, he was so beautiful."

Kiah seized Jedar by the collar, shaking him violently.

"Wake up! Jedar, I was successful in finding the passage out of the black hole. You blacked out on me long ago but we made it through safely. Brother you must have had quite a dream."

"No Kiah, the Unni gave me a vision of the Golden City. I now believe in all things that Boeski instructed us concerning the Unni. Didn't you see it Kiah? When I return to my command, I am going to spread the laws of Unni throughout the galaxies."

"How are you going to accomplish such a feat Jedar?"

"I will establish a central headquarters on the Zedor planet and from there, I will set up sister branches throughout each colony, starting from the Sixth Quadrant, even unto the Eighth. I will even involve father and your new mother, it might make them feel useful during their declining years, and you Kiah, can also do your part on Durran."

"Jedar, we have a lot to talk about, but for now, let's get some needed rest, for I wish to discuss some important issues with you when we arrive at our destination."

## INDECISION ON THE WAY HOME

It was morning aboard the Galuppa as Jedar walked briskly into the breakfast area, spoke Quinia, and instantly the beverage was available at his fingertips. Kiah had just finished opening his packet of pills, when Jedar walked in the room.

"Good morning young commander, you're just in time for a nutritious breakfast."

"Kiah I hate these pills, I have visited star systems where foods are extraordinarily tasteful, providing amazing sustenance for the body."

"Little brother I also am familiar with these delightful and fruitful planets, I also recall from father's early recorded data that the Feramas was of this unique classification. In Ceylon, what little food we produced was grown in soil that had been contaminated by nuclear waste, and later when the ground regained some normality, we continued to contaminate the soil with an over abundance of pesticides in our efforts to kill off the invading locust and insects. This forced the academy to begin experimenting with genetic food substitutes. Jedar if it wasn't for the great wisdom of our scientist creating the miraculous pills that you hate so much, Ceylon would have ceased to exist long ago."

"Ok Doctor Kiah." Jedar winked at his brother as if he had learned a valuable piece of sagacious information. "It's back to the pills for now, my wise and all knowing brother. After all, I want this body to stay healthy at least until I finish my present mission for the Unni."

"Jedar, I am beginning to feel, you have been right, for it appears there was a marvelous plan set in motion, which lies beyond rational consideration. Little brother, I am sorry for my many harsh words, but growing up in Ceylon has hardened me, perhaps it was due to the aversion I held against father."

"Jedar will you and father return with me to Durran? Old Ceylon is a distant memory and our former home also no longer exists. Jedar I have the authority to order father to return with me, no longer to waste his time intervening in the affairs of the Feramas.

On Durran, father could occupy one of the honored positions, such as Guardian of Durranian History & Preservation."

"That is interesting Kiah, so enlighten me, what is this preservation of history?"

"Father loves historical research, especially that relating to Ceylon's antiquity, and he would be placed in charge of all historical archives. Can you envision it Jedar? Father would take great pride in his accomplishments, and I consider this to be an honored position for him."

"Kiah, what position does your intellectual mind have in store for me in this complicated universe?"

"Well my young and high-strung friend, your present line of work as academy commander, is the most honored profession throughout Durran, every senior officer would cut off their right arm to be promoted to your high ranking. Jedar, if you were to get any more recognition, you would be sitting on the Durranian council, or my seat as governor, and I am not quite ready to give it up, so tell me brother, what do you have to say?"

"First of all, I know you mean well Kiah, and for some strange reason, I feel I will always have a strong kinship to you. But father will in no way leave the Feramas, that is where his heart lies, it is his love and life. The Unni led father to the Feramas to set in order, his marvelous plan for the universe, and there he nurtured the planet since grandfather presented it to him as a gift. If the Venduras War had not taken place, then Borkia would not have been there on the Feramas to save the Children of Chaldoc from the Hunsha. If these invaders had been successful, then the prophet would not have been born and the Unni's light may have gone out, never to return on the Feramas."

"The great love of the Unni was embraced by the children of Chaldoc, being extended to father and myself, and those serving aboard the Tri-Star, who also chose to believe. It is important that I tell you," spoke Jedar with tears in his eyes, "father will never leave the Feramas, even if you command him to do so. Your offer to me sounds enticing but I also have been changed. I was born into this spiritual environment, and taught under great spiritual advisors such as Boeski, Treeka, Simka and Medoa. Kiah if you can permit me to maintain my beliefs, I am more than willing to devote my life to the Durranian cause and serve you faithfully as my supreme military commander. I also feel within my heart that all life is about to end, and just as the light became extinguished on Zorber and our former homes, soon there will be no Kronos, and no Durran. All creation must pass away so that life can begin anew, just as it always has. I discern that this is too deep for you to comprehend, but big brother, I perceive that you feel within your heart that what I say is true. You have seen enough and heard enough, you have even been used as an instrument of the Unni to carry out his divine plan."

"Perhaps you are right Jedar, these ideas will take time to ration out, but no matter what your decision is for now, I would like my new found family to return with me to Durran for at least a short visit."

"Kiah, I will speak with father about your kind request, I believe father needs to get away from the Feramas for a short period of time, to relax."

While the Galuppa soared through the galaxies on its return home, Kiah and Jedar had time on hand, to discuss their experiences and become more acquainted.

Upon returning home, they united together, fighting new battles, and they successfully strengthened alliances throughout the quadrants. Jedar established religious headquarters on the neutral colony of Zedor, which made it possible for ambassadors to spread religious material throughout the quadrants. The citizens embraced salvation, and new converts by the millions were brought into the knowledge of the Unni.

Even Dreara, who had been so headstrong, felt the zeal of her faith and did everything she could, even in spite of her advanced age. Ral somewhat paralyzed, confined to a mobile carrier, shared in spreading the word of the Unni. In spite of his limited physical condition, he still had the physique of a citizen of lesser age and his eyesight was nearly perfect.

It appeared to Jedar, that no matter how much good he accomplished, evil was always present, seemingly outweighing the good. Albeit Ragan was incarcerated in the black hole, the spirit of Waki was still manifest throughout the colonies. Jedar knew that the Waki's evil influence would eventually be eliminated, but until that time, he had determined to devote his life to fighting the spiritual forces of darkness.

## RAL CHASTISED, HIS BLESSINGS PASSES TO KIAH & JEDAR

Ral realized his life would soon come to an end, desiring in his old age to see his family reunited on Durran. The trip would take a few days, but Medoa took the opportunity to once more encourage Ral to remain faithful to the Unni.

"Ral," spoke Medoa, "your final days are fast approaching and I must speak with you in regard to the Unni. I realize that you have repented of your sins, yet you are not to be held unaccountable. The Unni instilled in you the wisdom to balance the scales of justice, and you chose to follow your mind rather than your heart."

"Commander the glory that should have been yours, is now passed down to your sons, they will be blessed to witness the Unni's universal destruction in your stead. Your iniquity was the result of laws, which was passed down by Ceylonian leaders before you were born, and that is why you are privileged to remain in the divine will of the creator."

"Medoa why was Ragan permitted to reap his evil upon the land? I realize you have told me about philosophic ideas, such as good cannot exist without evil. What was it? Oh yes, the negative and the positive forces are interdependent upon each other."

"Ral, I do not know the complexities of his intentions, but I can tell you that the Unni holds a special place in his heart for the citizens living on the Feramas. His love extends to every citizen that acknowledges him as their creator, and they are indeed destined to live with him in, what you call, the Golden City."

"Medoa, when I die, will I see you again?"

"Ral, I will be serving the Unni for eternity, singing praises around his throne of mercy. The Unni desires that you continue to enlighten citizens everywhere, telling them if they continue to rebel, they will be in danger of eternal damnation. Ral also tell them they are to love and to be loved, for the Unni is love."

"Ral, stop by the medical lab for a needed tranquilizer, I do feel when you arrive on Durran, you may need it, because tomorrow may well be your greatest day."

"Yes Medoa, I will visit the doctor and then I will take my rest. Goodnight my friend."

## RAL ON DURRAN

Kiah escorted his family into the Durranian capitol, at first Ral appeared to be highly impressed, but after closer observation his countenance began to diminish, but he was not going to let his discouragement ruin this special day for Jedar and Dreara who were caught up in the excitement of the celebration.

On Durran pollution had been virtually eliminated and the ban on contagions was now sternly enforced by the Council of the Twelve. Today's population was equipped with an apparatus that could fly them above the hustle bustle of the city. To protect each citizen from accidents during their excursion, each flight jacket was supplied with backup computer chips, in case one of the primary chips would fail. When the citizens traveled to near each other in flight, a computerized voice would make them aware of the danger, and automatically redirected their flight pattern to protective zones.

Jedar was taken by surprise, when someone placed a flight jacket on his shoulders. As Jedar soared awkwardly just above their head, Ral could see his excitement, and at least for the moment, Ral became caught up in the thrill of the day.

When Ral look around, he considered that the citizens were still, just as calloused and cold, as those that had dwelt on Ceylon. He detected how everyone remained aloof from their neighbors, and rarely spoke, unless there was a reason. Ral realized that they were working totally to perpetuate the idealism of their honored society, but there was little motivation for achievement. He felt they were more like androids, which slaved under the governmental system. This was troublesome for Ral, and the day's events only served to remind him of the reasons he had left Ceylon so long ago.

Suddenly, Ral had a flash of spiritual enlightenment and he began to examine the citizens in a different light. "If the prophet could change the hearts of the disbelieving citizens on the Feramas, perhaps the Durranians might also bask in the Unni's glorious light." Yet, he was dismayed as he looked at their faces because there was no smiles, only complacency. They appeared to be lost, and they reminded Ral of sheep that had gone astray.

As the festivities continued, Kiah introduced them to the eleven members of the council. They scarcely recognized Acerera, and Keeksonn due to their advanced age, the rest of the members was not known to Ral, because they were elected after Ceylon's horrific destruction. Jedar looked handsome in his new uniform, which displayed his medals of valor, the one that he cherished most, the commander medal, was the smallest.

Ral watched lovingly as Jedar tried to act with some degree of sophistication, while Dreara was becoming very tired, no longer enjoying the activities. Ral realized Dreara would not stay content in her outlandish environment. She had grown accustom to life aboard the Tri-Star, and to her, it was home and her only safe haven.

Kiah could not wait to show Ral all the latest technology, but at least for the moment, Ral opted to bypass the sky ride, instead accepting his first ride on a less imposing means of transportation.

Kiah could not wait to show his family the City of Tribute, which had been built to honor his father. When Ral beheld the city with all its majesty, he could hardly speak. Citizens from colonies throughout, not just Durran, but the entire Seventh Quadrant, would stop off on their planetary travels, just to enjoy the wondrous City of Tribute.

There in the midst of the city square stood a statue of Ral, which was higher than the tallest buildings on Durran, it was indeed stunning. There was also a recorded message that repeated over and over, telling how the son of Atar, Ceylon's governor, had risen in ranks to colonize several planets in the name of Ceylon.

Jedar was also surprised to see a less imposing statue, that was erected in his honor, but he was more surprised to hear that that the city had been erected long before Kiah's recent visit concerning the Zorber.

"This is the greatest day of my life Kiah, I can now see that you truly loved father in spite of all the ill feelings you had harbored against him. If anything ever comes out of this, it will be that our family has finally been reunited."

When the celebration came to an end, they adjourned to the Galuppa for a light snack and a cup of Durranian tea. Kiah was just about to ask his father concerning his future plans, when the sirens began loudly to echo throughout the starship.

## DESTRUCTION ON THE FERAMAS

"Commander Jedar, there is an urgent message, immediate response required." Issued forth from the ship's computer.

"Yes Simka, how are things on the Comatra?"

"Jedar you must depart for the Feramas, there is an extreme emergency that needs your immediate attention."

"Simka, have the Comatra readied, I will be there possibly before night fall."

"Kiah, I hope you understand that I must immediate depart, but when circumstances merit, I will return and continue our present conversation."

"Yes Jedar, I do understand, and I will make arrangements to speed you on your way to the Comatra, and little brother, keep me informed of the developing conditions on the Feramas."

"Kiah, please take care of father till we return, his health has been failing and his final days are near at hand."

"I am aware of that and we will await your return, now go in peace."

Jedar arrived on the Comatra, and true to his word, Simka had prepared the ship for immediate take off.

As Medoa had always served at the side of Ral aboard the Tri-Star, Simka was now, second in command and advisor to Jedar aboard the Comatra.

As the Comatra soared above the Feramas heavens, Jedar could not shake the eerie feeling that something was terribly wrong.

"Simka switch on the image scanner." Spoke Jedar. Simka was extremely quite.

"Simka I am awaiting your report!"

No response was given as Jedar walked over and began to observe the screen.

"In the name of the Unni, what is going on!"

To Jedar's disbelief, everywhere he glanced throughout the Feramas, there were millions of citizens that had died in mass. He looked on in disbelief at decomposing bodies that were heaped upon each other throughout the land. The crew was horrified, watching in bewilderment as the Feramas survivors voraciously ripped out the hearts of those that had most recently died, drinking the blood of the maggot infested bodies in their last effort to stay alive.

"Computer provide a detailed analysis of probabilities that could have led to this mass extermination that is taking place on the Feramas."

"Commander, my data banks are on line with the universal information system and my report is not encouraging. Disease has destroyed life throughout the Feramas and the lower quadrants, and because these planets had been contaminated, the citizens sought shelter, trying to escape the scourge, which followed them."

"My god, I am glad father isn't here to see this, why such carnage? Simka how about Durran, will the pandemic touch her?"

"Yes commander, but it will not be soon."

"Simka, how long, please tell me now!"

"Jedar it will not take place in your lifetime, for according to the Unni's promise, the seed of Ral is not to perish until just before the ending of all cosmological life. But the true time lies with the Unni. It appears the creator needs Durran for a few more seasons to accomplish the last phase of his divine plan"

"Simka, we must immediately return to Durran, and Simka, please notify Kiah of our situation, but I emphasize, this must not be mentioned to father."

## CHAPTER 16

### THE DEATH OF RAL

By the time Ral had grasped that his beloved Feramas was no more, time seemed to slip away as events kept moving toward the ending of all existence. The years caught up with Ral, because he was helpless and unable to move in his final days of life. As Ral waited for death, his mind became filled with memories, especially that of his father's death, and the scene kept occurring over and over in his mind.

"I seem to recall one of the officers." Ral briefly paused as he tried to remember the envoy's name, he then continued to ramble on. "Yes, it was Leaoka that had informed me of father's death." Ral fought hard to keep the images in his mind, but because of the congestion in his lungs and his weakened condition it was difficult to hold on to his thoughts.

"Oh yes, I felt terrible when I heard of father's death, and there were so many questions that flooded my mind and I recall that I inquired of Medoa and the prophet. Their answers was a source of refreshing, especially when I realized that father continued to subsist in the presence of the Unni. "Oh prophet, where are you, now that I have need of you? Yes, with all the questions that I challenged you with, perhaps I should have received a degree from one of Ceylon's more affluent universities. Well, I must quit rambling, because I must share my final time with my beloved family."

Ral asked Dreara to send in Medoa.

"Medoa, my old and trusted friend, to you I want to make my final request."

"Yes Ral, I would be much obliged to honor your wishes if it should lie within my power to do so."

"Medoa, I desire to be buried under the brown dirt of the Feramas, if perchance you could ascertain the burial plot of my old friend the prophet, I would be most indebted, for I cannot think of a more hallowed place and I desire that Dreara be placed beside me."

"Ral the record books do not disclose where Boeski was buried. The holy books revealed that at Boeski death, his body was transformed, and taken directly into the Golden City, an event that was witnessed by hundreds of citizens. We do have computerized records of where the prophet's father, your old friend Borkia, is buried, if that would be acceptable to you."

"Yes Medoa, so be it. I have loved its blue skies since the time my father first gave it to me, I provided for it, just as I did for the citizens, whom I grew to love."

Medoa could not bring himself to tell Ral that the plague remained a constant threat and Kiah could not chance spreading it to Durran. But true to Medoa's promise some future date if conditions were to change, Ral would then be removed to his beloved Feramas.

"Medoa, they were my family and I presume that is why I never left its outer sphere, even when Ragan reaped his mayhem. I still think of the good times we shared at the academy, Ragan was so full of life in those days, and did he love to sing. He always had a different female at his side, it seemed he was never without one. He really wanted the Feramas for his own, and Medoa, why is it that I still miss him? Perhaps if I had not given him such an important position at such a young age, maybe Waki, would not have obsessed him to do the evil deeds, which caused me such grief. Medoa I have forgiven him, do you think ill of me for it?"

"Love and forgiveness are two qualities that the Unni has asked of all who serve him. No Ral, I admire you for all of the sweet thoughts, which you have for every citizen. Ragan will receive his divine punishment, as all citizens who fight against the spirit of the Unni. Ragan shall forever dwell in isolation and his constant wish will be that he was never born. Ral it took you a long time to accept Unni, but look how far you have come, also consider your family, they are believers because of your example. Ral because of your works and those of your family, consider how many millions of citizens on numerous planets, including Durran, will share in the glorious light of the Unni."

"Medoa my time is passing quickly, so perhaps you should begin sending in the others, so that I may bless them."

Dreara never left Ral's side, constantly holding the hand of the citizen she had loved so long. She made an attempt to smile as Medoa left the room but couldn't, Jedar then entered the room.

"Father, it's wonderful to see you again." The last time they had spent time together, was at the City of Tribute, but it was obvious to Jedar that his father's health had quickly deteriorated and this would be their last goodbye.

"Jedar, you don't look to well, perhaps we should change places?" Ral spoke, trying to add a little levity to the conversation, he was fully aware of his deteriorated appearance and his weakened condition, but he did not want to make his son feel uncomfortable.

"Jedar place your hand in mine for I wish to bless you."
The more Ral tried to speak, his words came slower and slower.

"My son may the Unni bless you." Ral desired to further speak, but could not, he was too weak.

"Thank you father, but do not try to speak, please try to conserve your strength. I am going to ask Kiah and the others to come in." As Jedar departed, tears began flowing freely from his eyes, he knew death was very near and he did not want to cheat the others out of their final goodbye.

When the door opened, Kiah entered, and when he saw his aging father's emaciated condition, his spirit was so weakened that his knees almost buckled. The room had been darkened, except for a dim light that cast a sparkle to his father's eyes.

"Father, I came here today, not only to see you, but to ask forgiveness for all those years that I loathed you for leaving mother. I have learned from watching you that you are a great man, and just as your father's achievements have survived, the history of Durran will be the history of Atar and his son Ral, Space Colonizer."

Dreara could not be restrained as she broke down and fell to her knees, hanging on to her husband. When they heard her cries of anguish, everyone in the room could not keep from weeping for Ral, for their love was just too great. Because of Dreara's weaken condition, Dr. Rhear gave her a shot in order to sedate her, desiring not to remove her from Ral's presence before he uttered his very last breath. The monitors indicated the worse was about to take place and everyone moved close to Ral.

"Someone turn the lights down, it's too bright, and it hurts my eyes."

Ral, in his weakened condition, could not comprehend that those around him could not hear his faint words.

"Who is there? Boeski, is that you? I prayed I would see you before I died."

Everyone knew Ral had seen something, for he appeared to be speaking to someone and his countenance was most heavenly. The family and friends could not see the prophet as he reached for Ral's hands, and together they stopped for a brief moment, looking at the tears and compassion expressed by Dreara, the family and the host of friends. Boeski asked Ral to take one final look at his lifeless form, and as they departed, he spoke to Ral. "You have earned your rest, you are now free to walk with me into the eternal light of our creator."

"Did you feel that Jedar?" Spoke Dreara, "It was as if the wind touched me."

"Yes mother, I also felt it, it surely was father letting us know that he is now content in the spirit world. We will see father again and grandfather will also be there. Mother, I wish I could be with him, I can't wait."

## RAL BURIED ON DURRAN

"Medoa to transporter room, please respond."

"Yes Medoa, continue your transmission."

"Immediately begin to prepare commander Ral's body for burial and make arrangements to transport, coordinates to follow."

The capsule containing Ral's body was of a unique design, it contained an alloy that once sealed, could never be opened and it was impregnable. This was done so that the memory of Ral and his family would live on, if discovered by some distant space traveler.

Original embalming was developed by the prophet on the Feramas. In the early days of mummification the inner organs were removed and replaced with wet mortar, which completely filled the insides of the deceased, and dried as hard as stone, there were still a few mummies on display throughout the quadrants. Techniques in mummification had become technically advanced, going through a complicated purification process. All the inner corporal organs were removed, and replaced with genetically replicated organs, never to decay, the synthetic tissues were soft to the touch, making the body appear youthful.

Enclosed in the capsule were recorders that showed visual images of Ral, providing detailed records of his family, just in case there would be a need for proof of his genealogical lineage.

Medoa had found the location of Borkia's abode on the Feramas and erected a replica on Durran. The academy set aside 100 acres of land to be fenced in as a shrine to the commander. A garden was planted and a full time attendant was assigned to its care, and Ral was buried in the fertile ground of Durran with his friends and loved ones in attendance. Dreara never recovered from the death of her husband, and within just a few shorts weeks, she was buried beside Ral in the family plot.

David B Kingman

## KIAH & JEDAR'S FINAL CONVERSATION

So much had happened in such a short time that Kiah and Jedar still could not believe what had recently taken place.

"Well Jedar, isn't it strange how events have come about since I first came to visit you and father, when I solicited your help against the terrible Zorbers?"

"Yes I recall Kiah, the Unni works in mysterious, but interesting ways. Look at the beauty of Durran's six moons and the dancing lights in the sky. I feel the Unni placed their unending array there, just for us to behold. Perhaps father's spirit is entwined in the lights, and he along with Atar is speaking to us, telling us wondrous things concerning the Unni, but we are not spiritual enough to hear their voices, echoing gently through the Durranian winds. Wouldn't that be something Kiah? Wouldn't that truly be something?"

"How about you Jedar, can you believe it is about to end?"

"No Kiah, I believe that long after we have gone from here, the Unni will start all over. He might even reuse the Feramas, why would he waste a perfectly good planet? He would cleanse the land by his mighty hand, and then create a male and female citizen. They would populate and fill the land, until they expand out in search of distant planets, then in given time there would be a new Atar, and his sons will also be distant space colonizers. And then, when life begins to end, their sons will be discussing, just as we, how the process will be repeated, over and over throughout eternity. Why do I say this Kiah? Because the Unni loves his creation, it is his nature to create. He has lived without beginning, and with him there is no end. He loves all of his creation and he cares for it, just as a mother loves and protects her young."

"That sounds wonderful Jedar, let's go and get some well deserved rest. By the way, I never did get to tell you, I still think you're a wimp."

"Why you arrogant Durranian snob, I'll rub your nose in this red sand that you love so much."

The two brothers, with arms upon each other's shoulders, walked home across the wet sands of Durran, wondering what new and wonderful experience they would encounter when they awake to greet the dawning of the new day.

# THE END

## INDEX OF CHARACTERS & EXPLANATION OF TERMS

**ACERERA**   A member of the Ceylonian Council.

**ADRADA**     Eldest son born to the first couple that inhabited the Feramas. It was through their seed that the Children of Light, traced their ancestry. Zehon, the father of Majia and her son, the prophet, were of this lineage.

**AGREG**   The **Agregleourite** giants formerly resided on the small and distant planet of Groga, but eventually, after the food supply ran out, they settled on the planet of Zerena. This new land was mostly comprised of rock and limited natural resources. In a remote area of the planet (Agreg) the Groga giants were able, because of their physical constitution, to work in the tar pits, selling the minerals throughout the far reaches of their star system. After Captain Atar placed the Zerena under servitude, he offered the descendants of Machiaz employment as prison overseers.

**ATAR**    The second Governor of New Ceylon and father of Ral. Just as Abraham in the Bible was called out by God to establish his chosen people, the Unni selected Atar and his family to establish faith throughout the star system, before the final destruction of all cosmological life. (See Ral)

**ATRA**     The planet set aside to accommodate burials for Ceylon's most prominent citizens. Military leaders were buried by order of their military rankings, their wives were privileged to be located in a select area of Atra. Ral went there to pay his respects to Mylia, his Ceylonian wife.

**BRAKA**     Ral held a lot of admiration for his uncle, they were friends at the academy until Braka married Atar's sister. Braka was killed by Gormia, commander of the Zecra Nation but because his spaceship was blown asunder, there was no DNA left so that he could be brought back to life in the Regeneration Chamber.

**BRUDDA**   Served as Chairman of the Ceylonian Council

**BAISHA**   A member of the Ceylonian Council.

**BANURK**  Brother of Chaldoc and a son of Adrada on the Feramas

**BOESKI**  The Prophet was the son of Borkia & Majia. He believed he was the son of the Unni. When Ral invited the prophet and the Chaldocians aboard the Tri-Star they became close friends. Boeski made many journeys through the galaxies with Ral, logging every event. He also studied the computer's technological data banks and was permitted to us this knowledge to help bring about scientific development on the Feramas. (See Borkia & Majai)

**BORAVIAN MAGISTRATE**  He contrived a plan to get Ragan and the escaped prisoners from Agreg, drunk, in order for them to be easily arrested by Kiah and Jedar.

**BORKIA**  He was an Officer and a close friend of Ral aboard the TRi-Star. He married Majia on the Feramas and they had one child, Boeski the Prophet. Many years after Borkia was murdered, he was regenerated by Ral in an effort to please his friend the Prophet, but his remains had been contaminated after burial, and the regeneration cycle left him deprived of his mind and soul. Boeski became quilt laden, realizing he had not honored his father and mother and was unworthy to enter into the Golden City. (Heaven) The prophet asked Ral to place his father's shell in the crematory and once again place him beside his mother on the Feramas. (See Boeski& Majia)

**BRACHAR**  Atar sent Ral to the Bracharian star base to gain the military experience that would demonstrate to the council that Ral was worthy to manage the affairs of the Feramas.

**BRUGULA**  He was the leader of the ruthless Hunsha tribe on the Feramas. His clan attacked the encampment of the Chaldocians and would have marched them on a long and perilous journey if Borkia had not intervened. (See Victar)

**CEEKRA**  The planet where the Interplanetary Games were held, often attended by Captain Atar as he observed the Groga defend the honor of Ceylon

**CEPPRA**  Treegra the Kronos, in order to form an alliance with the Zecra Nation had given his daughter Greeska in marriage to Gormia the leader of the Zecra. Her name on Zecra was Ceppra. The

Kronos women were known for their insatiable sexual appetite. They wore no clothing in order to attract male suitors, they were barbaric people lacking all sophistication.

**CEYLONIAN STAR TIME (C.S.T.)**    The Ceylonians utilized a different measurement of time than their planetary neighbors.

**CEYLON OLD**    During its early history, old Ceylon held on to a belief in a higher spiritual being called the Unni, but due to their decadence, the moral fiber of their colonies declined and religious passion was forgotten by the citizens. After the planet was blown asunder by the asteroid, Academy Officer Dreeska established the citizens on New Ceylon, naming it after its predecessor.

**CEYLON NEW**    Dreeska was made Governor of New Ceylon and the banishment of the religious belief system in old Ceylon was strictly enforced, causing the citizens to become calloused, with a not so caring attitude. Ragan was able to bring the Ceylonians of new Ceylon to a state of moral decline, just before the planet was destroyed in the same fashion as its sister planet, old Ceylon.

**CEYSAR**    Was one of the planets of leisure, and known for its exotic drinks prized by the citizens of Ceylon.

**CHALDOC**   The son of Adrada and progenitor of the Chaldocians. aka., Children of Light. The prophet was a direct descendant of this line.

**CHILDREN OF DARKNESS** (THE)    They were the offspring of Ragan and followers of the dark spiritual force called Waki.

**CITY OF TRIBUTE**    Kiah honored Ral and Jedar by erecting large statues in their honor on  Durran.

**COMATRA**    Jedar's Starship.

**COUNCIL OF THE TWELVE**    After old Ceylon was destroyed, Dreeska began revamping the Ceylonian council by appointing eleven of the most brilliant citizens who would rule and make all governmental decisions. The position of Governor was the most powerful political office, and there were only four that ever ruled, Dreeska, Atar, Gemaal and Kiah.

**CREESKA**    The son of Adrada on the Feramas and brother of Chaldoc.

**CRUEL**    He was one of the sons of Ragan on the Feramas. He offer a forbidden and vile beast upon the sacred alter in disrespect to the Chaldocian's religious beliefs.

**DADAR**    Served as an officer aboard the Tri-Star.

**DA ENDEN**    the planet of the small citizen that fought against Machiaz in the Interplanetary Games. He could puff himself up like a toad and was able to shoot electrical bolts at his opponents. This almost worked, but he died when Machiaz, the giant, crushed the small challenger in his hand, causing the electrical energy to go off inside his own body.

**DARMAR**    A distant planet that fought against Ceylon.

**DORKEA**    The religious leader of the Children of Light on the Feramas who told them of possible infiltration by their enemy, as Borkia hid close by while observing them.

**DOEKA**    Ral's mother-in-law and Dreara's mother

**DREARA**    The Tri-Star's Recreational Officer and the Ceylonian wife of Ral. She experimented with Ral in sexual acts that had been forbidden in Ceylon. Jedar was conceived by this illicit encounter. Dreara was reluctant to believe in the Unni, but late in her life she became involved in Jedar's ministry. (See Ral, Mylia @ Jedar)

**DREESKA**    The kind and benevolent military leader who saved the entire population of old Ceylon by removing them from the planet before it was destroyed by the run-a-way asteroid. After he detached them to the Recreational Planet for their safety, he was eventually able to relocate them on one of the newer planets, which was suitable for habitation. Dreeska was so admired by the relocated citizens that he was unchallenged in his election as Governor. After he died, the council maintained rule for thousands of years, until an evil politician, Gemaal, forced an election in which he deceitfully tried to steal the governorship from Atar. (See Atar & Gemaal)

**DREKKA**   Braka's wife on Ceylon and sister to Governor Atar.

**DURRAN**   The planet of Durran had long been held in reserve by the Ceylonians as a sister planet, just in case new Ceylon might share the same fate of old Ceylon. Kiah was appointed Governor just before New Ceylon was destroyed. Durran was destined by Unni to be the last planet to be inhabited before time and space ended. Kiah and Jedar would be privileged to be an eye witness of the Unni's final cosmological destruction. (See Kiah @ Jedar)

**EPARDA**   A lesser messenger (Angel) assigned to the Tri-Star.

**FERAMAS PROJECT**   Ral was given the Feramas as his first colonization assignment. It was a gift from his father who placed the first male and female citizens there in order to populate the land. Their righteous seed became know as the Children of Light, and the female's offspring through sexual relations with Ragan brought forth the Sons of Darkness. Ral loved the Feramas citizens and spent most of his life watching over and protecting its citizens from above the Feramas skies. The Feramas was among the last planets to be destroyed before the Unni's final judgment.

**FLOACRE**   The Floacre planet was able to use their minds to perform many great accomplishments like the mind meld which could short circuit various electrical devices. But Gemaal used it to trick the council members to vote for him during the election for governor. In reality, he had just merely found a way to short circuit the dreaded electroshock mechanism.

**FRANNAU**   Brother of Chaldoc and a son of Adrada.

**GALAXY EXPLORATORY DIVISON**   Military headquarters in charge of colonizing new planets throughout the Seventh Quadrant and beyond.

**GAUNKA**   A distant relative of Dreeska who had the right but never chose to run as Ceylon's Governor. He was too involved in the affairs of his world being obsessed with eating, drinking and sexual improprieties.

**GATALINA**     A member of the Ceylonian council who cast his vote for Atar during the election for governor.

**GEMAAL**   Believed that Atar had cheated in his bid to be Ceylon's new governor, vowing revenge on Atar and his future descendants. After the death of Atar, Gemaal became governor and continued his harsh judgments against the house of Atar. Gemaal died with his beloved citizens on New Ceylon, rather than seeking safety on Durran. He appointed Kiah to succeed him as  Durran's governor, even though he hated Kiah's grandfather, Atar. He repented of his injustice against the Ceylonians, but he repented to Kiah rather than to a  so called God.

**GLENNA**    A Ceylonian term for sweetheart.

**GORMIA**     Leader of the barbaric Zecra, and brother-in-law of Teegra the Kronos. He was later successful in killing Ral in battle, ending Ral's first life cycle.

**GORNOR**    Engine room officer aboard the Tri-Star.

**GROGA**    The former home of the giants that dwelt on Zerena. They served as prison overlords in the tar pits, which were located in Agreg, a remote sector of Zerena. (See Agregleourites)

**GYRO-CRAFT**    Housed in the belly of Ceylonian Starships the Gyro-Craft was the parallel of the biblical wheel in a wheel. The messengers could ride it on air, land and water. The Gyro-craft's central power came  from inside the belly of the mother ship, yet it could also operate under its own power source of energy called Patriska. It could only move straight up and down or directly right and left at sharp angles, it was also able to travel at high rates of speed.

**HUNSHA**    A barbaric tribe dwelling on the Feramas, enemies of the Sons of Light.

**JEDAR**   Ral and Dreara's son born aboard the Tri-Star. Jedar and his half brother Kiah were destined by the Unni to physically see a glimpse of the ending of all cosmological life. (See Kiah)

**JEMAAR**   One of the two sons of Kiah on New Ceylon

**KATRANE**   A captain aboard the Tri-Star. He filed charges against Ral for injuring him in a scuffle when Commander Ral was possessed by the Waki (Satan) aboard the Tri-Star and on the Feramas.

**KEEKSONN**   Member of the Ceylonian Council, he favored Atar in his bid to become governor of New Ceylon.

**KIAH**   The eldest son of Ral on Ceylon was raised by Atar his grandfather, and was later befriended by Governor Gemaal who appointed him to serve as Academy Commander, eventually Kiah became his replacement as Governor of Durran. From the days of his childhood he had hated his father for leaving his mother, but he came to understand that everything that happened was providential and in the will of the Unni.

**KOREACHE**   A distant sector of the Seventh Quadrant that had spread disease throughout New Ceylon the year that Kiah was born.

**KRONOS THE**   A warring and barbaric planet lying under Ceylonian servitude that occasionally rebelled against them, but their power was so weak in comparison to the mighty Ceylonians that they were looked upon as the proverbial thorn in the side. Their leader was Teegra who challenged Ral during his first space battle.

**LEAOKA**   A member of the Ceylonian council.

**LEARDAR**   Navigator on the Tri-Star.

**LEKRAAL**   A planet that waged war against the Ceylonians.

**LOUFA**   Transporter Officer aboard the Tri-Star.

**LOUPA**   Brother of Chaldoc and a son of Adrada.

**LOUSKA**    Doctor on the Ceylonian Council. He was almost killed by the Waki after he boarded the Tri-Star for the birthing of Jedar.

**MEDOA**    He was a angelic spiritual advisor, assigned as Ral's second in command. The messengers were created to serve the Unni and to serve citizens throughout the galaxies. Before making his manifestation before the throne of the Unni, he would pinch his nose and twirl at the speed of light. Medoa was privileged to serve as the Unni's personal envoy. He was of a higher spiritual order. Simka and Treeka were messengers of lesser authority. (See Messengers)

**MACHIAZ**    The father of Mondor the Agregleourite. Captain Atar entered him into the Interplanetary Games establishing the Groga as Ceylon's galactic champion. After the giant was victorious in combat against the citizen from Da Enden, the future sons of Machiaz were also appointed as overseers of the Agreg Penal Colony. Machiaz was so obsessively concerned with wealth and power that he had little time to worry that Atar had killed his father during the surrender of the Zerena. (See Mokaz and Mondor)

**MAJIA**    She was the daughter of Zehon, a priest on the Feramas and the wife of the Ceylonian officer, Borkia. Their son, Boeski, the prophet, became the most prominent figure in the early days of the Feramas. Majia maintained faith in the words of her husband, always believing that he was truly a traveler from a distant planet. (See Borkia, & Boeski)

**MASKRA**    A son of Ragan on the Feramas.

**MESSENGERS** (Angels) There was no remembrance of how the messengers came to be advisors to the Ceylonian government, but their service was so beneficial that they were merely accepted, no questions asked. Some of the messengers were assigned to serve as spiritual warriors to fight off the evil forces of the Waki and others served as starship advisors. They were also created to serve citizens throughout the galaxies that humbly asked for their guidance. Medoa was an advisor to Ral and his closest friend. (See Medoa, Simka & Treeka).

**MOKAZ**    A Groga giant, grandfather of Mondor the Agregelourite. Mokaz once killed two Ceylonian officers with his bare hands and was himself killed by Captain Atar during the surrender of the Zerena. (See Machiaz & Mondor)

**MOLECULAR FIELD**   The crematory on Ceylon where millions of citizens forfeited their lives for crimes committed against the government. For the vilest citizens death in the Molecular Field was circumvented and the transgressors were sent to Agreg to suffer horrendous death at the hands of Mondor.

**MONDOR**   Overseer of the Agreg Penal Colony, whose whip was so fierce that many of the prisoners died by their own hand before ever reaching the sulfer and tar pit hell holes. Mondor was a Groga giant, his ancestors had long ago relocated to Zerena after devouring the food supplies. Mondor held a special hatred for the Ceylonians because Atar, Ral's father, had killed Mokaz's, grandfather. With so many prisoners on Agreg to choose from Mondor could afford to be selective. He was cannibalistic and the prisoners would delightfully bring about another tasty meal.

**MYLIA**   Ral did not realize till after her death, how much he really cared for his Ceylonian wife and for his selfish inconsideration he suffered dreadful mental anquish because he had left her behind on Ceylon Kiah, their son, while he remained away for years searching for new planets to colonize.

**PANCHAR**   A member of the Ceylonian Council.

**PATRISKA**   A limited and highly prized nuclear fuel that had long been imported to Ceylon from the outer quadrants. The Ceylonians believed their reserves of Patriska had long been exhausted, but when Ral was held prisoner on Ceylon with his family he found a rich supply of the needed fuel and was proclaimed savior of the land. The citizens influenced Gemaal to restore Ral to his former status in the academy.

**PECHKA**   The home of one of the prisoner on the Agreg colony.

**PEIDA**   A training officer during Ral and Braka's stay at the academy.

**PEISTOID COLONY**   Kiah negotiated an alliance of peace with them during the governorship of Gemaal.

**PHALO**   The native planet of Zareen, the telepath serving aboard the Tri-Star.

**PLUATA**   Son of Ragan on the Feramas.

**PLUMA**   Jedar desired to leave the confines of the Tri-Star and look upon the face of citizens like the Pluma who had two faces and two sets of arms.

**PNEPE**   The starship that Ral and Braka were assigned to on one of their academy training sessions.

**POGRON**   A favorite past time game of Ceylonian nobility.

**POKAR**   When Ral was in his private chamber he spoke "Pokar" and the drink was made to his liking.

**PRALOR**   A planet noted for its beautiful music.

**PROPHET, THE**   Boeski was born on the Feramas, to Borkia and Majia. Boeski being the son of a Ceylonian had a natural lifespan of 1000 years, he had far outlived his contemporaries on the Feramas who lived less than 100 years. (See Boeski, Borkia & Majia)

**PUELL**   The god of the Zecra.

**QUINTOEA**   Member of the Ceylonian Council and a distant relative of Atar. When Quintoea cast his vote for Atar in the election for governor, Gemaal lost the election and hated Quintoea because he was a relative of Atar. Gemaal also held nothing but contempt for Atar, and made a vow of vengeance upon the new governor. Gemaal had Quintoea murdered for his suspected betrayal.

**QUINA**   Beverage served on the Tri-Star.

**RAGAN**   His home planet of Zylon was one of the planets that fell under the jurisdiction of the Ceylonian, and Ragan, who was born there, believed that he was better than those that kept his people in servitude. When Ragan's father became Mayor of Zylon he asked permission of the Ceylonian council to accept his son into their prestigious military academy. It was in their early days at the academy that Ragan met Ral, becoming close friends. Ragan believed that Ral was promoted above him, because Atar, his father, was governor. Hatred began to fester in his heart and Waki, the black spirit, was soon able to take complete control of Ragan's mind. Ragan represents the evil influence over universal citizenship.

**RAPADO**    Atar placed the first female citizen on the Feramas and her name was Rapado.

**REGENERATION PROCESS**    The Ceylonians designed a Regeneration Process, where they could extend the natural age of their citizens. They were endowed by the Unni with a natural age of 1000 years, but at the time of death, they could be brought back to life in the Regeneration Chamber, six additional life spans of 1000 years each. They had also developed a method of cultivating newly developed planets with a process that accelerated land development making it soon habitable for colonization. Both the Regeneration Process and the land regenerations were an abomination to the Unni.

**RENOUNA**    Kiah's wife on Ceylon, they later settled on Durran after Ceylon's destruction.

**RAL**   The central character of the book is Ral, the son of Atar, who desired that his son follow in his footsteps. But Ral could not adhere to Ceylonian laws or the social structure of the government. Ral could not comprehend that he was being led by a higher calling, the god of old Ceylon that had long been abolished. Ral spent most of his life mothering over the affairs of his beloved Feramas. After the planet was destroyed by a cosmological pandemic Ral spent the final days of his life on Durran with the assurance that even though he had lost favor with the Unni, his sons Kiah and Jedar would blessed by the Unni to witness the end of all existence.

**RHADDA**    God of the Feramas, same as the Ceylonian god, the Unni.

**RHEAR**    Doctor serving aboard the Tri-Star.

**RENNA**   The Tri-Star's hologram computer was designed to include a female voice, which featured human qualities. Renna was also programmed to interplay with the commander in a flirtatious manner, which seemed to please the Commander.

**ROGAG**   Bridge Commander aboard the Tri-Star.

**ROGARA**   He was Kiah's security officer aboard the Tri-Star, and accompanied Kiah to the Tar and Sulfur pits on Agreg where Ragan was to suffer at the hands of Mondor.

**ROKAK**   The mayor of the Durranian colonies just before Ceylon's Destruction.

**ROPRIER**   A member of the Ceylonian Council.

**SAIR DREESKA**   Interpreted as, The City of Dreeska. Prominent citizens had many cities named after them, statues were also erected throughout the districts in their honor.

**SABRA**   Tailors of fine clothing, dwelling outside the Seventh Quadrant.

**SEED TUBES**   The females on Ceylon were impregnated by having a long tube inserted into their vaginal cavity. Only top ranking officers and politicians could donate their sperm for the continuation of the species but only the most noble military officers like Atar, were permitted to store sperm for the impregnation of their Ceylonian wives. After the proper indoctrination period their offspring were released to live in the home of their parent. The idea of enjoyable sex had long been abolished so the citizens living in such a stringent environment grew up to be cold and calloused in all personal relationships and appeared to be more akin to the androids which heavily populated every Metropolis throughout Ceylon.

**SEVENTH QUADRANT**   Ceylon's solar system. There were eight known quadrants, but beyond the inner sector of the 8th Quadrant, where the merciless Zorber dwelt, the Ceylonians could only speculate concerning any possible of life. (See Zorber)

**SIMKA**   A lesser Messenger who was assigned as a personal tutor to Jedar aboard the Tri-Star. When Jedar received his command, Simka was assigned to be his advisor and second in command.

**SHASHENNA**   A member of the Ceylonian Council

**STRAPPA LEAVES**   Herbs that when smoked produced euphoric states of consciousness.

**STRIKA**   The father-in-law of Ral's first wife, Mylia

**THE SONS OF LIGHT**   The Chaldocian believers in the Unni.

**SUDARIN**   A nation that waged war against Ceylon during Ral's campaign against the Venduras colonies.

**TANNER**   Alcoholic drink that was highly prized by the Celonian aristocrats.

**TEEGRA**   He was the leader of the Kronos, who hated the Ceylonians for placing his people under servitude. Teegra and his people were barbaric but they were never a real threat to the mighty Ceylonians. (See Kronos)

**TEESKA**   Son of Ragan on the Feramas.

**TONKOR**   A member of the evil Hunsha tribe that attacked the Chadocians on the Feramas. Tonkor surprised Borkia & Majia after Borkia killed Victar. Majia believed that Tonkor and his men were about to kill her, but suddenly Tonkor and all twenty enemy soldiers lay dead at her feet killed by Borkia's lazier.

**TREEKA**   A lesser Messenger serving aboard the Tri-Star.

**TRI-STAR**   Ral's prototype starship that was given to him by his father, just before he departed Ceylon to oversee the development of the Feramas.

**UNNI**   During the early days on old Ceylon, there was a belief in the existence of a god called the Unni, but later leaders such as Dreeska banished this theology as nonessential to the good of the colonies. It was Ral, thousands of years later that without realizing it, would be instrumental in reestablishing this ancient belief system. The Unni guided and protected Ral so that he and his sons would play a part in the eventual destruction of not only the Feramas, but all life. The Unni was the Ceylonian god and the Rhadda was the god of the Feramas.

**VENDURAS**   When they waged war against Imperial Ceylon, Ral had to leave the Feramas in control of his friend, Borkia. Ral was able to subdue the Venduras colonies winning many medals for his service there.

**VENTURA**   Allies of Ceylon that reported Zorber's unrest to Kiah.

**VICTAR**   After he raped Majia, Victor was killed by the strong hand of Borkia.

**WAKI**   The negative universal force that often exercised his power over gullible Ragan to do his bidding. He tried to prevent the birth of Jedar by preventing Doctor Louska from materializing on the transporter pad. The Waki was also manifested to Ragan on Zecra, a turn of events, which led to the death of Ral. The Waki's messengers were forever fighting with the Unni's Messengers in a battle of good over evil. (See Unni)

**ZAREEN**   The telepath aboard the Tri-Star. She was a dark skinned female born on the planet of Phalor. Ral raped her when he was under the influence of the Waki.

**ZECRA**   The Kronos formed an alliance with the Zecra to fight against the mighty Ceylonians. (See Gormia & Teegra)

**ZEDOR**   A neutral planet in which Jedar was able to establish his religious headquarters. It was on Zedor that Ral and Dreara, in their old age, distributed religious materials throughout the various quadrants.

**ZEHON**   Father of Majia and grandfather of Boeski, the Prophet. It was Zehon that discovered the murdered body of Borkia.

**ZERADIN**   He was a sage and friend of the prophet who taught him astrology and higher spiritual values on the Feramas.

**ZERENA**   The Groga giants imposed themselves on the Zerena citizens after they destroyed their own lands on the distant planet of Groga by devouring all green vegetation. The Zerena citizens were very small in comparison to the Groga such as Mondor, but it seemed in comparison to be a workable arrangement. (See Groga & Mondor)

**ZERESS**   A planet that supplied much of the synthetic food supply to New Ceylon.

**ZIANA**   The Zecra had severed relations with the Ziana Nation.

**ZIDIO**   A sacred mountain located somewhere on the Feramas.

**ZORBER**   The Zorber dwelt in a solar system lying outside the Ceylonian jurisdiction and their acts of terror were questionably recorded in the Ceylonian Archives. Kiah sought help from Ral and Jedar when the Zorber threat was thought to be serious but in reality he just desired to see his long lost family.

**ZORN**   Original home of the first couple on the Feramas.

**ZYLON**   Home planet of Ragan.